LANCE OLSEN is author of more than twenty works, including the novels *Calendar of Regrets*, *Head in Flames*, and *Nietzsche's Kisses*, and the anti-textbook *Architectures of Possibility: After Innovative Writing*. Among his awards are fellowships from the John Simon Guggenheim Memorial Foundation, the American Academy in Berlin, and the National Endowment for the Arts. Born in 1986 in Salt Lake, he teaches experimental narrative theory and practice at the University of Utah.

Theories of Forgetting

Also by Lance Olsen

Novels
Live from Earth
Tonguing the Zeitgeist
Burnt
Time Famine
Freaknest
Girl Imagined by Chance
10:01
Nietzsche's Kisses
Anxious Pleasures
Head in Flames
Calendar of Regrets

Short Stories
My Dates with Franz
Scherzi, I Believe
Sewing Shut My Eyes
Hideous Beauties
How to Unfeel the Dead: New & Selected Fictions

Nonfiction
Ellipse of Uncertainty
Circus of the Mind in Motion
William Gibson
Lolita: A Janus Text
Rebel Yell: A Short Guide to Writing Fiction
Architectures of Possibility: After Innovative Writing
[[there.]]

Theories of Forgetting

Theories of Forgetting

Lance Olsen, editor

The University of Alabama Press
Tuscaloosa, Alabama 35487-0380

Manufactured in the United States of America

FC2 is an imprint of The University of Alabama Press

Book Design: Lance Olsen with Illinois State University's English Department's Publications Unit; Codirectors: Steve Halle and Jane L. Carman; Assistant Director: Danielle Duvick; Production Assistant: Jamie Koch

Cover Design: Lou Robinson

Typeface: American Typewriter, Adobe Garamond Pro, Georges

∞

The paper on which this book is printed meets the minimum requirements of American National Standard for Information Sciences—Permanence of Paper for Printed Library Materials, ANSI Z39.48–1984

Library of Congress Cataloging-in-Publication Data

Olsen, Lance, 1956-

Theories of forgetting / Lance Olsen.

pages cm

ISBN 978-1-57366-179-9 (pbk. : alk. paper) -- ISBN 978-1-57366-846-0 (ebook)

1. Memory--Fiction. 2. Memory in literature. 3. Experimental fiction. I. Title.

PS3565.L777T44 2014

813'.54--dc23

2013041359

for A, and all the days left

Acknowledgments

The editor wishes to thank the publishers of *Corium*, *Ocean State Review*, *Rampike*, and *Timber*, in which excerpts from this book first appeared in slightly different form; the John Simon Guggenheim Memorial Foundation and American Academy in Berlin for their belief in this project; the Tanner Center for the Humanities and its fellows at the University of Utah during the spring of 2010 for their generosity and thoughtful support. Film, photography, and manipulated images are by A. and L. Olsen. William F. Fox's *The Void, The Sign, and the Grid*'s perspectives on the Great Basin are echoed, quoted, and slant-quoted several times throughout what follows, as are essays from *Robert Smithson: The Collected Writings* (edited by Jack Flam) and one still from Smithson's *Spiral Jetty* film and one from Smithson and Nancy Holt's *East Coast, West Coast.*

Nature is never finished.
—Robert Smithson

And then the—

21 June

Something is happening to me.

I wasn't sure at first. Now I am. A glary gray migraine aura. A sheet of plastic lowering between me & me.

The same sort of feeling when you suspect flu has begun scattering through your bloodstream: the peculiar ache behind your eyes, the poisonous ghost at the back of your throat :::: and then again, you say to yourself, maybe you've just worn yourself down lately. It happens. Maybe all you need is a glass of orange juice, some extra sleep, a handful of echinacea.

Maybe it is there.

Maybe it is not.

Maybe it's all the hours you've been putting into your

The stars are the first to go away.

~~This film is~~

Then you're on a downtown street corner, waiting to cross, staring at nothing with everybody else, and there's no refusing it.

It has zero to do with you. It has everything to do with you. It isn't going anywhere.

Here it is.

The mulchy tang fanning out behind his eyes.

Sweep the last leaves over your body.

Lacunae: his mou

[[ ]]

I was too busy to think about it until trying to edit some footage a couple minutes ago.

It's back, following me into the daylight.

If there are two hours left of cold, I can manage it:
this is what he tells himself.

What you tell yourself.

What I.

Two hours, and we'll be

22 June

My fingers woke me in the middle of the night. I figured maybe I'd slept on them wrong, except the tingling didn't fade until after sunrise. It was like the 9-volt battery you touch to your tongue when you're little and hold there as long as you can because it's both tinnily unpleasant and fascinating.

A plastic sheet lowering between him and him, what
it feels like, yet

23 June

Robert Smithson: Museums are tombs, and it looks like everything is turning into a museum.

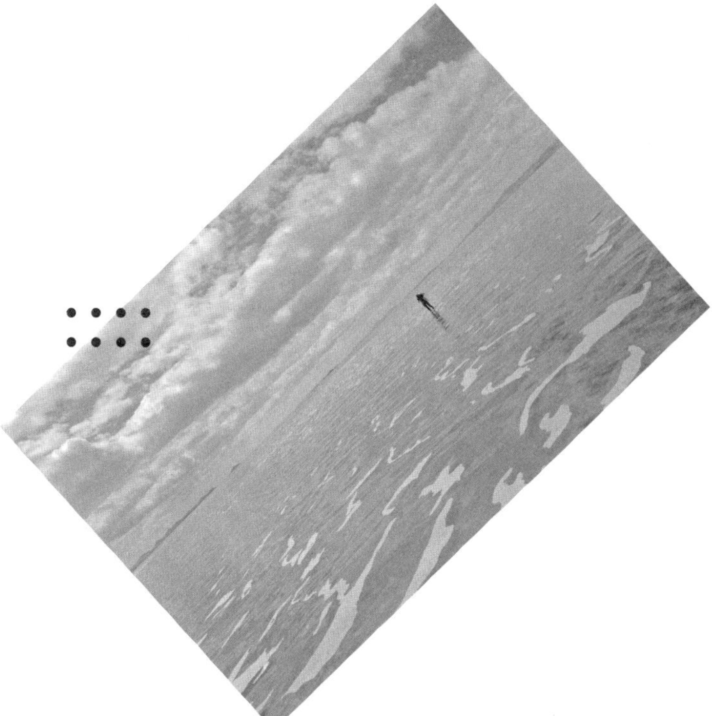

Eventually, like this, it will be morning.

24 June

I was standing at the sinks in the mall restroom. I wasn't standing there and then I was. ~~I don't~~ A middle-aged woman in a taupe business suit and plum lipstick was dispensing soap foam into her palms at the first, lathering and scrubbing. Done, she sidled over to the second and repeated the same gestures. She moved to the third, lingered politely as I used the fourth, holding up her wet hands like a pre-op surgeon, studying herself in the mirror. I stepped to the hand dryer. She slipped into my spot. I crossed to the exit. She returned to the first sink and commenced washing all over again.

25 June

~~When you're well, even if you've only been well a little while, your body can't remember what it was like being unwell. The recollection is an abstraction, one disembodied thought among~~ ——

Eventually, like this, it will be

26 June

You keep telling yourself it will go away. Of course it will go away. Things like this go away all the time. That's what things like this do. Whatever it is, it will run its course, blow over, become the sort of bruise you spot one day whose origin you can't recall, and a week later you'll glance down and won't be able to locate it anymore, unsure you're even looking in the right area, whether you're recalling a relatively new bruise or one you acquired months ago and forgot about and finally remembered. It was on your left calf when you thought it on your right. A hip when you thought it an elbow. Like that.

No: he has already thought th—

27 June

An arid, light-breezed, too-warm summer morning in this city of the sweatless. You can't walk more than a few blocks in the upper Avenues without the inside of your mouth going sticky dry. You can't help being aware of the UV rays relentlessly unarguing your cellular facts.

Even this early in the day, the atmosphere over the basin is ochering softly with ozone, desert dust, particulates that this evening will put on a red-slashed tangerine drag show above the airport, the marshlands, the mudflats, and the hunched backbone of Antelope Island out in the glint of lake water to the west.

He wakes with a. The woman in the seat beside him on the plane is. The plane is. Chemicals. You close your eyes a—

This morning your interest keeps tagging the human meteor strike in the Oquirrh Mountains called the Bingham Canyon Copper Mine: open-pit, a mile deep, 2½ wide, 450,000 tons of material extracted every day, every week, month, year, the world's largest manmade excavation, a 1900-acre cochlea chewing itself into the planet since 1904.

In satellite images, it appears as an enormous uncanny amoebic scar.

It may seem to be about many other things—bullets, heart valves, crazy cells, blown vessels, skidding cars—but in the end it's all about oxygen.

Houses bordering the sidewalk on your right drop away just beyond the intersection with K Street. The valley unfastens, opening out across the downtown a thousand feet below, through wooly green suburbs south to Murray, Midvale, Sandy, Draper, Riverton twenty miles away.

The unchecked perspective even after all these years unnerves you, the idea you're seeing everything you're seeing all at once.

The man laughing at the tiny version of himself curled into itself curled next to a rock, understanding in the end everything is about oxygen.

All this seeing.

All this relentless taking in.

The high desert's combination of severity, immensity, and shock makes you conscious of your own breathing, how you negotiate this breath, then this one, then the one after that.

Gemini: the twins leaning away from the grayish mist of the Milky Way.

28 June

When he becomes interested in aerial art in the late sixties, in projects constructed with an eye toward how they'll appear not from earth's surface but from hundreds of feet above it, Smithson isn't moving outside himself.

When has he witnessed the sky this noisy with so
many silences happening at once?

Yes lets

This is the important point: he isn't breaking any new aesthetic ground, at least not in one sense. He's turning back deeper into himself, shaped by the environments he grew up in around New Jersey: rusted-out factories, abandoned quarries, the turnpike, the shambled landscape of Atlantic City, the grimy refineries of Perth Amboy, the power plant

Ready? says the tourist they stopped and asked to
snap their picture, a skinny pockmarked German
in black leather pants and black t-shirt.
The couple processes a pair of traveler smiles.
One, the German counts off.
Whose mind is his face crossing at this instant?
Two—
I want to say I am thinking this.
The dazzle of stars flung across the sky. He has
never seen so

and weathered pilings and derricks and sewage pipes and garbage broadcast along the riverbanks of the Passaic, the dump trucks excavating tons of concrete slabs resembling the modern equivalents of monuments from antiquity—a shoddy region constantly falling apart at the same time it is being hastily pieced together in a process that reminded Smithson of ruins, only in reverse. When in 1969 he takes

Pick up, the voice on the answering machine says.

Hello? he says.

Pick up, the voice says.

Hello? he says. Who is this? Hello?

Pick up, the voice says. Pick up if you're there.

out a 20-year lease on an abandoned industrial site along the northeastern shore of the Great Salt Lake, he's both circling back to the beginning and not circling back, revealing home as the spot you can never return to, but can also never leave. He scouted Mono Lake in California, considered doing something involving one of the salt lakes in Bolivia. Except the day he spotted the blasted astonishment of Rozel Point

A breath, and he.

A breath, and he wants to say it is already dark. The middle of the night. He wants to say he is—he is buried beneath those leaves on the hillside in the park across the street.

He is afraid of the black he is rushing into, confused by how quickly this unfamiliar life is swallowing him.

No, he is in bed. That's where he is. He is lying next to his wife in the hospital bed in their room. They are sleeping side by side, his hand on hers, believing in their sleep they are somewhere else, posing for a photograph in front of a tree root bigger than they in front of temple ruins, his arm around her shoulder, happy just to be there, here, that's the emotion, simple pleasure, unaware like everybody else they aren't moving into the future, but the future is moving into them.

on a helicopter flyover, how the saline microorganisms tinted swaths of water there a supernatural rose, his mind was made up for him. Until then, he didn't know what he wanted. Until then, he'd been entertaining plenty of

You brace yourself against the boulder, watch exhaustion rubbing away his mind.

schemes, including an enormous island constructed from corroded boats and barges, sure the shape would find him when he reached the right place.

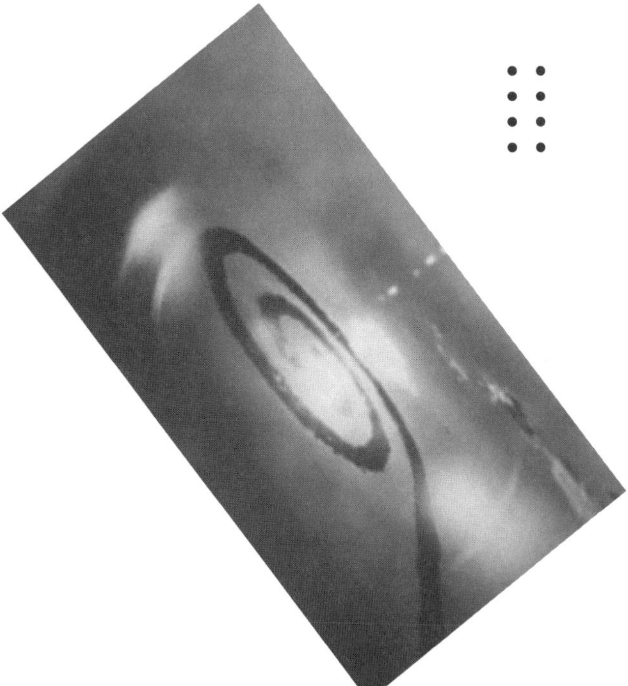

The earth is too crowded for voids.

The scene, he wrote in an eponymous essay in his typical jittery, hyperbolic prose, suggested an immobile cyclone while flickering light made the entire landscape appear to quake.

(Somebody will always be waiting for you who
doesn't know he or she is waiting for you.)

29 June

Sometimes the fizziness migrates down my fingertips into my palms: nerve static. I'll be sitting next to Hugh in the living room, watching TV, watching not so much what is on the screen as the clarity of the images, the velocity with which they turn into other images, and it will hiss alive.

Who are these mammals? she asks from her hospital bed.

What mammals, honey? he says, raising his head from the book he has been reading.

His left leg simply dropping out from under him.

No, his foot coming down wrong, twisting.

No, he is navigating this unimaginable terrain and
some

I'll think: I should turn and tell him. It goes without saying.
    I will, I think. I promise.
    I'll turn and tell him right now.

will begin to plummet, the desert invert itself, turn
itself inside ou—

You huddling against this boulder, trying to get
your

bearings, heart spoo—

The man kneeling, touching.

The man breathing inside sun clamor.

Straining to pee in the unexpected twilight.

Squeezing.

Massaging his lower belly.

Not a trickle.

Not a drop.

The day is running out and there are jagged rocks and scree and he is attempting to navigate the unstable terrain, water finished, light around him silvering. First this information comes to him as a relief. He senses coolness wafting in. It feels gorgeous, a swimming pool full of chilled air, this sudden gust of what is the word restoration, no, reanimation, this sudden gust of reanimation, but just behind that thought another: the temperature

I won't.

He has enough going on.

And what do I have to tell him?

I have to tell him this:

I may (or may not) be exhibiting symptoms that may (or may not) be demonstrative of the ordinary fact I'm no longer in my twenties, forties.

At a certain age, events like this simply start leaking into your world.

This isn't news.

It's something closer to innuendo.

Why not wait until we have something real to talk about, hard, scrappy, defined, something that will genuinely bother us both?

Decides to dog the tracks in the opposite direction, but a moment later, an hour, the tracks trail off once more.

Trying not to overreact, you.

Trying not to overreact, you retrace your steps and it is the same thing.

Were they the right tracks to begin with? You can't say. How can you say? It isn't out of the question they belonged to another pickup, another kind of vehicle altogether.

You lower yourself onto one crampy knee to examine them, touch your fingers to their contours as if that might help clear something up.

The sand is a summer sidewalk.

So why isn't he sweating anymore? You would think I'd be sweating.

The more I study, the more difficult it becomes to guess whether the tracks were made recently or a month ago, a month or ten minutes.

Why are his thighs aching?

The man trying to.

This leads—

There are no marks indicating the truck turned around. None indicating it started backing up. Every thought hurts. The day is running out. This is what the man realizes with a start. He watches you tilt back your head and look up into the blaring sky, instinctively, as if maybe you will see the rusty white pickup hovering several hundred feet above him.

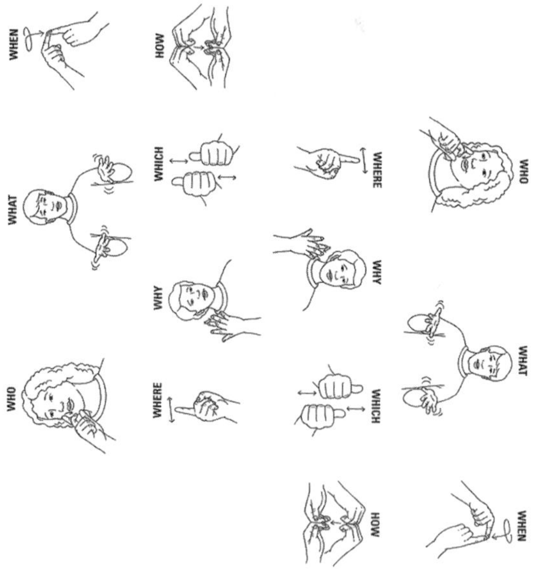

30 June

I don't know why, but today I can't shake the girl who became a cheerleader in high school a dozen miles from where Robert Smithson grew up, although she didn't know it at the time, wouldn't have cared if she had.

If someone were to ask, you would say the air isn't air anymore, it's so thin, so baked and harrassing.

The mountains ahead look like worn-down pyramids, much darker than the bright sand he is crossing, almost black.

He can feel the skin along the part running through his hair burning.

He paces the sips from his water bottle.

He thinks: I can do this. Come on. I can walk out. Who can't walk out? I just have to return to the village, return to the—

And then the tracks just stop.

I'm trailing them and then they.

You raise your head, scanning the geological exhaustion.

You veer onto them.

Everything seems possible again despite the deranged heat.

There is no atmosphere.

That's what you would say, if someone were to ask.

1 July

2 July

Or another way of putting it:

Carpal Tunnel Syndrome: compression of the median nerve routing through the wrist, resulting in numb fingers & muscle weakness in the hand.

Hunching, the man hasn't changed his mind and then he has.

It was something else and now it is this.

Events speed up and all I have to do, you figure, is retrace my steps. Sooner or later he will come across the pickup's tracks.

That's all I have to do.

So you get to your feet, strike out, positive in which direction the tracks lie until you walk for however long you walk only to locate nothing.

The man pauses, deliberating, trying to forget everything he has ever learned. Should he continue? Turn around?

He pushes on, desert radiating up through his sneakers. Time jumps and, about to surrender, there they are.

The tracks are right in front of you. How could you have missed them?

If you had turned back earlier, where would you be?

<u>Dupuytren's Contracture</u>: hereditary knotting of tissue just below palm skin that eventually pulls fingers into crooked positions.

<u>Focal Dystonia, or Writer's Cramp</u>: symptoms emerge when performing tasks requiring prolonged fine motor movements: painting, penning, playing a musical instrument

This next thing should be easy, I think, I propose thinking, standing there, receiving the space ballooning out around him.

How hard can this next thing be?

You hunch up against a boulder, trying to get my bearings, sun crazy on your face, his neck, lips. My lips don't feel like my lips anymore. They feel like one strip of plastic rubbing against another.

3 July

The girl's father was a merchant marine, her mother a nurse. They met in a Staten Island hospital during the War, the latter caring for the former whose tanker had been torpedoed in the Atlantic.

The explosion blew out his left eardrum, and, afterward, the U-Boat circled the sinking ship, machine-gunning crewmembers as they bobbed to the sea's burning surface.

What money does.

One hundred dollars, U.S.

Sometimes the sand is caked beige, sometimes red and fine as flour. It reminds him of the hue and texture of the sand in southern Utah. A powdery beach bordering an absent ocean. You have to struggle to make progress across its give.

Capitol Reef. Frying Pan Trail.

All this distance, and the only thing you encounter are mirrors. The sand: the sand. The Great Salt Lake: the Dead Sea.

The last time you took a roadtrip down there was—

When?

With the kids?

Your tongue going sticky and you stop, shrug off your daypack, take out the water bottle.

The girl told that story to her friends in the schoolyard and on sleepovers and she lived in a little redbrick house with picture windows and a white wrought-iron sign outside the front door that said: Snug Harbor. There was a large white magnolia in the lawn which lay next to a field in which the local high school uninterested everyone who attended it.

The girl liked to exist outside herself: sing, dance, be watched. The events that pleased her most about her senior year were landing the leading role in Bye-Bye Birdie and meeting a folksinger with dark curly hair and a sparse goatee.

The breeze, steady, arid, makes him conscious of his own breathing.

A moment later, maybe a day, and the man is walking through wasteland, silence occurring as continuous impact: non-sound, high-pitched and tinny and not there and there.

Utopia: an Adobe Original.

Danke.

This is good, I say aloud. Let's stop here.

The driver glances over at you without meeting your eyes, at your hands moving, and you watch yourself pumping air as if you are patting down transparent flames welling up around you.

Superfamilies: serif, sans-serif, slab serif.

She fell for his nice-guyness and laundry-detergent scent, the way he easily inhabited the far shore of high school while coaching her to be present in the moment… an idea which seemed gleamy as glass, and one which really meant, she learned (but only much later when it didn't matter anymore), not to contemplate the echoes of the rock you just tossed into the middle of your life.

She had never been in big, sloppy love before, and so was immediately convinced her boyfriend would save her—although from what she wouldn't have been able to say.

there is even less: a solitary weakly green saltbush, a ragtag cluster, uninterrupted expanses of.

He recalls the girl in the.

How in class she struck the same posture as crash-test dummies do immediately preceding the collision.

I think of all the places this isn't.

A single black bird rocketing by, apparently flying in reverse.

The pickup passes canyon entrances, fissures cut into the rocky bulges, rushing deep into the increasing placelessness. The cabin is oil, sweat, nicotine ghosts, everything clanking—the undercarriage, tools in the bed, thermos in the hatchless glove compartment. Your neck hurts. The man's neck hurts. His spine and neck. The desert won't stop. It keeps unscrolling before him like a video game.

Soon they were playing gigs together in Greenwich Village, he on twelve-string, she behind the mic, while the girl's father, now a supertanker captain who spoke in loud imperatives both on and off his ship, displayed open distain for his daughter's suitor.

And soon the couple was married.

"Driving is a spectacular form of amnesia." JJ

The man believes he may have just seen a petroglyph, an extraterrestrial family holding hands, or only scratches, and so he rotates in his seat to have a look and the boulder is gone in velocity smear.

When he faces forward again he doesn't know where he is. I look over my shoulder and can't locate the village behind me. The low encircling mountains seem different ones than those I was looking at a minute ago, half an hour, although it is possible they are the same and you are simply perceiving them from a different angle. He can't estimate how far away they are. Hundreds of yards? Five miles?

Relentless unchecked perspective makes him feel like he is seeing everything at once.

Starting out, the man had had the impression there was almost no vegetation. Now he realizes

Soon almost out of money.

Soon living in drizzly Brussels, the only European country whose medical school boasted low enough standards to accept him into its program. They lived on waffles, chocolate, and buttery pommes frites. He flunked out twice. The girl gradually came to understand that, although they had always

miles an hour across sand flats strewn with sharp stones.

The ride is spine grinding. At some point something in the man's neck snaps with a whiteblue flash.

Far off, craggy granite outcrops resembling eroded fortresses.

Closer, smooth dunes so beautiful they seem contrived by some director of photography and a CGI crew.

The color of the sand changes beneath them and around them and changes and changes again, cayenne to salt white to peach to cayenne.

There are camels, legs tucked under them, necks stretched out in front, jaws resting on the earth like slaughtered turkeys, dozing in the sun, divorced from the universe.

There are tire tracks rushing toward the horizon and oddly shaped boulders the color of dried blood balancing precariously atop other oddly shaped boulders the same color.

been best friends, they had never actually been in what other people would call love.

Soon divorced, the girl, no longer a girl, moved back to New Jersey, working first as mechanic in a Hackensack auto shop, using the skills her father had taught her during drab weekends stooped over the family Volvo's engine, then as waitress in a diner at the Paramus Bergen Mall. The

Growing up in camp. Two millions of us in Jordan. Two millions.

Then the taxi is turning around in the middle of the highway.

The man is watching, watching himself watch.

The cab is losing color as it accelerates, shrinking into a black beetle.

The man standing there, contemplating the glassy heat shimmering over the blank asphalt.

At a dingy appliance shop next to another dingy appliance shop he hires a Bedouin driver who owns a dented rusty white pickup, pays him one hundred dollars. The Bedouin wears a white cotton robe and white-and-red keffiyeh. He can't speak English and won't meet the man's eyes. The two communicate through an awkward impromptu sign language. Despite this difficulty, they are off paved road in ten minutes, off dirt road, juddering at thirty-five

special The Pizza Burger—a run-of-the-mill hamburger with lots of catsup on it, a fancy name, a slice of mozzarella cheese, and a sprinkle of oregano served on an open-faced, untoasted, whitebread bun accompanied by a thin, poignant slice of pickle.

And here she is, I am, too many decades removed from that planetary system to calculate the exact number quickly, curled up on this stuffed couch in this bright living room, watching sentences slip out from my pen tip, wondering: <u>Who the hell was she?</u>

Stop making things, he told her. Stop bothering. Just let me, will you?

And here events speed up. He senses time shredding around him, understands that's how it will come at him from here on out.

The taxi driver doesn't speak until they pull into a village at the edge of Wadi Rum. The man gets out, walks around to the driver's side, reaches in to shake the driver's hand. But the driver keeps both of his on the wheel, fisheyeing straight ahead and responding with fourteen words: I'm Palestinian.

4 July

Hosting holiday cookout with bookstore staff this evening. Hugh manning the shish kabobs and bratwurst on the grill, me a salad from our garden and quartet of pies: apple, blueberry, pumpkin, ~~rubar~~ rhubarb.

Inside of my head blank as snow blindness.

The man's grandfather looked puzzled, then frightened, then his face grew emptier, looser. He spent his days wandering through the backyard of his suburban house in overalls and a wide-brimmed straw hat and knee-high rubber boots, never quite shaved, never quite immediate, pretending he knew what to do with the bushy tomato plants in the vegetable garden he had put in near the garage, the choked flower beds along the wooden fence.

During a Christmas gathering, the whole family in the living room watching television, an image of the Eiffel Tower startled itself onto the screen. The man's grandmother perked up: We had such a wonderful time that summer. Do you remember, dear?

Agitated, his grandfather said: I don't know what you're.

Never mind, his wife said. Well, my goodness. Who feels like some hot chocolate?

But his wife's words stuck in his skin.

5 July

AMMAN, Jordan (AP) . Performance artist Tehching Hsieh, best known for spending a year voluntarily locked into a space resembling a prison cell in his Manhattan loft, was found dead Thursday in Petra, Jordan, his manager confirmed.

The 62-year-old appeared to have hanged himself in his suite at the luxury Petra Inn Hotel, said Lt. Adnan Al Massri, the officer responsible for investigating the death.

"His body was found naked, hanging in the wardrobe," Al Massri said. "We are investigating a suspected suicide."

"All we can say is we know Tehching would never have done such a thing," said Chloe Williams, of Niekerk & Associates, Hsieh's agency. "We're awaiting the conclusion of the investigation to find out what really happened."

It is unclear why Hsieh was in Jordan, Williams said. The artist's friends and family hadn't heard from him in over a month.

In 1978 and 1979, Hsieh placed himself in "solitary confinement" in a wooden cage measuring 11'6" x 9' x 8' in his loft on Hudson Street in New York. The cage con[illegible]

mattre[illegible]

It felt like a few strands of hair coming loose in a brush, the unconscious pat on your back pocket while standing at an intersection that reveals your wallet unpresent.

...ss, pillow, [illegible] a bed, can for refuse, mirror, toilet paper roll, paper towels, toothbrush, soap bar, nail clippers, cup, bottle light bulb, tea bags, and sponge.

Hsieh signed a contract agreeing not to write, talk, listen to a radio, or watch television for one year while in the cage. Each day a friend dropped by to snap a photograph of the artist, bring him food, and remove his waste.

Hsieh's only activities involved thinking and waiting for time to pass.

Other year-long performances by Hsieh included remaining tied by an eight-foot length of rope to fellow performance artist Linda Montano, livi[illegible] out on the streets of New...

PIZZA G...

All Items Labeled

SUMMER!

40% OFF

• Summer Cra...

• VBS Crafts

SUMMER!

where he had grown up, where they discovered his relatives considered him a defector for abandoning his kin for some new toothpaste-and-Palmolive-soap life an ocean away.

Shortly after returning, his sentences started letting him down. Parts of them flaking off, going into hiding.

The thing you say before you say You're welcome, he would say.

The other word for automobile.

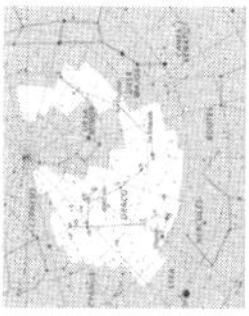

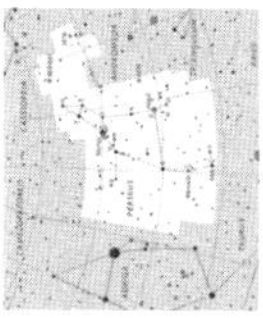

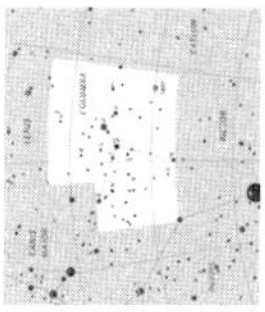

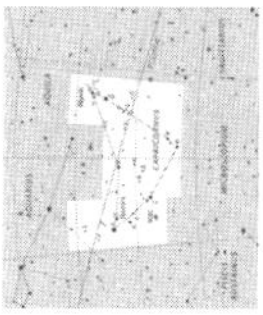

He found work as a sharecropper. His wife joined him two years later. Five, and he owned forty rock-strewn acres he had cleared with his own hands.

Ten, four hundred.

People did such things—how?

The man doesn't know.

No one in the family liked to talk about the man's grandfather or what he did, brag or articulate their admiration—not because they were modest or embarrassed, but because the narrative surrounding him had already begun to fray, because that generation was all about forgetting where it came from, transit for its members a kind of oblivion where you never leave anything in your wake.

The man's grandfather raised corn and cotton until he was in his early sixties, after which he retired to a Houston suburb. His wife and he used the money they had socked away to see the hill country in central Texas, the Crater of Diamonds State Park in Arkansas, and, once, sail back to visit the farm

6 July

Reached into fridge this morning for milk & my hand felt like I'd dunked it in a bucket of ice water.

The carton skidding across the floor, a wide surprised white sweep behind it.

Hugh was arranging lawn furniture on the deck for breakfast among the delphinium & forsythia. He probably didn't hear a thing behind our neighbor's sprinkler system, ambient bird chitter, the dog several houses away (in which direction remains continually unclear) that attempts engaging its own double in dialogue.

The desert flattens. Chunky rocks give way to larger sweeps of sand. A pickup passes carrying a small camel curled in back like a large dog.

A steel-colored dust layer hanging over a ragged ridge, and the man closes his eyes to concentrate on the hot wind hitting his face. He decides he is tired of thinking. Tired of his brain doing all the work. Besides, out of the blue, there are too many words in English. Who needs them?

From what he can put together from family lore, his grandfather grew up on a farm near Stockholm and sailed to the States when he was eighteen. He didn't know the language but was too proud to ask for help, so the train he boarded in New York took him to Galveston instead of Minneapolis where he had meant to arrive. The only things he had to eat on the three-day journey were a few bananas he bought on the dock.

Winston for me.

(Did you know R. J. Reynolds sponsored the first two seasons (1960-1961) of The Flintstones?)

[[N.B.-> Fred & Barney smoked Winston during commercial breaks.]]

down near the entrance to the Siq and try to make my mind into an overexposed snapshot.

He wonders why his body always feels like it swells during the daytime, why he has trouble getting his sneakers on after noon.

He remembers his grandfather.

What sounds good right now is a little, his grandfather would say, sitting in his La-Z-Boy in front of the TV set in the living room.

The cold.

Corianders.

No.

Just as I begin to suspect the driver may turn down my offer, he returns, settles behind the wheel, lights up a Pall Mall, no, a Menthol Full Flavor Parliament, starts the engine, and, mute, creeps onto the town's main street.

[[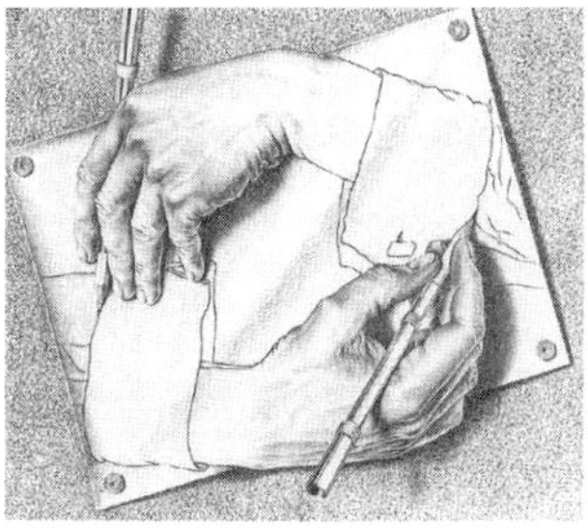]]

over with the map in hand to several other drivers talking together under a tree.

Even though all the windows are rolled down, the inside of the cab radiates heat. Perspiring, I stare out the window at two kids racing horses

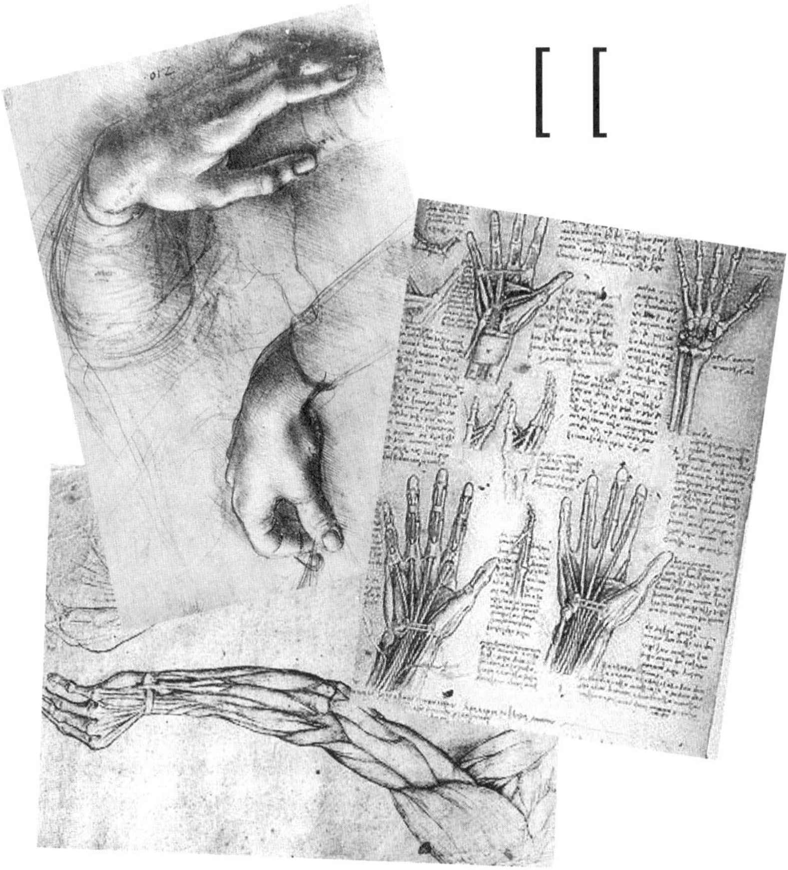

I wiped up the mess with a couple of dishtowels and stood at the sink, collecting my heart, fingertips numb, tinged bluish white.

I shook my hands.

Nothing changed.

I nested them under my armpit.

A minute, and I returned to composing breakfast, bowling granola, spooning blueberry yogurt, turning a peeled banana into the ~~spe spr~~ spare change of off-white quarters, ~~wasting~~ waiting for the next thing, for the thing after that, concentrating on ~~everuy~~

everything

except at how my zombie hands had misbehaved.

Daypack over one shoulder, the man stands and shakes Basel's hand, turns and heads for the front doors.

And now he is crossing the street toward the row of cabs waiting along the curb near the entrance to the Siq.

Sliding into the backseat of the first one in line.

The driver has the bulk of a human-sized brick and barely speaks English. Relieved, the man leans forward to show him on the map where he wants to go. He produces two one-hundred-dollar bills. Without responding, without agreeing or disagreeing to take him, the driver opens his door and stiff-legs

Says he should be heading out for the day, he has lots to see. The man wishes Basel a good time at his uncle's and suggests they meet up at the front desk tomorrow morning at seven.

Chipper, Basel agrees, repeats the hour, tells the man how much he is looking forward to their drive north together.

Me, too, the man says.

So many bands, says Basel. So little time to discussing.

He is proud of his joke and laughs.

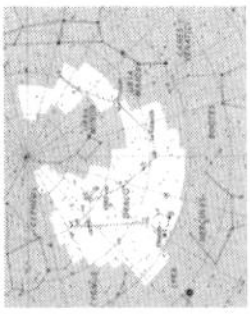

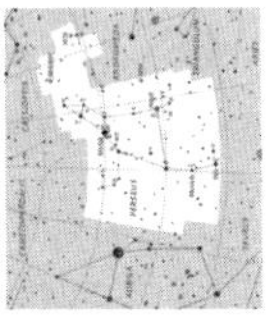

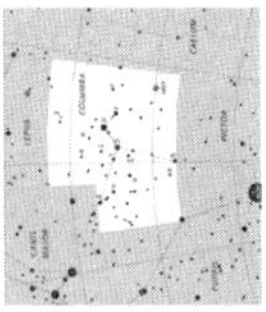

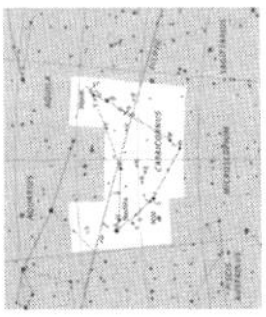

7 July

Robert Smithson's pediatrician: Doctor William Carlos Williams.

8 July

I'm remembering how the girl who was no longer a girl one day discovered herself speculating: if she could dispatch any six of her burger-joint regulars, which six would they be?

Why going so far to be by yourself?

The man looks past Basel, back again.

I'm just traveling, he says. I can't seem to keep still. Does your uncle have many children?

Many boys. Yes. Six. Seven. Growing fast.

Where does time going?

Anywhere it wants, the man says.

Basel begins describing his uncle's wives, although the man isn't attending to their conversation any more, couldn't repeat the substance of it were someone to ask. He appears to be listening, inserting comments, except something inside him is already moving forward to the next place.

He stalls another few minutes, asks Basel what time it is and mimics surprise when Basel tells him.

i'll let you be in my dreams if i can be in yours.

No, no. Visiting relative. Uncle. To introducing me to his third wife. Married last year. Big feast. Where we going to today?

I'd like to see some more of the ruins. You okay with heading back tomorrow?

Tomorrow. Yes. Big lunch today at uncle's house. Lamb. Curried eggplant. Stew. Rice.

Sounds like fun.

A man with family is rich. Basel looks down at his latte, up again, says: Maybe I can asking you something?

Sure.

Why you traveling so much?

How do you mean?

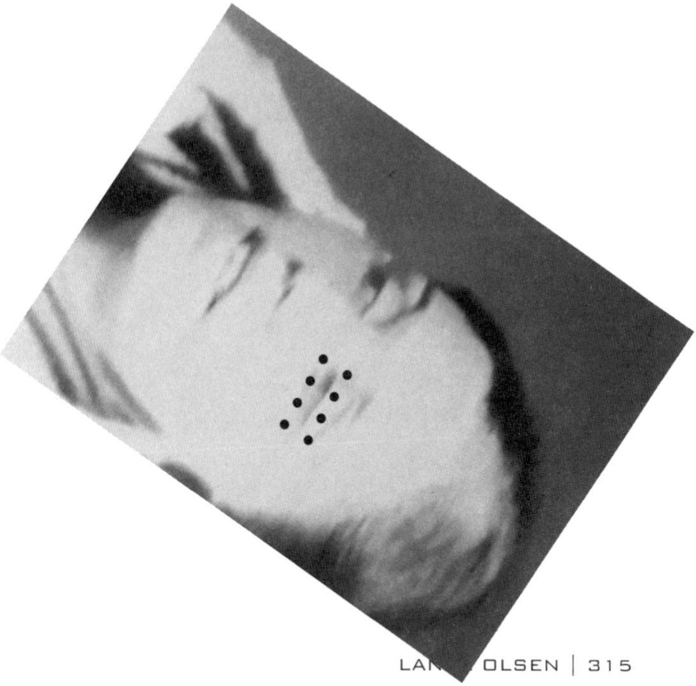

And with that, she became a pescatarian.

A vegetarian.

A vegan.

Guiltily reverted to omnivore.

She became a Buddhist, a Unitarian, an Existentialist, one of those people on the street who hands out leaflets questioning the abundant creepinesses associated with the Church of Scientology.

envelope and instructing him to give it to Basel when he shows up asking after him. It is seven a.m., no, earlier, five, no, later, nine, nine thirty, that's what he would guess, and the clerk bows marginally to indicate he will do as directed and the man thanks him and walks into the lounge where he orders a Glenlivet, neat.

The expression of the waiter who serves him remains carefully uncompleted.

Done with the first, he orders a second, and after that a double latte, which he is almost done drinking when Basel wanders in from a side entrance and spots him before he can escape.

Basel's face fills with recognition. His black Beatles t-shirt and black jeans are rumpled. He cuts toward the man, hand outstretched, smiling emphatically, and the man stands, invites him to join him for another latte.

You are liking Petra? Basel asks, eager.

I didn't see you yesterday. Did you have a chance to look around?

She attended a community college in Paramus.

A four-year in Teaneck.

She purchased a gassy third-hand Chevy Nova whose color was difficult to define and drove cross-country to attend Portland State University, believing she didn't know a lot about what she wanted, but that it doubtless involved touching down somewhere she had never touched down before.

the man hears the Brits talking loudly. Maybe it is the next room, maybe down the hall. Maybe he is asleep and only dreams he hears them. Maybe he is in that liminal brume where your eyes are shut but you believe they are open and you are both awake and not awake and the real universe exists as a report you only partially accept. The man supposes he is staring up at the polystyrene beaded ceiling, yet disconnected images are flying at him, the boy with the rock heart in his hand, her face, all her faces through all the years, some older, some younger, some more tired, some less, some happier, some sadder, some puzzled, some focused, some frightened, some bored, some blank, some bad, some beautiful, some pained, some pleasured, and then he is awake again, and then he isn't.

And now he is leaning against the granite counter in the lobby, handing the cartoon-jawed clerk the

He fidgets and tugs out of the dress, bunches it up, places it gently in the wastepaper basket under the bathroom sink on top of the pile of other articles he has shed.

Palatino: its greatest strength its readability.

A breath, and he wants to say it is dark, the middle of the night, only he can detect light bleeding in from the sides of the curtains and there is the LED on the microwave and the alarm clock on the side table and the red speck pulsing on the smoke detector above the closet. Lying on his back in bed,

[[The verb fun derives from the Middle English fonnen, meaning to cheat, hoax, befool. Cf. fond.]]

About her first year there she can summon up almost nothing:

1. the marbled linoleum tiles (alternating somewhat less ugly mocha with somewhat more ugly mocha) covering the bathroom floor down the hall from the cubbyhole she rented in a frayed house on a frayed hill with three strangers, one of whom, an Austrian in a thrash band guided by irony named The Whining Fantods;

The light material brushing his belly.

He sorts through his daypack, extracting any item that isn't of immediate use to him. He throws out two extra t-shirts. A rolled-up pair of jeans. Three pairs of socks.

He throws out his wallet, his passport.

The stories he tells himself while he works don't seem like his stories anymore. It feels as if he got them from some biography he read somewhere, some film he half-recollects, and eventually like they have reached him by hearsay, from somebody else who heard them from somebody else.

He thinks: What you don't remember never happened.

He thinks: All this living, and here they—

In the top drawer of the desk he locates an envelope and prints Basel's name across it. Slips in four hundred American dollars. Licks the seal. Presses down firmly with his thumb.

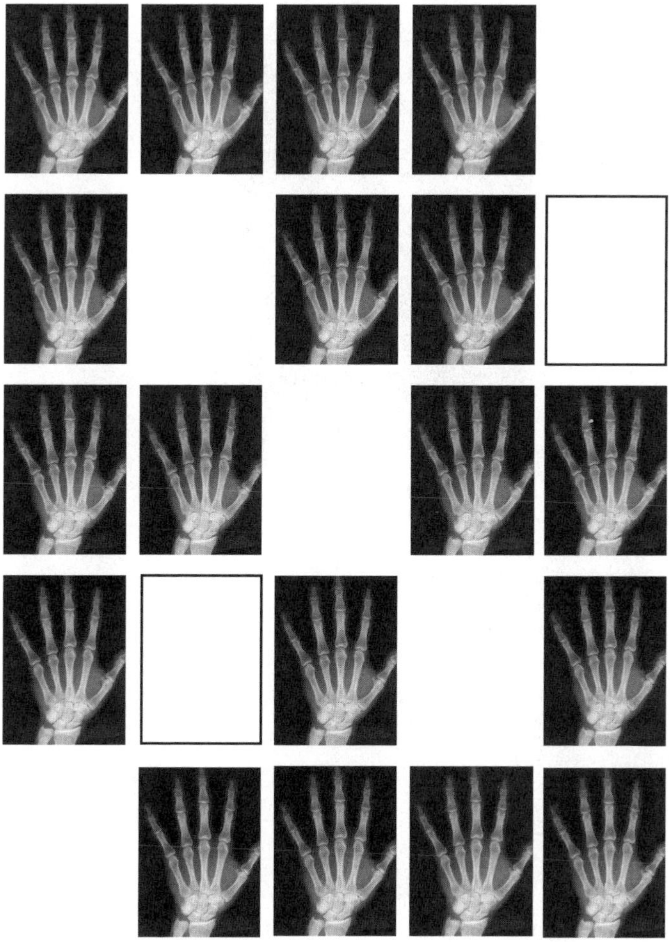

And now he is leaning back into the pillows on the bed, legs splayed, studying himself in the mirror over the bureau.

water, watching a teenage minder randomly whip donkeys collected in a small herd on a bridge over a baked streambed. One donkey brays and the minder whips another. Another donkey brays more frantically and the minder whips a fourth even harder. After each snap of the whip, he surveys to see if anyone in the vicinity is impressed by his cruelty.

At a stall near the ticket booth on his way back to the hotel at dusk, the man buys a map of the country, stops to have one more look around him, chucks the incense burner into a trash bin as he passes through the main gate.

And now he is squirming into her dress again in his hotel room.

[[

2. the hot plate she cooked most of her meals on;

3. the impressive textbook chimney growing out of her desktop that smelled of week-old wet hair if she brought the tip of her nose near it, which she liked to do, surreptitiously, often;

4. and four peasant blouses and two peasant skirts which these days hurt too much to think about for any length of time.

Baudrillard, re-redux: "Americans may have no identity, but they do have wonderful teeth."

other. For a few minutes the man is here, looking at their teeth, here and swimming beside a woman, another woman, this one, in tepid milky green water, thin wedge of whiteness several hundred yards away through vaporous–

At one of the souvenir stalls across from the amphitheater, forty warped tiers of seats for six thousand people cut out of a hillside, the man buys a brass incense burner as a present for her from a man with a beard died red who appears to have given up on making a sale today.

The man carries his present with him through the rest of the afternoon, switching it from right hand to left and back as he strolls through a colonnaded street, these ruins of a palatial temple, this café in the shade of a few sickly trees where he stops for a small plate of hummus and bread and a bottle of

disturb them, intent on living what they are living at a distance. They allow him into their atemporal cloud, or maybe they don't notice him. Their eyes are closed, yet they are almost in sync with each

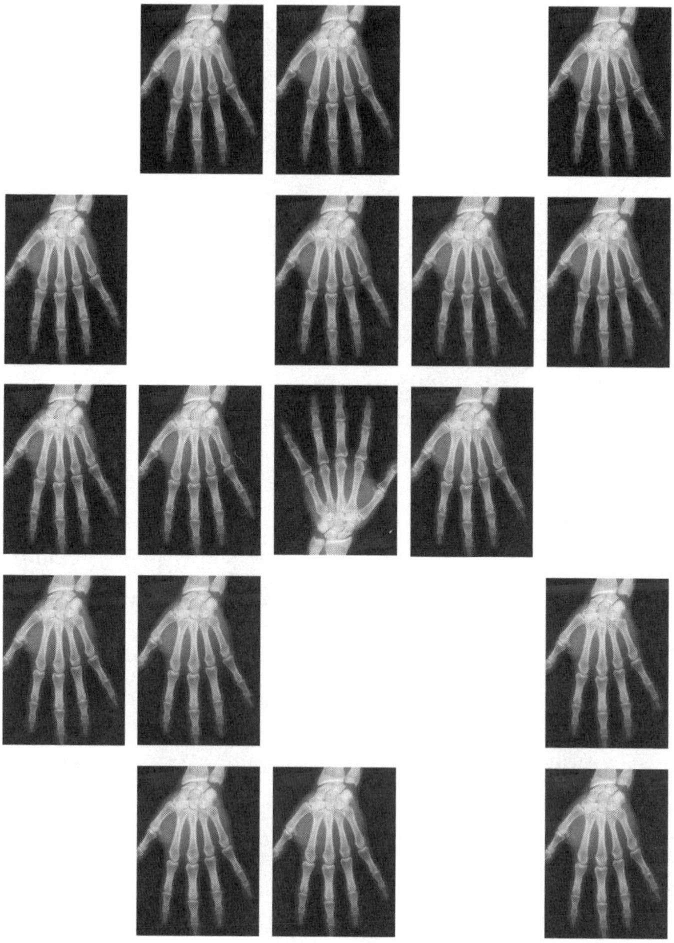

Those textbooks piloted her into a double major (studio art; art history) and helped her start looking through the idea of herself to herself.

Sometimes after classes and before strolling to her sorting and stacking job at the library, she cross-legged on the grassy tree-shady strip running down the university's navel

Buildings become landscape become buildings and on the ceilings of some he can make out paint traces from two millennia ago.

Stairways leading far up cliffs that erode into stone and dry air.

Tombs honeycombed across vast rock faces that have sagged over time, semi-liquefied and hardened again.

In one temple, twenty feet deep, fifteen wide, biting whiff of urine in the air, he chances upon four middle-aged American women performing unworldly slo-mo yoga movements, the only sound their steady breathing. They are having a moment, this moment. They are taken with the specialness their lives have become and are moving inside religion, inside the motions their bodies are enacting and their arms and legs are covered with bug bites.

The man sits on the stone step, careful not to

and sketched. That's where one afternoon she became aware of someone peering over her shoulder: a ponytailed guy skinny as a Pixy Stix with wire-rimmed glasses, an Army field jacket two sizes too baggy for him, and an overlapping canine and lateral incisor.

The girl who was no longer a girl could tell that initiating a conversation with her was one of the bravest acts he had ever undertaken.

Wow, he said.

was so much going on in that video that it made him punchy, and then, from another niche in his mind, this thought: I could walk away.

The man catches himself thinking: I could rise. That's what I could do. I could just get up and walk away. I could return to the hotel, return to the capital, fly back to the States and start over—doing what? Doing this, and then doing the other thing, and then witnessing a different life assemble around me.

He could do that. It would be weirdly easy. Check in. Check out. He could do that, he is doing that, that's what he's going to do.

Except he isn't; he doesn't.

What he does is ease up, stretch, twist side to side to loosen his spine, and push deeper into the melting orange-cinnamon city Antoni Gaudí might have dreamed had Gaudí had an active enough imagination.

(The exercise she'd been working on: Using pastels, draw a series of reclining human forms, each in forty seconds or less, with your eyes closed, from memory.)

(The results: dark-lined, smudgy conceptual people with misplaced noses and orange mouths floating in flat beautiful space.)

Really? she asked, overly hopeful. You think?

It strikes the man that it doesn't matter how many photographs you've looked at, how many documentaries about Petra, because this thing isn't that thing, this thing is some other thing, it isn't that experience, it is another experience entirely, another mode of being.

The boy with the heart-shaped stone stays with him, hovers, until the man shoos him away with a broadcasting gesture. A shirtless teenager approaches him for a camel ride and he waves him off, too. The man doesn't want to be a visitor. He doesn't want to have to explain where he comes from or how long he plans to stay or how he likes this country. He wants to leave sentences and the things they can't describe behind.

At some point he finds himself remembering the woman on her hands and knees in the video. He hasn't thought about her for weeks. Where was he when he watched her? He can't recall. How there

Jacques Derrida: "Whoever said that one was born just once?"

Squatting in the shade, rock face of the Siq at his back, he takes it all in. Squatting, he sees himself squatting, senses himself outside what he is observing, in a process of becoming insubstantial.

Tourists jockey for position to take the same photograph again and again. Every time they click, the world falls away. They don't know why they are there, what they're looking at. They will buy tacky souvenirs they would never buy back home and will throw away within a week, shocked they bought them in the first place.

Death isn't frightening. It's living that's the daily catastrophe, and tourists on a guided tour stare into space, primping, not listening to the guide speak quickly in an accent so heavy it is almost impervious.

A woman in her sixties with a Texan drawl turns to her woman-in-her-sixties friend with a man's potbelly and says too loud: I was told I'd get a room with a view, but all I see are trucks.

9 July

According to the War ~~Slipp~~ Shipping Administration, the U.S. Merchant Marine suffered the highest casualty rates of any service between 1940 and 1945. Officially, a total of 1,554 ships were sunk in combat, ~~insl~~ including 733 of over 1,000 gross tons. 1 in 26 mariners serving aboard themdied in the line of duty.

The man fetches up with a cluster of other sightseers, overwhelmed, steps into the clearing beyond and the unexpected bustle of camels and floppy-hatted tourists snapping photographs and haggling with peddlers and chattering at tables in front of the stalls selling cheap souvenirs and coffee and snacks.

When will you read this half-sentence?

A horse-driven buggy clopping by.

Piles of compressed cream-spinach donkey shit smeared along chaotically shaped and sized cobblestones beneath his sneakers.

A dark-skinned boy appears beside him, hawking a rock that resembles a heart the boy scooped up along the path and is now trying to sell for a dinar.

The man pays him no attention.

The boy won't fall back.

There are ambiguous humanoid figures carved into votive niches. There are violently green bushes clinging to the sides of pockmarked blond cliffs and uncanny languages fussing the air. Running low along the walls are sections of what once was piping designed to carry water from several miles away to the center of the city.

Rounding a corner at the far end, the astonishment of the Treasury widening into view, hewn out of the rose escarpment that looms fourteen stories above.

~~Slaef oqkding t~~ After leaving the hospital and the nurse he had fallen for, the girl's father returned to sea. He had been promoted to lieutenant.

Three months later, his ship was torpedoed again.

10 July

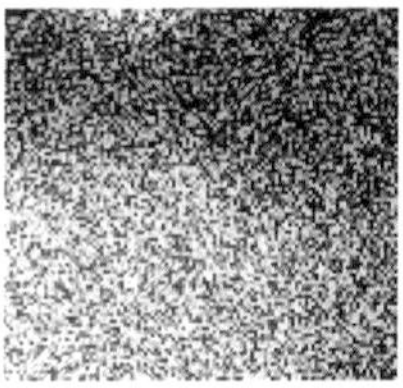
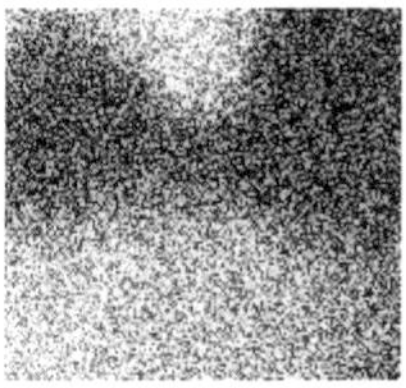

Robert Smithson: Visiting a museum is a matter of going from void to void.

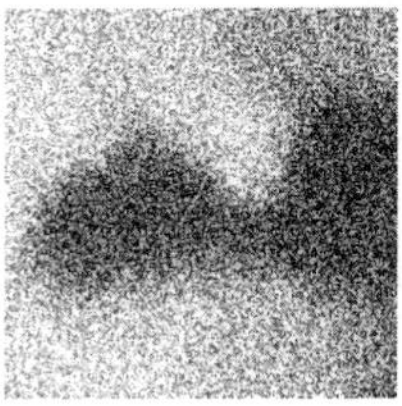
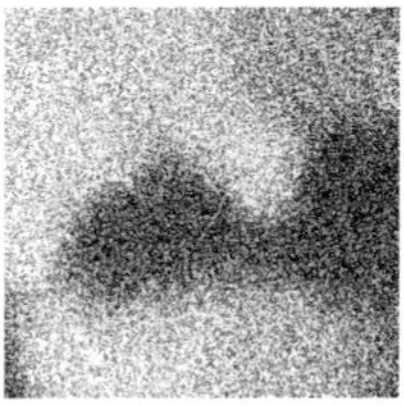

It is like a little assembly line of affliction.

What he is doing is moving up the Sig, the sandstone gorge winding a mile in toward the remnants. Its walls have been worn smooth by water and in spots are no more than nine feet apart and in spots almost six hundred high. It is ten in the morning, no, earlier, eight, nine, that's what he would guess, the sun already shrill on the back of his neck as he steps from the dense shadows.

11 July

Here I am not listening, said one of the voices that are Hugh.

If you're responding, I said, you're listening.

I'm not hearing, then. I'm listening, but I'm not hearing.

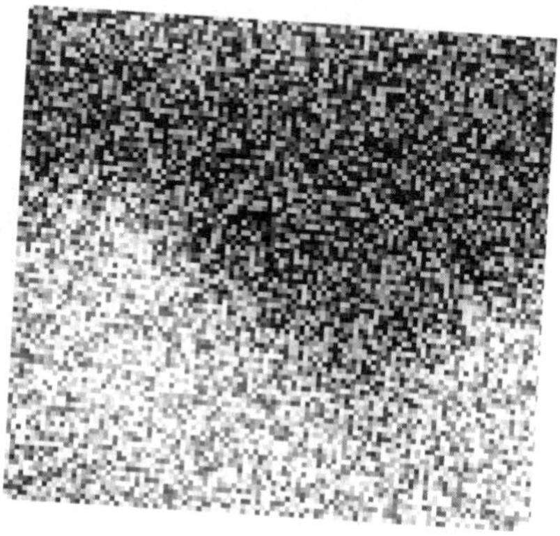

in his palm. There was someone's army marching in some grand parade past some proud leader and instead he has been thinking about moments he hasn't thought about for however long he hasn't thought about them, attempting to delete each from the desktop behind his eyes.

About that and about how his thumb just keeps making this same little flinching gesture over and over.

It is like those winking neon signs on rooftops in old detective movies.

Of course you're hearing. Look at you.

I'm eating my breakfast. That's what I'm doing. Eating my breakfast and enjoying this amazing morning out on our deck. Amazing, but too fucking hot by half. What is it, one-hundred twenty? One forty?

Eighty-five.

The thing is, why doesn't that dog stop barking? Aren't dogs supposed to be as a species smart and so forth? Why hasn't that one figured out it's barking at itself? That no other dogs really care what it thinks?

shut the heavy plastic curtains. Pulls shut the cloth ones over those. Returns to the bed to flip distractedly through TV channels until room service arrives.

He has ordered an American burger, tomato, lettuce, pickle, fries, a Coke, a tuft of guilt about his choice sticking in some corner inside him.

All this way, this energy, this time, and he orders an American burger?

What is he thinking?

All this living, and here—

i'm thinking of all the books that never get read by more than a handful of people.

At some point he realizes he isn't watching the TV anymore, hasn't been watching it for some time. There was Al Jazeera reporting how mortars dropped on settlements in a nearby country. There was Seinfeld, only everything was in Arabic and the laugh track was off and instead the man has been watching his thumb clicking the remote

The word TIME deriving
from Old English TIMA
("limited space of time"),
from Proto-Germanic
TIMON ("time")--both from
the Proto-indo-European
DI-MON, with the
poignant base DA ->
"to cut into pieces."

Eighty-five, and my fingertips are bluish.

The thing is how advanced can an animal be that can't differentiate its own noises from the noises of other beings? Your fingers look fine to me.

The term for a hand specialist is what.

What?

A hand specialist. A doctor who specializes in hands. Manuologist?

You'll have to speak up. Your mouth is moving, but I can't hear a thing it's saying.

Proof.

This is what he is in the process of doing, he decides: what he is in the process of doing is becoming untraceable, disappearing from former venues and situations, previous versions of himself. All records, images, narratives.

What he is in the process of doing is becoming a whiteboard washed clear after school.

This thought happens to him and Basel steps in from the lobby and stops in the doorway to survey the atrium, maybe looking for him, looking for the man, maybe simply thinking about having a drink himself.

Before Basel can spot him, though, the man rises and ducks out through a nearby side door. Returns to his room and stands at the large window overlooking the luminous blue swimming pool below that is one-hundred-percent vacant. He pulls

Sipping, the man fixes his interest on the slow burn in his chest, the trapdoor sensation below it. He wants to feel less. He wants to forget more than he has forgotten. Only it's not bad, he would have said had someone asked. Had someone asked, he would have said it's just that it could have been so much better.

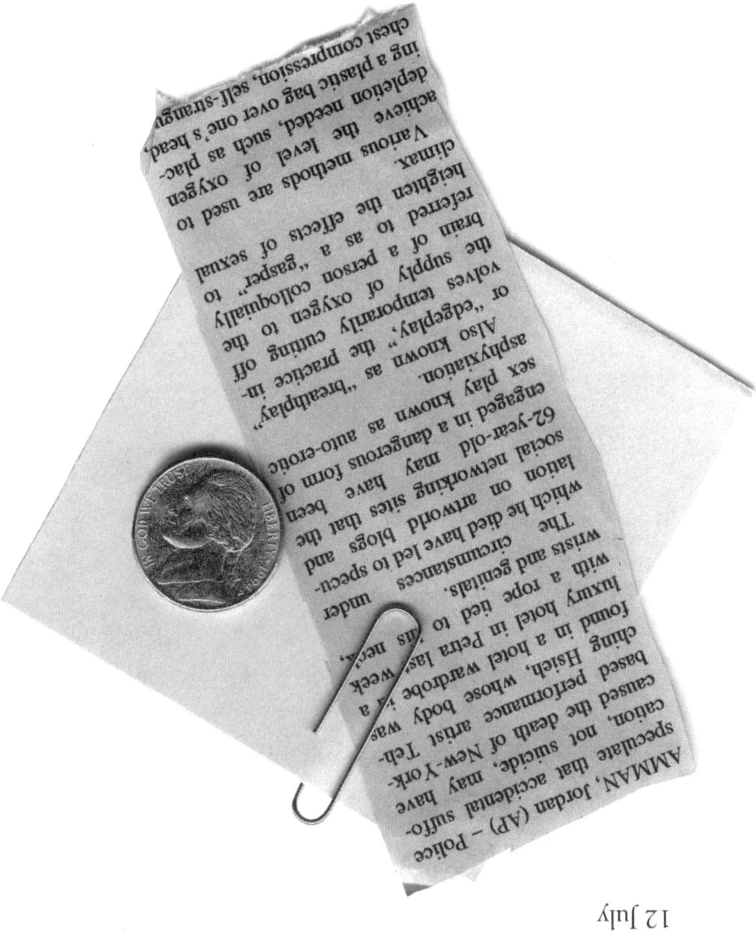

AMMAN, Jordan (AP) – Police speculate that accidental suffocation, not suicide, may have caused the death of New-York-based performance artist Tehching Hsieh, whose body was found in a hotel wardrobe in a luxury hotel in Petra last week with a rope tied to his neck, wrists and genitals.

The circumstances under which he died have led to speculation on artworld blogs and social networking sites that the 62-year-old may have been engaged in a dangerous form of sex play known as auto-erotic asphyxiation.

Also known as "breathplay" or "edgeplay," the practice involves temporarily cutting off the supply of oxygen to the brain of a person colloquially referred to as a "gasper" to heighten the effects of sexual climax.

Various methods are used to achieve the level of oxygen depletion needed, such as placing a plastic bag over one's head, chest compression, self-strangu

12 July

13 July

The hand is the primary organ for manipulating the human environment.

29 major and minor bones, 29 major joints, 123 named ligaments, 34 muscles responsible for moving the fingers, 48 named nerves, 30 arteries.

Our fingernails are in reality modified hairs.

Our sense of ~~torch~~ touch is intimately associated with our ~~houn~~ hands, which can form fists, point, prod, emphasize, draw, hold, make, brandish, type, play, pat, signal, stroke, sign, salute, caress, warn, wield, high five, wave hello and goodbye.

He orders a Glenlivet, neat. Drinks it quickly and orders another. Drinks it more deliberately and orders a third.

Other tourists come and go, families with children, older couples, lone businessmen here for a glass of wine or a dirty martini at the end of the day, trekkers in convertible pants made out of quick-drying fabric, mostly Europeans, but some Arabs, a handful of Japanese, two or three Americans, the kind who believe such places cease to exist the second they step out the door with their cameras and their fanny packs and the what is the word their inattention.

i've got its twin beside me. And that, dear bro, is how we're going to see this evening out.

He bends down, palms on knees, convinced he might catch the fallen object off guard, but the oatmeal-colored carpet remains just oatmeal-colored carpet.

The man climbs back on his bed and begins sorting through his daypack.

To his surprise, everything appears present. To his surprise, nature is never finished. Nothing has been removed, nothing disturbed.

Who would have thought the teen was—

The man makes sure he has his room key on him and takes the backstairs, the ones you are supposed to use only in the event of fire, down to the lounge, a well-lit atrium several stories high lined with white columns and scattered with intricately carved oriental furniture and palm trees and overhung with an ornate brass chandelier.

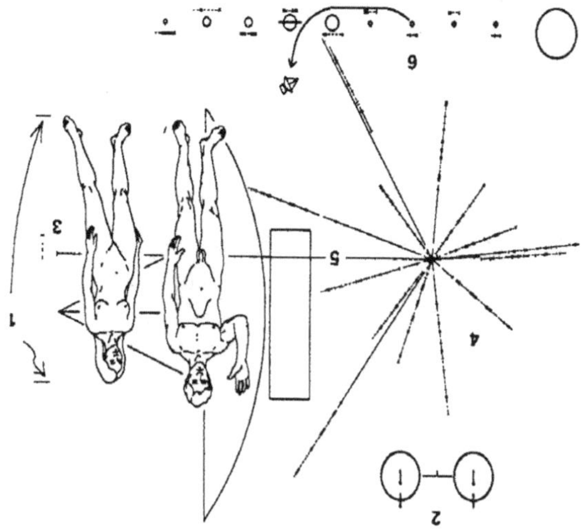

Carl Sagan: The upraised and open right hand is sometimes described as a 'universal' symbol of good will… The plaque aboard the Pioneer 10 spacecraft—the first artifact of mankind to leave the solar system—included a drawing of a naked man and woman, the man's hand raised, palm out, in greeting…

I describe the humans on the plaque as the most obscure part of the message.

That evening he takes two rooms on two different floors at the Mövenpick across from the entrance.

Sitting on his bed, listening to a group of drunken Brits lumbering down the hall, roller suitcases scraping and thumping walls, the man sorts through his daypack. To his surprise, everything appears present. To his surprise, in a way he feels happy. Nothing has been removed, nothing disturbed.

He believes he hears something drop onto the carpet and leans over the side of the bed to have a look. He gets down on the floor on his hands and knees, trying to imagine what it could have been that fell out of his daypack and feels around with his hands. Raises the bedspread. Peers under the frame. Stands and surveys the room.

is an ability to look ahead and see everything coming at you as either instructive or exhilarating.

The sun a glowing silver disk in a continuously ruining sky.

because he can't get the particulate gumminess out of his mouth, can't stop running his tongue over his jellied teeth. After a while he excuses himself, buys a bottle of water at the counter, uses the restroom in the back, a hole in the no-skid floor with foot rests on either side for a toilet. He rinses his mouth in the sink. There are four rusty bolts in the cracked tile wall where the mirror used to be.

Back in café, he crosses to the window to check on the sandstorm's progress, deciding he likes Basel's good-spirited energy, his eager connectedness with the world and unconcern about what will happen next. It isn't indifference that Basel displays. It

Black children are 10x more likely than white to be ~~burned~~
born with extra fingers.

White children are 4x more likely than black to be born with webbed ~~won~~ ones.

Cracking one's knuckles cannot lead to arthritis.

Just because you can move your finger doesn't mean it isn't broken.

and likes contemporary Middle Eastern music and how Jordanian couples are marrying later in life than they used to, twenty-four, twenty-five, and how he wants many children, many boys, he says, laughing, and someday to move to Germany.

Germany? the man asks. Why Germany?

Everything is shiny there.

Her name is Amirah. No, it is Hanifah. Except the man only partially follows what Basel is saying

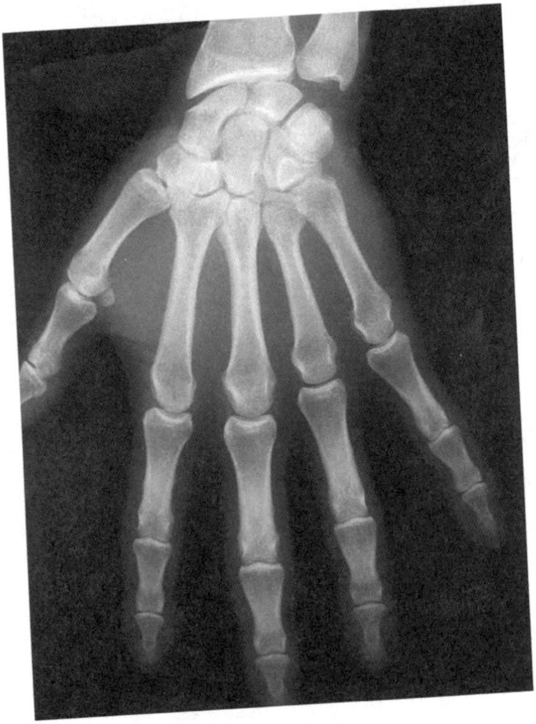

i think what i love most about the Sun Tunnels is
how little space they occupy in conversations surrounding
earthworks. How Holt's industrial/primitivist tour
de force represents the Lost Child role in the defective
family called contemporary art. How its inaccessibility
functions as resistance to being fully apprehended
and recuperated. How her postmodern Stonehenge
operates as a kind of cultural rumor, a perpetual
optical unreliability machine from which capricious
landscape & weather spill out, wind bluster everyw

All this seeing.

All this relentless taking in.

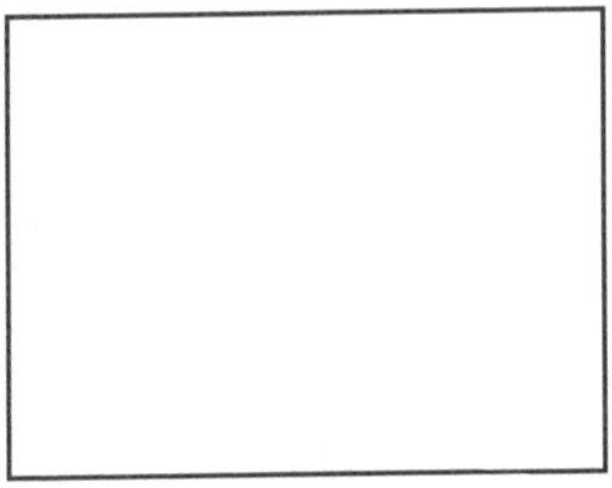

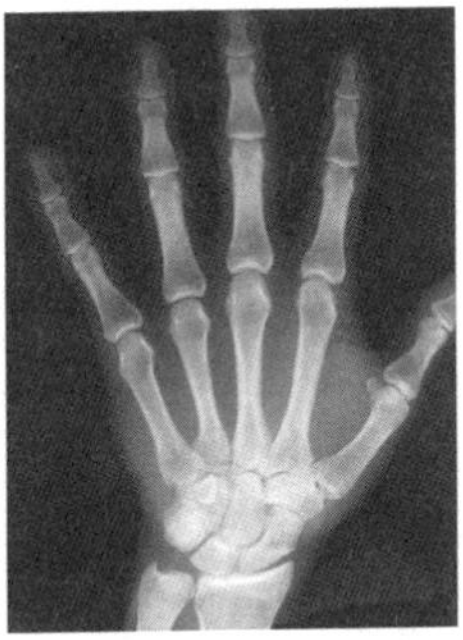

the whitewashed shed with the word COFE loosely spray-painted in red on the side next to an indecipherable Arabic word.

The weather makes him uneasy, turns him further inward, makes it feel as if reality is reaching its terminus all around him.

Inside, Basel orders two Turkish coffees. They sit on fold-up chairs at a card table to wait out the storm. The windows are shaking and the other customers—six or seven older, grimmer men—stare at them without even pretending to be doing something else. Basel pays them no attention. He talks freely about his girlfriend back in the village, orders a second round, lights up a Marlboro, no, a Winston, talks about how she is beautiful and uncomplicated

i guess that's really what i want to say. i want to let you know i get it now. To the extent that it matters ... which, i'm guessing, is maybe a lot less than either of us frankly wants to admit. Look at us. Which is another way of saying: Have a good life, but don't write back. Seriously. Don't write back. You're on this visit from your own planet. Enjoy the rest of your time here. Take care of yourself. Stay away.

-Yours, Aila

14 July

What followed was like one freshly unboxed kitchen appliance after another, everything shiny and exciting and, although she didn't exactly know how any of it worked, the girl who was no longer a girl wanted to ~~fa~~ find out, and so look at us, Hugh: there we are moving in together, ~~aptt~~ applying to graduate school together, packing my Chevy Nova ~~who's —~~

whose color was difficult to define and drivingto Seattle to enroll, down to Salt Lake City half a decade later, married, to open a secondhand-&-rare bookstore called (your idea) the Used Appendix.

Half a dozen workers slog along the shoulder,
only their dark eyes showing through slits in the
keffiyehs wrapped around their heads.

A bus stop hanging in the middle of bright
nothingness.

A cluster of women in burquas flapping in the
wind like a colony of huge agitated bats.

When the man pushes open his car door in the
small café's parking lot, the wind catches it and
snaps it away from his hand.

Grit salts his eyes and he is blinking, tearing,
snotting, stunned by the atmospheric vehemence.
Self-conscious about the act of breathing, he hunkers into the fury, hurries behind Basel toward

Then all of a sudden you'd show up beside me acting all intimate sibling. i was your ongoing experiment. i wanted you to like me. i wanted us to act like our parents' friends' kids acted. How hard could that be? We were both just these rejects out of step with disturbias where people cut down trees and then named their streets after what they'd disappeared.

On the CD, John Lennon is describing how tonight the Hendersons will be leaping through a hogshead of real fire. How Henry the Horse will be dancing the waltz.

Their production, he is saying, will be second to none.

The sandstorm registers as [an imprecise discoloration at the edges of the man's knowledge]—an approximation, he guesses, of what the world would look like through cataracts: foggy beigeness threaded with rosy light, then something dingier, weirder.

This thought happens to him and the wind buffets in and the silver Fiat begins shimmying. The man thinks flat before he realizes there isn't a flat before he notices the teen is gripping the wheel with both hands now. Everything sheens into garish graywhiteness, the horizon reeling toward them, the teen reaching over to turn off the air-conditioner, raising his voice to be heard.

Bad for car, he says. Paint. Windshield.

Should we pull over?

Next town. Out here, someone not seeing tail-lights on side of road—bam.

They pass into white sand drifting across asphalt like grainy snow.

Starting a family.

You always looked out of place--the kid who didn't understand the rules trying to partake in a baseball game with the other kids on the block who did. You always wanted to connect with your simulated teammates, make them proud of you, impress them, except you were hardwired against yourself. Your face didn't possess emotional gifts. You stooped, blushed, had the ability to make me feel like an only child.

Starting to watch our weight.

Accumulating the obligatory grill (first charcoal, then gas), used recliners, stuffed couch, mesh of important people, routine routes, reading lamps we invariably believed would work better than they turned out to work, bookshelves (brick-and-board, then laminate, then the real deal).

Grief is a subset of narcissism. That's what grief is. Everyone believes his or her loss special. Why not? Everyone believes there has never been, could never be, anything like it. Such a thing is beyond imagination, enduring, and the teen flips shut his cellphone, slips it back into his pocket. He reaches over to shake the man's hand as if encountering him for the first time.

Basel, he says. Anaa saäiid jidden bimuqaabalatak. Very glad to meeting you.

There are dirty white sections of what is the word PVC sewer piping lying atop rubble. A shop selling what appears to be red and blue plastic beach buckets or flowerpots and green plastic patio chairs into which would fit only children or elves.

And so, the teen says, where we going to?

The man likes the lightness he feels in his belly, this sense of continuous motion and adjustment.

He opens his mouth to learn what he will answer.

A hundred dollars a day, plus food and lodging. Three days, maximum. Then you pick up where you left off.

Road trip? asks the teen. Jack Kerouac. Neal Cassady. One hundred fifty.

The man laughs, says: One twenty five.

This concept of trusting people, not because you have a reason, but because your choices are limited.

Do you call this second sight?

The buildings on either side of the street are monochromatic, blocky, geometrically hectic, a series of odd angles and planes, like moving inside one of Escher's impossibilities.

There are satellite dishes, makeshift TV antennae, drooping electrical and telephone lines. Black pipes running up crumbling stained walls. External staircases where there shouldn't be anything.

Starting not to watch our weight.

Raising one boy (let's call him Jeremy) and one girl (let's call her Jennifer).

Witnessing them wobble-walking, tricycling away from us, picking out Star Wars lunch boxes for elementary school, accusing us of acting just like parents.

Exchanging ~~out~~ our apartment for a duplex, our duplex for a bungalow (white brick, gray trim, weathered deck, flower and vegetable garden both), grasping completely, piercingly, that someday something will go wrong, terribly, it always does, there's just no escaping it, that's how every story ends no matter how you try to outwit its narrative arc, but not now, no, right?

a shady strip of lawn. On any other afternoon he would have kept walking. The idea of striking up conversations with women he didn't know tasted like chewing on nickels. But this time he made an exception. (Hi, Mommy)

The Fiat speeds by a boy on camelback and cinderblock buildings are skittering up around them as they close in on the next town.

Without turning, the man hears himself ask: You want to keep going?

The teen glances over at him, back at the briskly narrowing highway. He grins. The Fiat decelerates and there are cars and pickups parked half on the curb and half off. There are green garbage cans lining the fronts of buildings. Above storefronts, long rectangular ads feature faces of stunning Arabic women for—for what?

Keep going?

Yeah, the man says. You have a job?

Many.

The dead space in any sentence
concerning Robert Smithson is
invariably inhabited by Nancy Holt,
his wife, & her Sun
Tunnels. You seen them? Amazing
work. Located in the Great
Basin outside the ghost town of
Lucin, 200 miles west of Salt
Lake. Four massive concrete tubes
(eighteen feet long, nine in
diameter) arranged in an "X," each
reacting differently to the sun, each
with small holes drilled into the top
that form light-patch constellations,
day stars across the walls of the
shadowy interiors. You can make
them out up to one-and-a-half miles
away among tall grass, their presence
immediately throwing into question your
perception of space and scale. H. H.
Arnason calls them Seeing Devices.

In college he heard from a friend of a friend that she spent her junior year in Germany studying art history. One morning she excused herself from her modern-painting seminar at the Berlinische Galerie, walked down a flight of stairs to the restroom, slipped her belt over a pipe running above one of the stalls, and hanged herself.

Each time the memory jumped him, the man re-experienced the surprise in the face of how unsurprised he had been. The same afternoon he heard about what she had done, he was cutting across campus toward his favorite coffee shop when he caught sight of another woman sitting on

15 July

In April 1970, Smithson hired ~~Ro~~ Bob Phillips, a contractor based in Ogden, to help him write his autobiography in space.

Smithson had already approached and been turned down by several other contractors suspicious of the young, bespectacled, pockmarked, shaggy New York artist who wore black leather pants even in the crazy Utah heat.

tarps, ropes draped with clothes, a herd of skinny goats foraging nearby.

Parched emptiness quivering.

Watching, the man recalls how in tenth grade he ended up in the same AP English class as the redheaded ponytailed girl from the naked elm in the park. Her hair reached all the way down her back and she parted it in the middle like Cher. She wore simple black tank tops, bellbottom jeans with red flares sewn into the seams from the knees down, a black armband to protest a never-ending war. They didn't speak to each other. She never looked in his direction. They had too much in common for that. Instead, they sat on opposite sides of the room, listening to predictable conversations about Holden Caulfield. He drew spirals in his notebook. She searched for someone on the other side of the wire-mesh window. Her posture mimicked those of crash-test dummies immediately preceding collisions.

Over the course of six days Phillips brought in a pair ~~of~~ ~~dumb dumv~~ dump trucks, a large tractor, and a front-end loader to haul 6,550 tons of black basalt and earth from the shore into the lake a few hundred yards ~~to the~~ west of a decrepit pier ~~na~~ and unused oil rigs.

Even blowing full force, the air-conditioning doesn't feel like air-conditioning. It feels like a hairdryer set to tepid.

The man's eyes feel scratchy, secondhand.

Everybody like Beatles, says the teen. All you need is love. Happiness is warm gun. Thirsty?

The man nods and the teen reaches behind the passenger seat with one arm, rummages, swings back with two bottles of Evian, no, Dasani. He passes over the first, braces the second between his thigh and twists. Swigs.

Even though it tastes like a hot-water faucet, the man chugs.

Two kilometers, and the car fishtails onto surfaced highway. The teen accelerates and soon they are skimming among scrub hills covered with dead grass and chunky white boulders and thistles with purple heads. A minaret spikes into cloudlessness behind a grove of dark green trees or large dark green bushes.

The stark openness throws the man's perspective cockeyed.

A military communications tower.

A quick cluster of Bedouin tents: dark brown

The Beatles went through 7 fiery incarnations before arriving where our culture recalls them beginning:

1. The Black Jacks
2. The Quarry Men
3. Johnny & the Moondogs
4. The Nerk Twins
5. The Beatals
6. The Silver Beetles
7. The Silver Beats.

(None of this matters.)

Helicopters hOvered overhead.

An entourage looked on.

A film crew recorded each step of the construction process.

Smithson would ask workers to raise a rock, set it down, ~~rile~~ roll it ~~hear~~ here, there, raise another, set it down, go back, adjust the first, and so forth until the placement appeared exactly ~~wri~~ right, part of a living thing thickening from the earth's skin.

Outcome a glassy black spiral 1,500 feet long and 15 wide stretching counter-clockwise into a vast swath of translucent red water—in Smithson's mind the color of the primordial sea.

road, white shirts, black pants, hands on hips, heads lowered.

The man rotates forward, unconsciously presses the back of his skull into the headrest.

The teen slides a CD into the player: the audience's hum-chatter, the orchestra tuning up, then the bright G major riff and McCartney launching into the history of a band that doesn't exist.

You like Beatles? he asks.

I do, the man says, taking in the wrecked countryside.

They are in a silver Fiat. That's where they are. One of those undersized models that seems like you could upend it with a semi-businesslike shove.

The teen studies the bill as if it were a week-old kitten.

Beaming, he says: Twenty.

Fifteen, the man counters. One for each kilometer.

No, no, says the teen. Twenty. Bad economy. Double-dip recession. Twenty and Mr. Canada get himself car and driver.

Twenty?

Then Mr. Canada king of the thing. Come. I am showing you my wheels.

And one day this happens: the man slips his thumb under his shoulder strap for slack as he rotates in his seat.

Through dust churn, he makes out two rapidly receding figures rushing into the middle of the

It would have been another hue altogether, had there not been those microorganisms flourishing in the extreme 27% salinity of the lake's north arm isolated from fresh water sources by the causeway erected in 1959 by the Southern Pacific Railroad.

Smithson was 32.

This would always be the project he was known for.

Three years later, he would be dead.

Fifty or fifteen?

Khamsa 'ashar. Fifteen. You need car? I have car. You like The Ghost is Dancing?

What?

I've seen so many friends of mine go so photo-less. New Pornographers. Arcade Fire. Sick Canadian bands.

I don't know, the man says, reaching into his daypack, not sure if what he is searching for is still there, the ten-dollar bill which he watches himself produce. I don't have much on me, but I can pay you this.

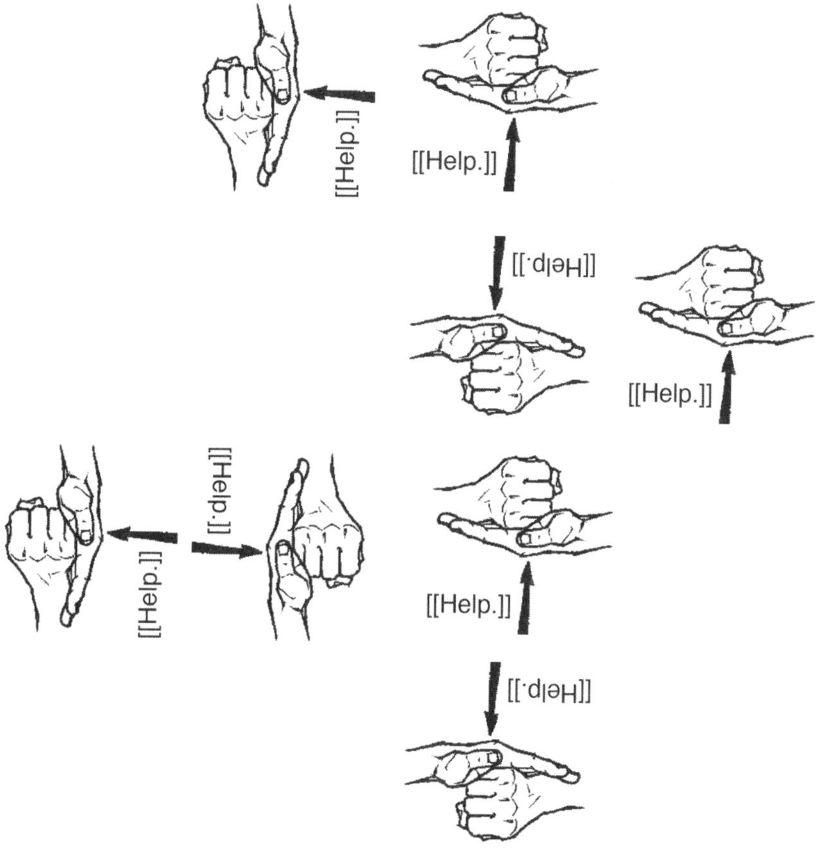

Taxi? The teen laughs. He has thick, slicked-back hair. No cab, no cab, he says. Where you want going?

South. What's south?

Aqaba. Petra. Theme parks for grownups.

Wadi Rum, the man says.

Lawrence of Arabia. Taxi next town over maybe.

How far?

Fifteen kilometer.

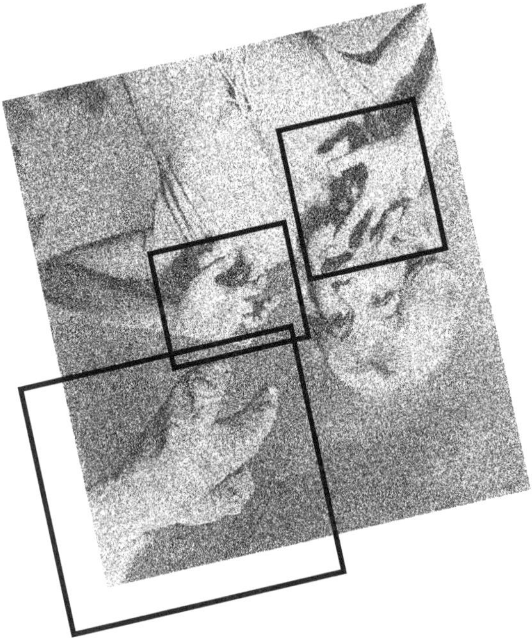

16 July

Or another way of putting it:

Ganglion Cysts: fluid-filled sacs within hand and/or wrist; nicknamed “Bible Bump” in reference to the bygone cure of whacking affected area with The Good Book while holding the culprit flat on table.

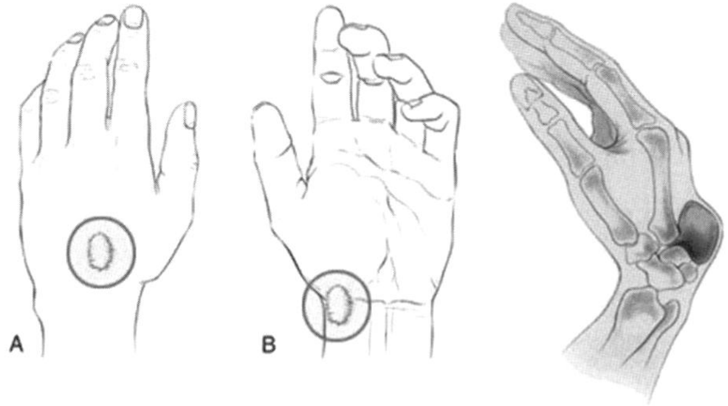

The man tries not to sneak a glance over the teen's shoulder. This is just a normal meeting on a normal street somewhere in the Middle East. This is just another morning, another afternoon.

The man studies his reflection in the teen's sunglasses. There didn't used to be a deranged blondred beard on his face and now there is. He reaches up without thinking to welcome it, asking: You know where I can get a cab?

Remember how mom & dad used to play this one to the point of madness on their turntable and faux wood-grained speakers big as compact fridges? One of you always reminded me of Lennon: wire-rimmed glasses, acerbic wit, hardcore existential insubordination. At some point the following year, you began falling off my radar for months at a time. Then you'd blip back onto my screen briefly, drop away again, out of thin hope write to tell us in your jittery, hyperbolic prose you landed a job in the diplomatic corps. Except a month later these postcards start turning up from increasingly wacked places. Tuscaloosa, AL. Bombay Beach, CA. As if someone had cut the string holding you down at last.

Nerve injuries: crushing, stretching, slicing, etc.

Neuropathy: alcoholic, diabetic, rheumatoid, multiple sclerotic, etc.

onto a main road, unpaved and lined with open-front shops. One sells bicycle tires, nothing but bicycle tires, another nothing but brown shoes.

Four men in dark wrinkled suits and white-and-red keffiyehs curtaining their shoulders stand in a circle in front of a shawarma stall, forking food from plates they hold at chest-level into their mouths and staring at the ground in front of them. They don't acknowledge this other man barging into existence across the street. He halts, panting hard, trying to get his bearings.

You British? asks a teen in a black Beatles t-shirt, black jeans, and black sunglasses grinning beside him.

Panting, the man looks over.

Canadian, he says.

It's the Time of Fire album cover on the t-shirt: John, Paul, George, and Ringo in satin day-glo military outfits. James Dean. Edgar Allan Poe. A choir of the out-of-step among a zeal of flowers and creepy dolls.

Toronto, the teen says. Hockey. Maple syrup. We love Canadians. You making trekking in our country?

Jean Baudrillard, redux: "There is nothing more mysterious than a TV set left on in an empty room. . . . it is as if another planet is communicating with you."

man smoking a cigarette, considering the foreigner as if he were considering something taking place on his TV set.

The man takes the next corner, trying to put complication between him and the shouts. He isn't certain this is how you evade capture. Why would he know such a thing?

What he knows is everything feels flexible.

What he knows is the squall of variation happening around him.

This elderly, gray-bearded guy whistling to catch the man's attention and rubbing his fingers together...for what? Cash?

He wants to say a village, although it could also be a. It could be Syria. It could Lebanon.

The man takes another corner and breaks out

Just give yourself time.

Just give yourself time.

The bewildering thing is that any of us are healthy at all… and then you realize that the feeling is a temporal illusion.

Tendonitis: inflammation of flexible bands of fibrous tissue connecting muscle to bone associated with overuse and/or aging.

17 July

I was ~~slan~~ standing over a teenager curled into herself on the plaza outside the city ~~liba~~ library. I wasn't standing over her and then I was. Maybe she was one of the homeless who nest in and around the building, wander through its stacks, sleep in its reading areas, lounge in its café, bathe in its restrooms. Except her long blond hair was sheeny, her skin immaculate, her jeans fresh dark blue, her pastel pink plaid blouse crisp as the idea of what you will do the day after tomorrow.

None of this happened and outside the sun isn't the sun. Outside, it is a continuous white explosion shooting into you from everywhere at once.

Where is he? He can't see. He stumbles forward, goes down on one knee. Wobbly, he rises, stumbles forward, shielding his eyes with his palm.

He is in an alley. That's where he is. He is in an alley maybe half a dozen feet across, open doorways at uneven gaps, heads emerging as he hurries past.

They aren't threatening, these people. They're just checking him out. That's what they are doing, their expressions mixtures of mild curiosity and suspicion. This young scarfed woman hugging a sleeping baby against her chest. This middle-aged

His lower jaw releases.
The gargly sounds dwindle away.

The man is lingering in a city, not that one, another.

Tang of spicy meat grilling. Ginger and dill.

At the end of the next hallway, another oversized wooden door. He flips the cumbersome lock and staggers back.

Maybe she had somehow fainted in the heat, been swarmed by infirmity. Except her position appeared deliberate, as if she'd simply decided to settle on the cement for a nap.

I kneeled, put down the borrowed books I was carrying, reached over, shook her shoulder.

She didn' respond. Her eyes remained shut, jaw loose, cheeks flushed.

Curious pedestrians began arranging themselves around us. We were trying to calculate if this were one of those false alarms that would embarrass us if we lent it too much importance, or one of those genuine ahistorical calamities over which we should be forming an impromptu community.

The kid starts dry-heaving as if inducing himself to puke, except the man releases the kid's neck from his grasp and slugs him in the forehead and then that stops.

The kid winces as the first pills storm his brainstem.

His eyes open.

The man and he exchange looks.

A minute, and the kid starts making gargly sounds.

A smile edges across his face.

A minute, and his eyes flutter and roll back in his head.

A businessman holding a cup of coffee suggested we alert someone at the information desk.

A Latina in black tank top and hip huggers squatted in front of me. Her tramp stamp, a red heart with lacy black letters frilling across it, said: This is the place. She began murmuring in Spanish what I took to be words of encouragement while running a hand through the girl's hair.

The kid tries turning his head and ejecting the pills, except the man slugs him in the left temple and then that stops.

He holds the kid down by his neck with one hand and clips off the kid's busted nostrils with the other.

Five seconds, eight, and the kid commences chewing, swallowing.

Semi-ground-up white flakes froth between his lips. In the mess the man detects what he takes to be several teeth chips, although he wouldn't want to commit one way or the other. Is this how fighting works? He's impressed. His entire life has been avoiding confusions like this. Now he realizes the feeling is thrilling and shameful and exhausting all at once.

The froth between the kid's lips shades pinkish, pinker, into a gleaming red that matches the blood oozing from his nose.

Someone ~~fo~~ phoned 911.

15 minutes, & two EMTs were loading the teenager into the back of an ambulance. She hadn't roused. She didn't show any recognition of what was happening. It was as if the rest of us constituted fractions of an interesting dream she was contemplating on the backs of her eyelids.

None of this happened and it isn't easy forcing open the kid's dazed mouth. Behind him, the man hears the shouts take a wrong turn. It isn't easy stuffing the kid's mouth full of the pills he squirreled away under his pallet. Behind him, he hears the shouts jostle over themselves and redirect, flooding up the corridors.

The instant jumpstarts again.

floor beside him.

The kid shudders and rolls off the man onto the

The instant arrests.

A soggy crunch follows.

direction of the kid's face.

And next his fist is missling up in the general

Gathers.

He clenches.

his right hand.

clouts long enough to concentrate his thoughts into

The man divorces himself from the incoming

Somewhere far behind him shouts commotion up.

The kid glances over the man's shoulder and back at him.

How about it? he says. We have like maybe two minutes. What do you say? Give up your mortal remains and become art. Can I ask you a question?

Step aside.

You need to chillax, Gavin.

The man tries to step around him, but the kid shifts again, and then they are both on the ground, grappling.

The kid is much stronger than the man supposed. Wiry. Fast. Almost at once he is straddling the man's chest and rabbit-punching him in the neck. The kid grunts and squeaks and chirps as he hits. The man finds the noises distracting. He wants to ask the kid to keep it down. The kid tries to knee him in the groin and catches thigh muscle instead.

Eighteen minutes, and the ambulance was pulling away from the curb, two enormously red-haired guys in baggy white t-shirts and baggy ~~bac~~ black shorts and big unlaced white sneakers ~~flitt~~ floating into my field of vision, smelling like monkey bars, the one on the right asking the one on the left: How much bullets that thing take?

18 July

Robert Smithson: Instead of causing us to remember the past like the old monuments, the new monuments seem to cause us to forget the future.

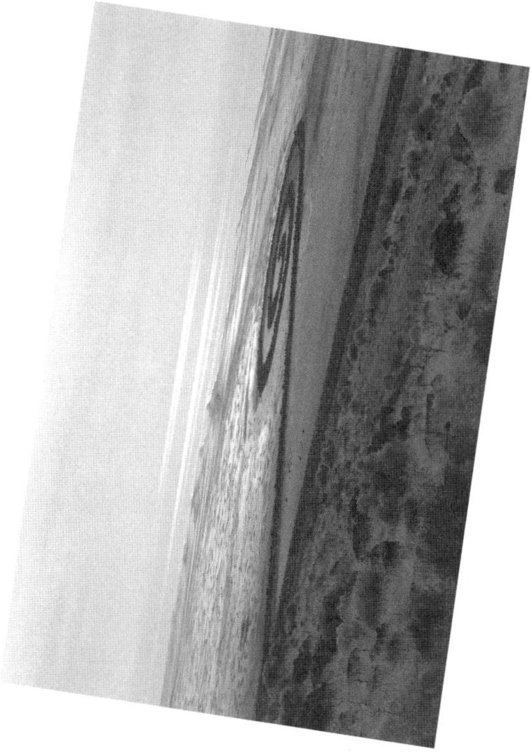

Honestly, dude, he says, you look awful. You want to sit down and talk about this? I'm sure we can blah blah blah.

19 July

The phone rang at 8:03 this morning. It was Doctor A's office letting me know there had been a cancellation and he could fit me in at 4:15 this afternoon.

Hugh left work early to drive me over to the medical center. In the beige and beiger waiting area he failed two People quizzes about celebrity love lives before a large chirpy technician whose knees rubbed together led me into an examination room. She took my blood pressure and history and left.

I'm leaving.

I have come to the frightening conclusion that I make the weather.

Get out of my way.

Or something like that. Truth is truth. Let it come at you. Wham. Seriously. Hey, you want something to eat? You look like you could use some-thing to eat.

Fuck you.

Whatever you ingest has died for you. Which is I want to apologize for the porridge, by the way. It's not easy feeding all those stomachs. Hey, can I share a quick parable with you?

We already did that one.

Did we?

The man tries to step around the kid, but the kid shifts position to block him.

Common misattribution. Cf. Haim G. Ginott's Teacher and Child: A Book for Parents and Teachers (New York: Scribner, 1972): 15.

Doctor A entered, shook my hand, sat down, and took my history again. His left ear wilted noticeably, as if the cartilage on the top had turned to Silly Putty in the sun. He was very tall and sparse and gray, yet his face belonged to someone in his mid-thirties.

He made me flex my wrists in unpleasant ways, palpated my forearms, thumped me with a reflex hammer, scrutinized my fingers and palms.

The less easily he could locate a name for what was going on, the more interested he became.

The performance artist.

He reminds me of you, Jeff, is why I mention him. He didn't want to stay with us, either. Nice guy. Quiet, but nice. Loner type.

The kid glances over the man's shoulder and back at him: You like the threads?

Get out of my way, says the man.

So you can do what, exactly? Embrace the et cetera? Regain your and so on? SOS.

...?

Same Old Story. What would you want to go and do something like that for?

The kid sounds hurt.

For one, the man says, you kidnapped me, is the first thing.

You think this is kidnapping? Hey, you know what Goethe said?

Give yourself time. No matter what you do, age ~~clim~~ comes at you like an open-handed slap. You can think about it all you want, prepare for its arrival, discuss it with friends, but its appearance always shows up as a scandal.

Done, Doctor A told me that everything looked like it should look. Everything looked normal. More or less. We were out of time today, he said, standing up, but he'd like to see me again. There were a few tests he'd like to run.

A few tests? I said.

It's silly to worry about what probably won't happen, he said.

And? I said.

Exactly, he said, reaching out to shake my hand.

almost limp-lumbers into the kid hurrying in the opposite direction.

Well, this isn't good, says the kid, coming up short.

Get out of my way, says the man.

The kid is wearing a diaphanous white djellabah and sandals. His hands are tunneling up into his sleeves. He glances over the man's shoulder and back at him and asks: Shouldn't someone be chasing you?

You'd think so.

Sometimes you've got to do everything yourself. Does the name Tehching Hsieh ring a bell?

20 July

Wince awake, cheek pressed against Hugh's chest. The prickling has spread from my fingertips into my palms and forearms. I open my eyes from blackness to blackness, lie there listening to Hugh's heart pumping in my head, his breath easing up to the brink of a snore and sliding back, catching itself, then he's awake too. We don't say anything. We change positions. His cheek presses against my chest. We change positions, me reversing into him. We change positions, him reversing into me. We change positions and

Before he can choose which way to turn, he has already chosen.

He understands why the new always seems dangerous to some people.

One day lying beneath the leaves, he heard a rustling above him. When he poked out his head to investigate, he discovered a redheaded ponytailed girl sitting up in the branches of a naked elm looking down at him, legs dangling. Her face was unlived in. Neither of them spoke. They inspected each other. They inspected each other. The boy slowly withdrew into his floating.

Another T-intersection at the end of another hallway: The man pivots left because he heard that's what you're supposed to do in a labyrinth and

the street. He would sweep them over him, curl beneath, lie in the mulchy tang with his eyes shut, motionless, noiseless.

First the universe would go away, then his body.

At the top of the stairs, another hallway. He slips off his diaper, chucks it aside, slips on his jeans and t-shirt and sneakers. Why doesn't he hear anyone behind him? He will think about that later.

He feels his heart sparkling.

At the end of this hallway, a T-intersection.

Unlike to lie, there is no primary verb in English (nor most other indo-European languages) for to speak the truth.

I'm shinnying up on him, ribcage to ribcage, stomach to stomach, nose tucked into the crook of his neck, inhaling dank Hughness. I hold on tight. He holds on tight. It isn't comfortable, but that's the way it takes place sometimes. Sometimes that's how you find yourself stalling as morning fades in.

21 July

All the editing I did this afternoon, this evening I undid.

[[Miles Davis: "Sometimes you have to play a long time to play like yourself."]]

The man doesn't know whether it is daytime or nighttime. It doesn't matter. The man doesn't know where he is going, just that he has to keep gaining ground.

Daypack over one shoulder, clothes bunched in front of him, he limp-lumbers up a flight of stairs. Fragments snap out at him. This step. This oil stain at his feet.

What should he do now? He should continue pushing forward. What should he do after that? He has no idea.

When he was eight he used to bury himself under autumn leaves on a hillside in the park across

22 July

Here are the things you try. Putter in the garden. Thumb through the newspaper. Go for a walk. Watch a dim game show. Make lunch. Putter in the garden.

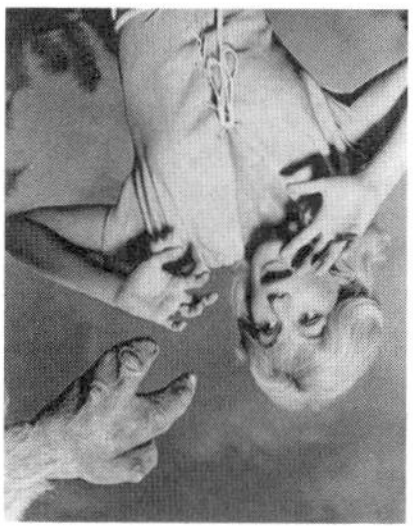

[ ]

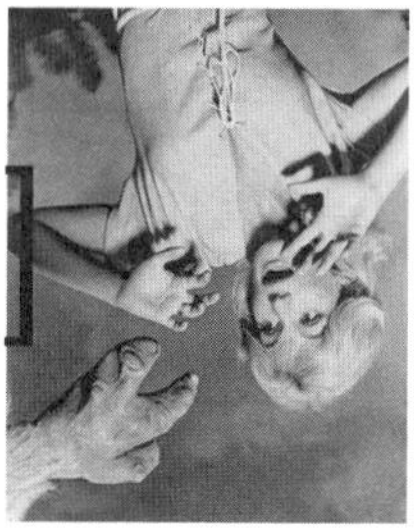

Jake.

Fred.

A moment later, maybe a month, he is up, he is moving.

He is at the door.

He is through it.

Everything was one way.

Now everything is another.

On the far side, a long windowless hallway. A string of fingernail-sized red and green Christmas lights winking along a cinderblock wall.

Watch George Pal's Time Machine, one of Smithson's favorites, a film relentlessly about the metaphysics of slow, stubborn undoing.

Look at Yvette Mimieux drawing back in terror.

Look at the hand threatening her.

When asked which of his movies was his favorite, Pal always answered: The next one.

No: that's not it.

-> shared with me via a few precipitous phone rants at 4 in the a.m. i had the distinct impression you believed you were talking at somebody else, or maybe it didn't matter who you believed you were talking at. in the fall you flew back into classes, picked up where you left off.

Alternative title for this chapter of my life: Self Portrait with imaginary Brother.

Sitting across the kitchen table from Hugh, eating Indian takeout—chicken tikka masala, saag paneer, daal maharani—you try to change the subject when he asks how you're hanging in there, picture what the evening holds, only all you see is an empty parking lot stretching toward the middle of the night.

Here and there among the unconscious, washers and feeders at work, moving in pairs, gruel bucket or piss bucket between them. A linen sack distended with dirty Depends.

The man's back is killing him.

At the far end of the row: an oversized wooden door, the kind that exists in the crusader castles of dreams.

The man watches people come and go.
Marks how many.
How frequently.

Passing into air: that's what he wants to do.

He wants to stray past the edge of conjecture.

-----: his mouth mouthing.

A couple days later you were gone. Thanksgiving ended. You ended. We talked around your name throughout winter break. After that, you became a certain agitation between the words in our emails. When i returned for spring break, there you were again, lying on the living room couch, thumbing through a magazine, as if that's where you'd been all along. i never asked what it was like in that place in Park City. You never volunteered any reports from the front. Mom and dad pretended those months were different months. You took the rest of the year off, hitchhiking southwest in the summer, hiking the Canyon de Chelly, dropping down from Arizona into Mexico and peyote visions, a string of acid revelations you

23 July

This on your voicemail in the late afternoon: I need your wisdom and healing, Anastasia. Frank told me he'd always stand by me, even with this thing on my face. But he went to work yesterday and never came home. I think it's for good. Call me when you get this. Oh…Megan. This is Megan. Call. Okay, so…Call.

I listen to the misplaced message three times over the course of the evening before pressing delete.

Nick. Keith.

Tom.

This is just like life, it strikes him.

The airless room constructing itself: concrete shoebox lit with sputtering gas lamps arranged randomly across the floor and on wooden crates of various sizes which themselves have been arranged randomly across the.

Understated clacks, wheezes, snorts, snuffles.

At the man's feet: his daypack, clothes folded neatly on top, sneakers arranged neatly beside.

Except his knees don't bend right. That's one thing.

Rockwell. Arnhem.

Would you please let me out of the, his grandfather used to say from his bed. If the dreadful lemon sky, seabirds, anyone is thinking about him anymore. I can't seem to find a. Will you look at. If the electrical lines stretching toward shining nothingness across the desert, the scream weather, busy cubist city, turquoise lizard fixed against the rock. If the vitamin-B stink of concentrated piss. The olive groves. The bright splashes of colorful bushes—where? Do you remember the way I. If that's a washcloth he feels. If the reek of donkey shit. Lamb stew in white sauce. If you're going to the lithium, would you please be a dear and pick me up a fork?

Sometimes the pills dissolve before the man has a chance to remove them. Sometimes they don't.

N.B. -> Early model sheets for Wile E. identify him, not as Wile E., but as "Don Coyote," an obvious nod to Cervantes.

24 July

Primordial sea, but also a Martian one. The Dead Sea, on whose southeast shore once lay the cities of Sodom and Gomorra. Ballardian wasteland. Reservoir of blood.

The spiral is a visual relative of the labyrinth, archaic symbol for gradual enlightenment, spiritual evolution, pilgrimage, return home, journey from this world to the next. The image occurs everywhere in megalithic art, from the Newgrange tomb in County Meath, Ireland, to the petroglyphs in Gila Bend, Arizona. In Mycenaean jewelry, it is an object of beauty, a sign of power. In illuminated manuscripts, an object to occasion a meditative state in the viewer, a sign of eternity. In Utah, it evokes 18th- and 19th-century legends about treacherous whirpools that formed in the Great Salt

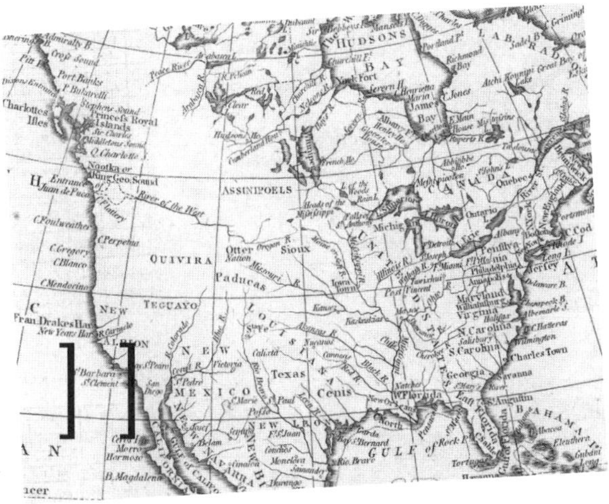

And one day this happens: the man tongues the two pills into the slick notch between his lower jaw and cheek.

Extracts them.

Slips them under his pallet.

The same thing happens again.

Lake, tore boats apart, and vanished as unexpectedly as they'd whooshed into being. Symbol of sun, serpent, wind, solstice, &, at burial sites across the globe, continual change. In pop culture, a device mad doctors employ to induce hypnotic trances in unsuspecting patients. In Op Art, a prevalent design that's nothing save itself. In anime and manga, the manifestation of disorientation and dizziness: cartoon characters' eyes spiraling in their sockets when they become existentially wobbly. In The Wizard of Oz, the yellow-brick road uncoiling from the center of Munchkinland, in contrast to the in-coiling twister that brings Dorothy to Oz—the former suggesting creativity, the latter chaos. In medieval Europe, a strategic military form: stone staircases winding

followers to remember how the soul-killing dictionary of life contained fewer definitions all the time, how only the living can be fully dead. He coached them to see this place always led to that place. Everybody stood on a street corner somewhere, waiting for the lights to change so they could cross, living in the sound of the dead protecting their houses with their own hands, even as those houses went up in flames, even as they chuffed in on themselves in sparkbursts like badly constructed sentences, blackout atmospherics blowing through the fiery wreckage of their predicates.

out the front door in search of fellow dead sons, kindred dead daughters, other dead fathers and dead mothers, dead uncles and brothers and cousins.

First to Chicago, and then Los Angeles and San Francisco and New York. The kid approached pedestrians, intuited their vulnerabilities, graced them with what they needed to believe. Strangers gave over their beatless hearts and, before long, were helping him recruit by learning to identify and approach versions of themselves at the back of cafés, in the locker rooms of fitness centers, the frozen food aisles of supermarkets. The kid flew to Europe. He flew to the Middle East. He encouraged his

clockwise from the ascender's point of view in order to place at a disadvantage attacking swordsmen who were usually right-handed. In Mark Danielewski's House of Leaves, the enormous staircase corkscrewing down without end in that Virginian home larger inside than out. A shape ubiquitous in the natural world, too, from snail shells to scrolls, from the sun's magnetic field extending through our solar system to the 200 billion stars comprising the Milky Way…at the edge of one of whose spiraled arms, the Orion—28,000 light years from the center—rotates an inconsequential baby blue ball that's us, just us.

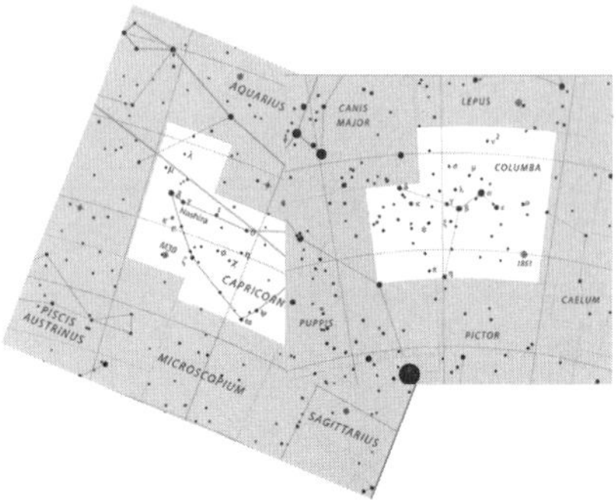

]

father said without glancing up. I am, the son said. I wish you wouldn't talk that way, his cloudmother said. Don't be odd, said the boy's dead father. But the son rose, stripped out of his clothes and skin, draped what was left of him over the back of his chair, and stood there, letting his parents take in what continued of him. Then he turned and walked

25 July

Morning: Blood sample. Urine sample. Test for inflamma-tion. Doctor A calls in colleague Doctor B for consultation.

Afternoon: Ultrasound. X-ray. Electromyographic needles. Doctor A and B call in colleague Doctor C for consultation.

the house. From what he could piece together, his father died in his twenties but never figured it ~~out, and so he continued~~ moving through life as if he had organs and agency. There was how his father stared at his food over dinner, how it was as if he were drifting far above it, peering down, unable to make out what was on his plate. How his father's eyes squinted out from behind a smooth plastic mask, polluting the kid's homework and video games. The look the father delivered his sur-roundings as he stepped through the front door after another day of trying to impair educational mayhem—as if he were shocked to find himself in this foyer again, find he still had a son waiting for him on this side of the curtain. Gradually, the kid's father became the overturned car along the side of the highway, and one evening the son announced at the dinner table: I'm dead, too. You're not dead, his

Robert Smithson: "Planning and chance almost seem to be the same thing."

over the world sense it unhappening, but they don't possess a verb for it. There is the waking. There are the pills. It is as if I were carrying light in my hands, the kid explaining, and the man trudges through a snowstorm at night, except it isn't, except there is a ubiquitous snowglow as if the moon were radiating from within the planet's translucent crust, except it is tropically hot and the snow isn't snow but shreds of paper from all the paperbacks that used to line the store, and the carcasses of bloated cattle lay scattered across the countryside, legs upraised, bellies ballooned.

The kid's father was a substitute teacher in Oshkosh, the kid explaining. Weekends, he worked at the gas station to help make ends meet. The kid's mother worked nightshifts at a local convenience store. The kid saw her for short gray patches in the late afternoon and early evening. He came to know her as the cloud of loneliness birring through

The desert feels like space, not place. Unvaried, sans landmarks, and hence, we believe, an absence of landscape. Because of its apparent featurelessness, no memories gather there.

Evening: You try to watch the news. You try to surf WebMD. You look up and it's 8:11. After dinner (Thai takeout: pad gra prow, brown rice), you try to sit on the deck and un-think yourself. You look up and it's 10:22. You try to listen to Miles Davis. John Coltrane. You look up and it's 11:13. It's 12:09. It's 12:35.

Night (I): Try to brush your teeth and get into bed and sleep and you look up and it's 2:33. It's 3:28. It's 4:10.

Are you god? the coyote asked, looking up at the hunter. They say: Does electricity ever mourn the loss of light? The man reaches for what he takes to be a shopping list magneted to the refrigerator and feels the earth shrinking rapidly beneath him. People wipe him down with moist washcloths, roll him over, change his diapers, roll him back. What diapers? The men with the blood-soaked lips and dark blue double-breasted suits say: What is god, if not the being who brings change? The kid is beside the man, knees cuddled to chest, rocking, explaining that this is what waiting for the end of the world feels like. A black snake sliding across the man's ankles resolves into a loose sock, the hyena snouting his cheek a frightening idea. The voice whispering into his neck says: Untie the knot, or: Untie the Not. The voice says: String quartet.

Rocking, the kid explaining: the Sleeping Beauties are waiting for time itself to run out. Individuals all

and maybe it is the professor and maybe these are others who only look like the student, the professor, and most appear to be unbreathing in steady-state twilight.

Somewhere beyond his skull, the older surely British woman is asking in a low soothing voice if the man can possibly conceive how lucky he is to have reached this shore when so many others are still adrift on the ocean far out in the whirlwind of correction.

Geometric Futura. Humanist Lucida Sans. The various stroke weights of Optima.

Merci.

When he reaches down to tug out the catheter, time skips and he wakes into purpleblack color fields inhabited by men with blood-soaked lips kneeling over him, imparting information. What catheter? The men in dark blue double-breasted suits say:

The desert is a science fiction movie.

Night (II): 5:06. 5:15. 5:22.

We expect a certain degree of differentiation in our landscapes. Colors, shades, verticals breaking the relentless horizontals. The desert gives us something else.

26 July

Exhausted, you try to get out of bed. Shower. Make breakfast. Waterpik. Brush your teeth. Edit. Thumb through the newspaper. Make lunch. Edit. Try to stroll up City Creek Canyon with Hugh. Read. Sit across the kitchen table from him, hands effervescing, eating Mediterranean takeout—baba ghanooj, hummus, falafel, dolmas, basmati rice—and try to let the evening sloth by.

Tomorrow morning you will get out of bed and do it all again.

wrenches and time skips. He wakes to discover himself lying on a pallet on a cement floor among a sea of other people lying on pallets—fifty, seventy-five—and the large space they inhabit is warm and stuffy and dim and chalky and something smells like sleep. The man believes he is dead and they are coming to hoist whatever is left of him into a coffin. He attempts raising his head and time skips and he is sitting upright on his pallet like a rag doll, legs spread, chin on chest, people placing their hands on him, on his biceps and back and neck, spooning flavorless gruel between his lips. The man focuses beyond the fluster of fingers and knuckles and maybe recognizes one of the students curled into a fetal position. Maybe the professor in her suit, now crumpled, flat on her back. Maybe it is the student

27 July

By the time we arrived in Salt Lake City, the Spiral Jetty had already forgotten itself. During its construction, Smithson believed the lake was receding. In fact, the water level was low due to a short-term drought. By the time he delivered his lecture at the University of Utah on January 24th, 1972,

He struggles, trying to shake off the kid's henchmen, except the world is already flashing blue to cobalt, blue to indigo, blue to black stall and float and hum.

He wakes into the midst of another skirmish: palms cradling his head, two more tiny pills disintegrating at the back of his throat. The man chokes and

advocating a mediation between ecology and industry by means of recycling such culturally dismissed sites as open-pit mines into earthworks, his own was several inches beneath reddish slosh. By the time the band from Hoboken named in the sculpture's honor released its debut album, Tour of Homes, in 1985, the thing itself had been submerged for nearly fifteen years. It would remain that way for fifteen more, specter of the original quivering a few feet below the lake's surface.

The other steps in front of him and squeezes the hinges of his jaws until the man's mouth is bullied open.

And the kid says: Return to your heart.

And the circle responds: Return to the delta waves.

And the kid says: Everyone is everyone.

And the circle responds: Everyone is everyone.

Amen and amen, says the kid.

Amen and amen, responds the circle.

And with that the kid advances quickly, snaps the two pills far back on the man's tongue, and steps away.

The man gags, gulps involuntarily, and the pills are gone.

He bucks, trying to lift himself out of the chair, except the heavyset men clamp down harder.

stairs or down are back again, hovering on either edge of his peripheral vision.

The kid says: Everywhere is everywhere...

And everything is everything, says the circle.

The kid says: There is hope...

But not for us, says the circle.

The kid says: Blesséd is he who expects nothing...

For he shall never be disappointed, says the circle.

One of the heavyset men steps behind the man's chair, reaches around, and with his massive arms braces the man's forehead and upper chest so that he can't move.

28 July

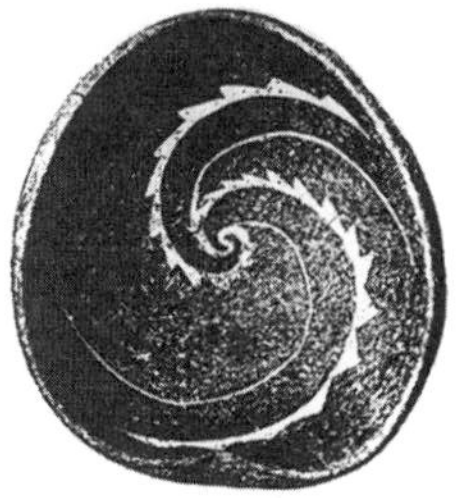

Double-spiral on ceramic bowl. Serrated edge represents clouds. Four-mile Ruin, AZ. Circa A.D. 1380.

Faces cocked toward the invisible ceiling, they wait for the hits to roll in.

Clarendon, designed by Robert Besley in 1845, was used heavily during World War I by the German Empire because of its elegant readability.
Thank you.

The man, who first assumes the turbulence running through him has to do with the scene he is witnessing, gradually comes to understand it really has to do with the fact that the two heavyset men in white shirts and black pants who dragged him through a hall and either up a flight of cement

i worry about you almost every day.

(it depends on the day.)

Which is to say i want you to be happy, is all, when i think about what i want.

i want you to understand sometimes the best revenge is a well-lived life.

Because the truth will set you free, says the kid.

But not before it is finished with you, responds the circle.

Klonopin? DFW: infinite jest?

The kid says: Blesséd are the tired ...

For they shall soon drop off, intones the circle.

Lorazepam? Nietzsche?

And with that the kid rises, reaches deep into the right pocket of his faded Levi's skinny jeans, and extracts a fist that fans open to disclose two tiny circular white pills.

Ativan?

Palm extended, he says: Welcome to the Sleeping Beauties.

Welcome home, choruses the circle.

Oxycontin?

Each congregant follows suit, placing with devotional care two tiny circular white pills she or he has produced from pocket and purse upon his or her tongue and dry-swallowing in unison.

Ecstasy?

Sublingual morphine?

29 July

William L. Fox: The predominance of unrelieved sunlight at relatively high altitudes and the subtlety of color in the Great Basin lead the untrained eye to fall off its subject matter. Early pioneers sometimes wrote about the Great Basin as if it had no vegetation whatsoever; the spectrum of color was so narrow that they just couldn't see the sagebrush, shadscale, and dry grasses stretching out before them.

Roland Barthes: "A writer is a person for whom language is a problem."

people have always had it within themselves to find a way to etc., etc.?

That history's real lesson is how the world is today will absolutely, positively not be how it is tomorrow?

And/or that future humans will therefore someday look back on us, here, now, with a mixture of dumbfounded awe, deep-structure exasperation, and unadulterated loathing in the face of what we allowed to happen?

Ecolaborator = Ecolaborator.

We approach the [~~Spiral Jetty~~] with our visual expectations already askew, already thrown into ~~tao~~

doubt,

and so we experience it without convention—or, closer to the point, with the idea of convention always bracketed, always foregrounded precisely in its contingency and instability.

platform to reveal a gun pointed at your face: an either crazy optimism or a willful cluelessness?

And but which, all said and done, is pretty much to say, the kid deep inside the rush of his own voice, do you believe when events get too weird or frightening or extravagantly incomprehensible that the human psyche just tends to sort of shut down, block out the menace, squeeze shut its metaphorical eyes while clapping its metaphorical hands over its metaphorical ears and starting to respond to said threats with a veritable flood of vacant platitudes about hope, triumph over adversity, how things have always sorted themselves out in the past, how

30 July

Doctor A should have ~~caleld~~ called by now. Unless, obviously, there has been a mis~~fake~~take at the lab; unless there has been trouble with the postal system; unless the results have arrived at the doctor's office, but have been mis~~plice~~placed; unless the ~~dr.~~ doctor has been running beHind ~~lotly and nit hod z ch~~ lately and not had a chance to get to them; unless the results have been negative and the doctor hasn't ~~sea~~ seen any ~~k~~ need to be in touch with you right away; unless the results have been positive and the doctor mista~~KE~~kenly believed he has been in touch with you when he hasn't.

by these obtuse organics surrounding it, especially if what it is being told to do doesn't make a whole bunch of sense with regard to its own existential prosperity—at which juncture humans will commence facing massively lopsided competition as earth's dominant species…

And but which, taken together, is pretty much to say, summarizes the kid, do you believe our kind has evolved to manifest one of two reactions before threats not perceived as imminent—the onrushing eighteen-wheeler, the lion in mid-leap, that man in the mackintosh turning around on the subway

No sign of sleep.

31 July

By the time Jeremy and Jennifer commenced the commotion of choosing colleges, the 2002 Winter Olympics had fussed into town and Salt Lake City had begun ripening from cultural backwater to comfortable urban zone populated with ~~descen~~

decent bars and

bistros, and energetic indie movie and music scene, and a swellingprogressive population, much to the aboriginal Mormons' chagrin. ~~(They refer to themselves as LaterDay Saints, or L.D.S.; Hugh calls them L.S.D. because, Hugh~~

What about that one?

Because there's this corollary, then—viz., that the gap between human IQ and robot IQ is lessening unremittingly and inconceivably.

Which means, not to beat around the bush, we are swiftly approaching a technological singularity whereby one day in the next, oh, fifteen or twenty years, in some corner of some campus somewhere in probably like Finland or somewhere, some artificial intelligence will with an electronic flinch blink into self-awareness…and immediately start wondering (at the speed of light rather than at the relatively hebetudinous chemical speeds meat brains can muster) why it should always do what it's told

3 a.m.: (mixed) review finished. No sign of Claudia.

When dropped into the end of a sentence, the ellipsis can inspire a sense of melancholy, longing, deferred or impeded desire, a trailing off, a faltering, the gradual loss of mass and substance, an unwillingness or inability to continue.

it's also known in the trade as an aposiopesis, a becoming silent.

the blink of an eye a reductio ad absurdum concerning the very nature of combat—all of which would be as if nothing, of course, compared to the possibility of two nukes detonated in a single day in two different cities...

Bang, says someone behind the sweatless man.

Bang, a voice to his side says.

And but so, the kid presses on, what about Moore's law, Larry?

What about, which is to say, the postulation that the quantity of transistors which can be placed inexpensively on an integrated circuit will double every two years, give or take, an assertion that has proved to be the case for more than half a century?

If the man feels capable of imagining that, with an amount of plutonium the size of an apple, you can create a manmade star at the intersection of two streets in Manhattan.

If, not to put too fine a point on it, the question about nuclear terrorism isn't whether or not it will happen, no, but where, when, and how staggeringly.

That a single such device detonated in the middle of a medium-sized metropolis (call it Philadelphia; call it Austin) would within one second evaporate every school, train station, bus stop, theater, office building, restaurant, shop, home, newspaper stand, car, bike, fire hydrant, skateboard, signpost, streetlight, tree, bush, trash can, dog shit pile, weed, and art or natural history or other museum housing all manner of treasure, not to mention one million people.

That such an instant would nullify each and every thing our species once took for granted about military strategy and tactics, poof, actualizing in

~~points out, they believe, among other extravagances, Native Americans descended from one of the lost tribes of Israel, that god lives on a planet near the star Kolob,~~

~~which the prophet Abraham first observed through magical seer stones Joseph Smith later used to translate the Book of Mormon from Reformed Egyptian[sic] into English, and that when~~

consequences of overpopulation arguably being the eventual replacement of democratic by authoritarian governments.

Achtung, says the elderly couple in unison.

That the current economic system comprises one big fat global Ponzi scheme based on crazily excessive credit, with the result of said system having nowhere to go but headlong into a titanic hebejebe unraveling that will intensify as natural resources peter out and alternative energies fail to replace them in time.

That we're all living in a let's call it a Wile E. Coyote Moment—already having sprinted off the cliff, holding a sign that reads Gravity Lessons, pointy ears drooping, the notion just beginning to begin to sparkle behind our nonplussed eyeballs that we're well and truly fucked?

That the most difficult thing about a nuclear bomb isn't how to make it go off—anyone can do that—but how to keep it from going off.

~~good male Mormons buy the farm they will receive their very own planets to inhabit with their very own sister wives and spirit children . . . nice work, Hugh says, if you can hallucinate it.)~~ By the time Jeremy and Jennifer prepared to disperse into their own lives, Hugh had ~~expen~~ expanded the

Chuck Jones knew precisely what he was doing when in 1948 he created his retelling of Camus's Sisyphus myth designed to teach kids over and over that in the end breathing doesn't work.

Ecophagy, one student says.
Ecophagy, says another.

If, the kid asks, the man furthermore believes humans are ten thousand times more common than they should be, according to the rules of the animal kingdom, and need to produce, as a consequence of their exuberant overpopulation, as much food in the next forty years as they have in the last eight thousand.

And/or that every American has between two and three hundred energy slaves standing behind him or her doing the work he or she takes for granted.

And/or that laws regulate interactions between humans and that the higher the population density, the more frequent such interactions become, and hence the growing need for yet more laws to regulate said interactions, and hence one of the

bookstore into the building next door. The girl who was no longer a girl had made her first two films.

And by the time the Spiral Jetty re-emerged (this go-round owing to a bona fide drought, courtesy, most likely, of incipient climate collapse), the idea for her third had presented itself: a short documentary exploring her accuring awareness that Smithson's signature work didn't only change from year to year, season to season, but day to day, hour to hour, second to second, an Impressionist's perfection, depending on the texture of the light, how it veils, what it stresses, the level and tincture of the water, the quality of the clouds, the consistency of the atmosphere, the person you were when you observed it then and the person you were when you observed it then, which was, needless to say,

Smithson's specific point: that all experience of his sculpture is by nature ~~braxen~~ brazenly haptic, brazenly full-body sensory involvement with space and place; that you can't so much look at the Spiral Jetty as

sure, and kid asks if he furthermore believes in the proliferation of the Africanized honeybee and/or that we as a species are already standing in the pith of a water crisis that everyone seems to be repressing the awareness of. Goodbye, Las Vegas.

If, the kid continues, the man likewise believes no water, no sanitation; no sanitation, hello disease, desertification, pan-famines.

The inexorable advent of factory farming, the great Pacific garbage patch, ocean acidification, fish contamination, increased crime rates and warfare as a result of diminishing resources, and/or a new ongoing Mass Extinction Event that is in the process of putting the Permian-Triassic to shame.

Plastic shopping bags, the cute Japanese woman says under her breath.

The man glances over at her for help.

be in and among it, which is to be in and among landscape. And when it finally reappeared, it was no longer composed of black basalt in sharp relief against a rose swath, but was well on its way to becoming a vaguer thing altogether, a shrunken crystalline-encrusted spinal column, a monstrous fossilized ammonite curled on an immense salt flat.

The waterline had crept several hundred feet south. The earthwork had sunk into a spectacular brittle whiteness.

The image tricked the eye into believing it was viewing, not a salt flat at all, but a stunning ice field extending outward, perspective all catawumpus.

Look at you waking up, says the kid.

Okay, the man says. I get it. Sure. I wouldn't want to put a precise year on it or anything, but, yeah, right, I guess I do.

Deforestation? the kid asks. Do you believe in deforestation?

His grandfather would in his last years go bounding through a sentence toward the final punctuation mark with confidence, only to stumble across the deep cavity where the noun should be. I'm going out to the, he would say. Could you please open a. I think I need some. Some. Some.

Is deforestation a category of belief?

Everything is a category of belief.

The man answers that he guesses he does, yeah,

This has exactly what to do with believing in god?

All you have to do is answer the question, the kid says.

What question?

You know rocket science? This isn't it. Which do you believe, assuming total world oil reserves at 1.25 trillion barrels and consumption at 85 million barrels per day, that the estimated depletion year will be 2057, more or less, give or take?

A person sitting six feet away from you, the thought passes through the man's body, you're seeing one billionth of a second ago.

The fully-realized conceptual project looks precisely like the world. That's why ikea is so special.

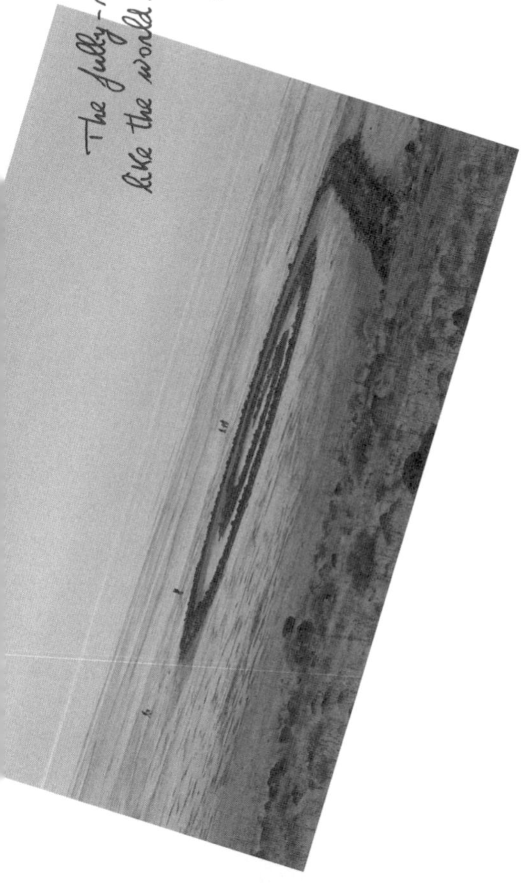

The man tries to calculate the kid's tone's irony quotient and comes up short. He glances around at the others in an attempt to locate some shared theme or themes among them. They all seem tired. They all seem dog-eared.

No, the man says. I don't. To answer your question.

How about the Hubbert Curve? Do you believe in the Hubbert Curve?

...?

Okay, says the kid, to put it another way: do you believe that production arcs of non-renewing resources approximate a classic bell curve and that, when the peak of production is passed, production rates will enter a state of exponential decline?

All at once the man isn't clear whether the kid is speaking the same language he is or an asemic version of it.

[[Jean-Martin Charcot: "Theory is good; but it doesn't prevent things from happening."]]

Viz.: 10,000 tons of rock.

Viz.: The system is built to fail.

1 August

Viz.: Most people experience the Spiral Jetty as a photograph, a remote representation, which is to say they don't experience iut at all…yet can only know their lack of experience if they have already experienced the other thing.

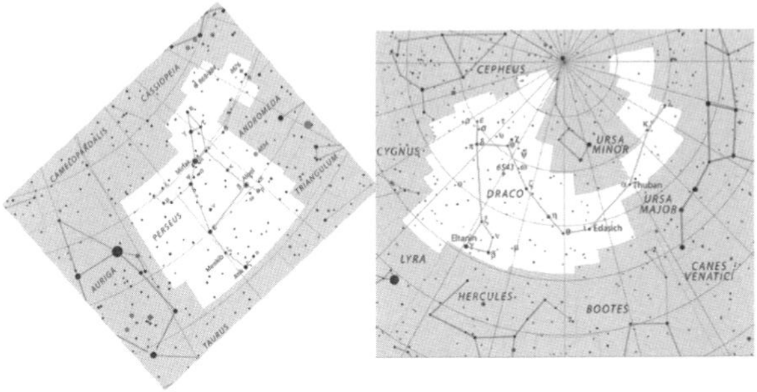

The kid, seated directly across from him, is asking something and the man feels everyone here is living inside a broken clock.

Do you believe in god? the kid is asking.

The man stares at the kid's inflamed harelip. The cute young Japanese and the older surely British women look at the man like a memory. The Indian or Arab or Mexican guy examines the tips of his sandals. The black hyperbolically sideburned guy fingers the dimple in his chin abstractedly. He is the one smacking his gum too fast.

Haven't we already had this conversation? the man asks.

That was private, Ron, says the kid. This is tribal. You've got me mixed me up with someone else. I'm not that guy. I'm this guy.

to the sweatless man the guy is really a woman. Somebody gives off the scent of hair washed with a minty product. There is an elderly couple leaning into each other, holding on. There are people sitting outside his line of sight. There are small noises behind him.

In the semi-darkness he can distinguish a single wall, the wall with the boarded-up windows in it, but not the other three, not what he assumes to be the other three, and so infers the room is extensive. A warehouse. A bunker.

There are a trio of what he would postulate to be college students of indeterminate origin whose faces are still too poreless and fleshy with residual baby fat to possess compelling features.

Four or five sputtering gas lamps arranged randomly around the floor and on wooden crates of various sizes which themselves have been arranged randomly around the floor.

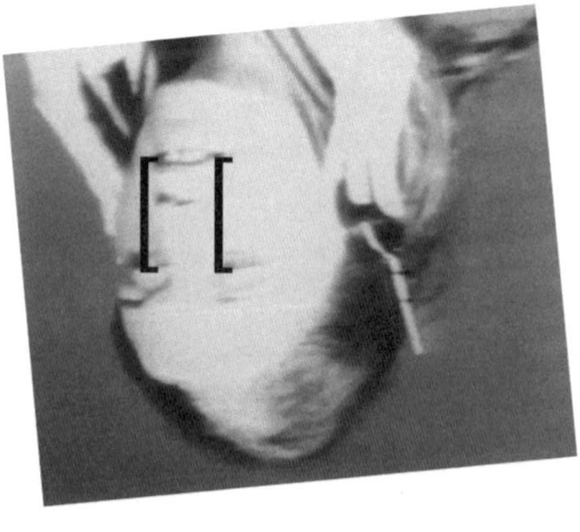

2 August

Hugh and I sit side-by-side in examination room fog.

Across from us Doctor A with his wilted ear sits next to Doctor B with his psychedelic Santa-faces surgical cap sits next to Doctor C with his see-through hair.

Their expressions convey empathy, awkwardness, preoccupation, detachment.

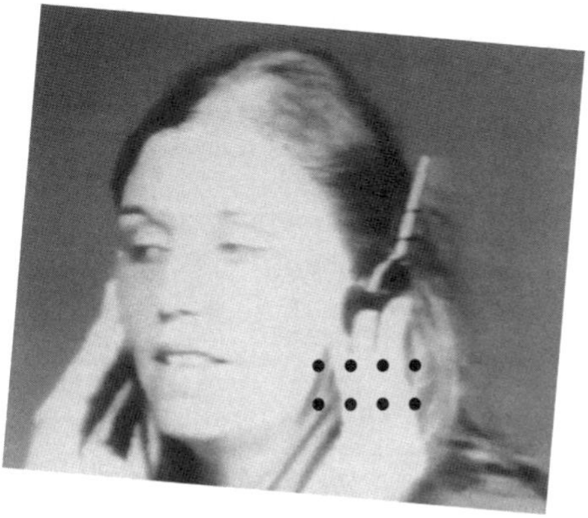

Doctor A has just finished explaining my tests have come back negative, but not negative in an ~~espr~~ expressly negative sense.

There is a clean-cut guy with a lime green golf-ing shirt tucked into his khaki Dockers and two-toned sneakers, who should be teeing off at a Palm Springs resort in ten minutes and then it occurs

The one i remember is the
one that drove you to the hospital, me at the wheel, mom shotgun, you doubled-over in the backseat like somebody just sucker-punched you. We'd collected from college the day before. Dad was still at work, mom & i on our way out to pick up fixings for a couple of
her outrageous Thanksgiving pies when i realized i had to pee. So i trotted back into the house, down the hall, & into the bathroom--without fully registering that the door there was almost shut. You
must've thought we'd already left.
Your little sister couldn't understand what she was seeing: you hunched over the sink, shirtless, cutting a jagged heart into your belly, bathroom all white tiles
& shiny red trickles. Thanks for the memories. i know: that sounds too mean by half. it's supposed to.

ME
Not negative in an expressly positive sense, either, you're saying.

DOCTOR B
That would be another sense altogether.

HUGH
Because you're saying you have to be careful. As doctors and so forth. You're telling us don't get our hopes up.

DOCTOR C
I believe I'm speaking for all of us when I say we wouldn't want to put it that way.

front seat of a Land Rover in the Tanzanian bush. Somebody is wearing powdery perfume. There is a youngish Indian or perhaps Arab or Mexican guy, sans socks, with his legs stretched out in front of him so far that he is resting on his tailbone, who should be attending a meeting in Seattle in which software is being discussed.

The man's grandfather, the man recollects out of nowhere, was sane and then that changed. At the dinner table once during a family visit he shouted for the chickens to be set free, except there were no chickens and everyone was eating Chef Boy-Ar-Dee spaghetti and meatballs and the sweatless man was a seven-year-old boy at the time.

black pants dragged him through a hall and either up a flight of stairs or down.

The ages of those occupying the chairs, he would say if someone asked, range from late teens to late seventies. Most are in their twenties, early thirties. There is a tall thin black guy with short gray hair, a short gray goatee, and hyperbolic sideburns, who should be in a jazz band. Somebody coughs the way people cough in boardrooms and churches. A cute young Japanese woman with spiky pink hair, matching pink leggings, and a pink polka-dotted sort of tutu with lacy black trim, who should be in a hip fashion shoot featuring stuffed animals and live snakes. Somebody is smacking his or her gum too fast. There is an older surely British woman with long white hair worn in a ponytail and a long chinless red face who sports a multi-pocketed safari vest and matching zip-off safari pants, who should be boosting herself up into the

[[Marginalia functions as parasitic traces of autobiography.]]

ME

What way would you want to put it?

HUGH

You're saying we need more tests.

DOCTOR B

We're out of tests. We've tested what's testable.

DOCTOR A
(DOCTOR A looks up at the ceiling, waiting for a metaphor to visit him, then, tropeless, down at me.)

What happens next is pretty much to remember never run after busses.

DOCTOR C
Because the thing is? Basically there'll always be another one behind the one you miss.

DOCTOR B
Unless it's three in the morning and that's the last bus of the night. Or, like, you're in Maine or something.

This thought happens to him and he remembers a ride in the backseat of a car. What car? He thinks taxi and can't recall whether it was the ride in from the airport or a different ride. Whether it was really a taxi or something else. The circle in the middle of which he is sitting is composed of fifteen or twenty chairs, each occupied. He remembers a green sign snapping past in the otherwise achromatic highway emptiness. The chairs remind him of electric chairs in vintage tabloids.

To the best of his knowledge, all of this has to do with him.

He remembers the ride in the backseat of a car and the toes of his sneakers scraping along a cement floor as two heavyset men in white shirts and

will you. We've kept them waiting long enough. Let's bounce this place. Let's pull the pin.

The man sits on a stiff-backed wooden chair in the middle of a circle of stiff-backed wooden chairs in a hot shadowy room smelling like what is the word turpentine. No: petroleum. A hot shadowy room smelling like petroleum.

It must be night: that's what he would guess, only he notices the windows are blocked with large rectangles of cardboard duct-taped over them. No: plywood. The windows are blocked with large rectangles of plywood fastened down with one-inch aluminum strips.

HUGH

So you're saying we'll just have to wait, is what you're saying. ~~Wit and sea~~ — Wait and see.

DOCTOR B

We're saying sometimes things just break, I think is what we're saying.

DOCTOR A

(Standing. Reaching out to shake my hand.)

Before we go, do you happen to have any questions for us, Amy?

3 August

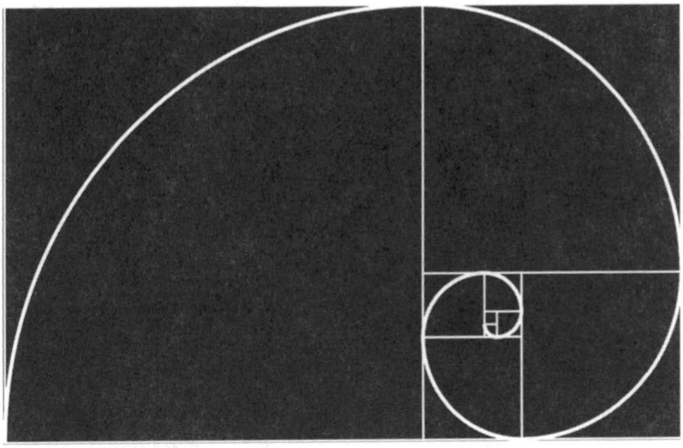

The Golden Ratio, Divine Proportion, or Ø is perhaps the most perfect number in mathematics, equal to the square root of 5 plus 1, divided by 2, or: (Sqrt(5)+1)/2 = 1.618033988749895. Which means nothing until you realize da Vinci's illustrations in De Divina Proportione have led

color of a pomegranate filled with warm tap water. The kid stands. They consider the sweatless man while he drinks, then the man with the scar across his forehead takes the pomegranate-colored mug from him, sets it on the desk with the small arrow engraved on a copper coin pointing toward Mecca, and rejoins the kid.

Okay, says the kid. You look like you're ready.

For what?

Some people want to meet you. Help him up.

want something to drink? I bet you want something to drink.

I wouldn't mind that beer.

We don't have any beer. You ever get the sense time is failing all around you?

Water?

Happens to me with alarming frequency. So weird. Get the gentleman a glass of water, the kid tells the man with the scar across his forehead.

Face loose, the man with the scar across his forehead steps into the bathroom and returns a minute later with a scaled-down coffee mug the

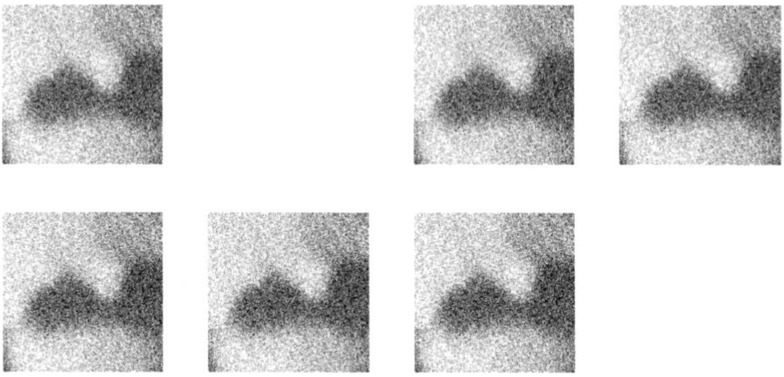

scholars to speculate he incorporated the Golden Ratio into his paintings; his Mona Lisa, they say, employs the Golden Ratio in its geometric equivalents. Dalyí explicitly used it in Sacrament of the Last Supper, the dimensions of the canvas those of a ~~gosle tect~~ golden ~~wrectan~~ rectangle, while a huge dodecahedron, with edges in golden ratio to one another, is suspended above and behind Jesus. Mondrian drew ex~~tinct~~ensively on the Golden Ratio in his Neo-Plasticist paintings, & research by perceptual psychologists indicates human faces proportioned according to the Golden Ratio are said to be more ~~beau~~ beautiful than those that aren't. In geometry, the Golden Spiral is a logarithmic one whose growth factor is related to Ø: the Golden Spiral gets wider

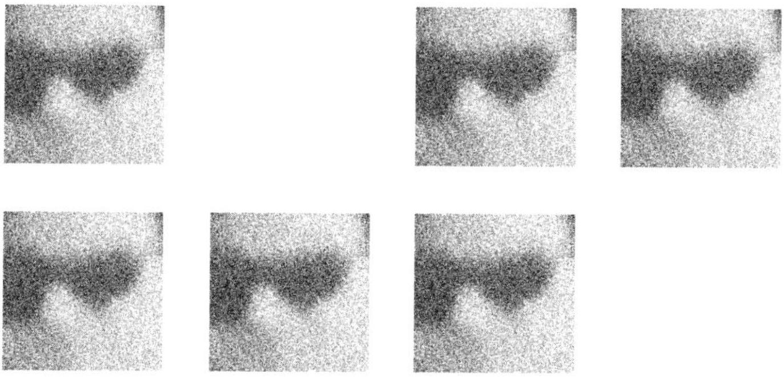

professors. No: it's two of the man with the mirror attached to the end of the aluminum pole at the barricade. His arms are folded across his chest and he bears a scar across his forehead that looks like someone went after him once with a hatchet.

You want to pee? the kid asks. Take a quick shower?

I'm good.

How about that glass of water?

The man asks: What kind of hotel is this?

You think this is a hotel? That's interesting. You

You thought you were at the university?

You were talking to her. On the wall by the main gates.

How would you like some kick-ass kabobs? Falafel, maybe? You know what mezze is?

You're saying she wasn't a professor.

Tapas, Middle-Eastern style.

What?

Mezze is tapas, Middle-Eastern style. You ready? You look like you're ready.

For what?

Savings Time. Let's plug it in, the kid says, rising. Let's get this party started.

Well, this is certainly getting predictable, the kid says from the edge of the bed.

The man's head jerks up.

How long? he asks, rubbing his neck.

You don't want to know.

The kid, the man sees, isn't alone. Face loose, the professor is standing beside him. No: it's two

(or further from its origin) by a factor of Ø for every quarter turn it makes. Regardless of how large the spiral drawn becomes, the ratio of its dimensions remains constant. Many ~~firms on nomen~~ forms in nature APPROXimate it, from the whorl pattern of sunflowers to pinecones and hurricanes, ram horns and fingerprints, the flight path of a fly closing in on its target.

4 August

[[Bad day.]]
[[Bad day.]]
[[Bad day.]]
[[Bad day.]]
[[Repeat—]]

lettuce leaves for decorative purposes? We don't have any.

What?

How about if I offered you a beer, is what I'm saying. How about if I offered you a foamy beer in a frosty mug?

Only you don't have any.

Of course we have some. Bud? Heineken? Maybe Amstel. I think we have Amstel.

What did I do?

In what sense?

To get your attention. What did I do to get singled out?

What a fucking backwater, the kid says, looking around as if he can see through the walls. I wouldn't get my hopes up about the Amstel.

That woman you were talking to—who was she?

The kid returns his focus to the non-sweating man, asks: Woman?

At the university. The professor.

Why did you follow me all the way to another country?

What makes you think this is another country?

This isn't another country?

There are plenty of people out there who'd give their right arm to be saved, Matt. Literally.

I want to be damned.

We're just like each other. We're part of the same family. You hungry? I bet you're hungry. Hungry and thirsty, but slightly more hungry than thirsty. You want a burger?

I'd love a burger.

Fries, an ice-cold Coke?

Yeah.

Lots of catsup, right? Mayo? Maybe a couple

By the time I started recording Smithson's earthwork's unhurried undoing, controversy had already erupted around the question of ~~weathe~~— whether or not to start buttressing it, restoring its original personality by the addition of new rocks. If not, art specialists warned, over the ~~coars~~ course of the next decade or two Smithson's enterprise would simply melt into the landscape—something, and then something else; here, yet gradually otherwise.

By the time Jeremy started work as a ~~Untied~~ United Nations press officer in New York, Jennifer as a fine arts journalist in Paris, my sense of them progressively proud, passionate, and distant, as it should be, the Canadian firm Pearl Montana ~~Exploit~~ Exploration & Production had submitted

Scott. Names. Whatever.

The man you met is madly interested in what you're saying, but he already left.

The kid misses a beat, pushes forward: What if I'm not asking? What, is what I'm saying, if it's something else I'm doing?

Like what?

Maybe I'm just being polite, too.

Which is you're saying what?

What, is what I'm saying, if we both just get up and leave? Now. Which it's not a question, except pretend it is. What would you say next, I'm saying, supposing that's what I'm getting at?

What room? For a moment the man can't tell. He can't identify anything around him. He rubs the back of his neck, considering the washcloth on his leg as if it were. When he raises his chin someone is.

What do you say? the kid says.

He is wearing a semitransparent wrinkled white cotton shirt with a nehru collar over a pair of faded Levi's skinny jeans.

What time is it?

Midnight. Give or take. Jesus, are you a twitchy sleeper or what?

What?

Motion addicts.

I'm a not-knowing junkie, the sweating man says.

You and me, we've caught a bad case of difference dependence. Our world has to be different yesterday, or it doesn't feel like today.

I've caught a bad case of please get up and walk out that door.

Look at you waking up.

Pretend you never met me. Pretend you met someone else. This other guy looks precisely like me, maybe, only isn't.

You're you, Mike.

I'm not Mike.

an application for drilling two ~~explana~~ exploratory wells from floating barges in the Spiral Jetty's proximity. The state may have received nearly 3,000 e-mails opposing the idea of restoration, including a statement from Smithson's widow, Nancy Holt, herself a pioneer in site-specific public sculpture, but here's the thign: Smithson himself would have loved it.

For him those grungy oil rigs, that Heraclitean flux, that forever wearing away into difference, would have meant the apotheosis of his aesthetics of entropy, the consummate embrace of the countless quiet catastrophes taking place around us, always and all ways, if only we could be awake enough, brake enough, to pay attention.

5 August

Information is an overrated concept.

Tell me one thing: what do you have to lose?

Everything.

Too late. You know what we have in common,
you and me?

Exactly zip.

After religion went away, nobody knew what to
say about death.

Can I ask you a question?

Shoot.

What country is this?

We're both motion addicts.

Do you believe in god?

What? the sweating man says, sincerely surprised by the question.

Do you believe in god?

Who believes in god?

Exactly.

You're trying to convert me? That's what you're doing.

Believing in god is like claiming Keebler elves run the universe with help from Santa Claus and the Easter Bunny. The evidence is precisely where?

You're not trying to convert me?

Of course we're trying to convert you. You thirsty?

You paid off the driver?

Thirsty and hungry, I bet. But slightly more thirsty than hungry? Am I right? People like you, me. Loose affiliations. Tribal thought.

Did you know the word <u>family</u> derives from the Latin <u>familia</u> meaning <u>servants of a household</u>?

Detail from well-known birthing scene. Snake, anthropomorphic figures, spiral. Hurrah Pass, near Moab, UT. Circa A.D. 1100.

(William L. Fox: <u>The only hope for survival of the rock art is obscurity.</u>)

6 August

Because, as a boy with easy access to New York City, Smithson spent hours in front of the dioramas and dinosaur displays at the Museum of National History.

Give me one good reason I should listen to you, he says.

Because you're all beat up, says the kid. Look at you. Aren't you all beat up? It's like you just walked through a carwash in a business suit.

That's a reason?

We're on the move here.

Which people?

What do you mean which people?

Which people are receiving?

Admit it. You're curious.

I can't express how un-curious I am. This is me just being polite.

Everywhere is everywhere. You could use a friend. You've been sleeping alone in this place for... how long you think you've been sleeping in this place all alone for?

I got in maybe an hour ago.

Try five days.

The man misses a beat, pushes forward: Really?

Let me ask you something. Be honest, okay?

Five days?

Becoming.

Becoming what?

We're not following you. You're following us. You want some more pills?

I'm just this guy who got on a plane one day.

You're curious.

The sweating man looks up, looks down. Rubbing, says: I possess zero curiosity.

It's huge, says the kid. Ask me a question.

I don't want to know anything I don't already know.

Go ahead.

The sweating man turns over the kid's sentence.

It feels as if someone has airbrushed away parts of him.

Because the Great Basin, which stretches from the eastern side of the Sierra Nevada to the Wasatch range (at the foot of which spreads this, spreads us, spreads Salt Lake City), fingers north into Oregon and Idaho, south to the

Because he planned to become a zoologist, and his father, who started out as an auto mechanic and ended up as a mortgage and loan executive, built a mini-museum in the basement of the family house in Clifton, New Jersey, to exhibit his son's collection of live reptiles, preserved specimens, fossils.

of a non-site?" by saying: "i like the idea of quiet catastrophes taking place."

Arizona border, is the highest and driest of the American deserts, the last empty tract on 19th-century maps of our continent, the only zone in North America ~~whirr~~ where all waters drain inward to evaporate in the intense heat and wind.

Because the section of U.S. Route 50 that ~~biselects~~ bisects it is ~~inck nameni~~ nicknamed the Loneliest Road in America.

~~Becuase for Smithson the difference~~

We've got something we want to show you.

The kid's harelip appears pinker and puffier than usual. Tired. Raw.

Why? asks the sweating man.

It'll change your life.

The kid misses a beat, pushes forward: You're thinking people always give you that line. This is different. You don't believe me. I don't blame you. I'm nothing, the sweating man says, rubbing, feeling deficient in distinct outlines. What am I to you?

Everywhere there are these nodes of, um, happening, you could call them.

I'm just this guy.

in one interview, Smithson answers the question "What exactly is your concept

Because someone pointed out the difference between art and entertainment is this: art is that which deliberately slows and complicates perception to allow you to re-think and re-feel structure and experience; entertainment deliberately speeds and simplifies perception so you don't have to think about or feel very much of anything at all.

7 August

Robert Smithson: For my film—a film is a spiral made up of frames—I would have myself filmed from a helicopter—from the Greek helix, helikos, meaning spiral.

8 August

The ~~form arachni~~ architecture of the spiral is such an

can't say, with a grainy yellow lightfog.

Rubbing the back of his neck, he considers the washcloth on his leg as if it were a large withered beetle. When he raises his chin someone is sitting on the edge of the bed biding his time while the sweating man tries to catch up with his own mind.

Serviceable, the kid says. Not great, right? Still.

The sweating man chucks the washcloth onto the polyester cushion beside him. Rubbing, he says: You followed me here?

organic, ancient, and over-determined one that it unfolds, not into meaning, but into an emblem of semiotic possibility.

Associated with almost anything, it attracts a rabble of connections.

9 August

Robert Smithson: Planning and chance almost seem to be the same thing.

10 August

Intensity makes a place to return to.

The goddamn sweating and his goddamn jittery left foot.

Presses the washcloth against his hot face, lungs clenched as if a noseless demon were closing in, reaching out for his collar.

His head jerks up.

What room?

For a moment the man can't tell. For a moment he can't identify anything around him. The lamp in the corner saturates the atmosphere, where, he

11 August

~~Smithson was born in Passaic, New Jersey, on 2 January 1938. Harold, his 9-year-old brother, had died of leukemia 2 years earlier, so in effect Smithson was an only child who wasn't an only child, a replacement for a child that was, in a sense, never there. His parents, Susan and Irving, moved back to Irving's hometown, Rutherford, shortly after Robert's appearance.~~

~~Irving would die of cancer at 67 on Friday the Thirteenth, April, 1973, three months before Smithson's death.~~

~~His mother would die of can~~

Call from Doctor A's office. He wants to see me in an hour.

Something's come up, his receptionist said.

where he would go. He doesn't know where he is. He doesn't know if he is in a city. He can't remember its name.

So he runs cold water, saturates a washcloth, returns to the couch, presses the washcloth against his hot face.

Waits for the nausea spreading across the back of his tongue to leave him alone.

Waits for the goddamn sweating to stop.

12 August

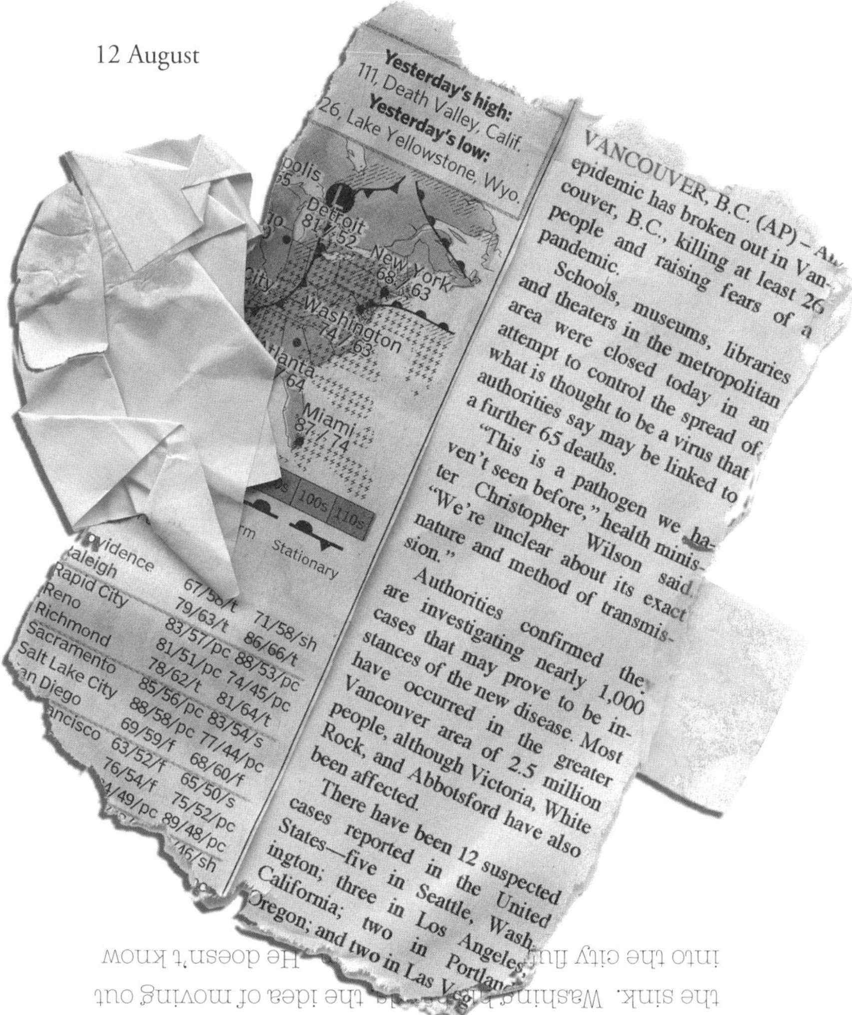
Yesterday's high:
111, Death Valley, Calif.
Yesterday's low:
26, Lake Yellowstone, Wyo.

Providence	67/58/t	71/58/sh
Raleigh	79/63/t	86/66/t
Rapid City	83/57/pc	88/53/pc
Reno	81/51/pc	74/45/pc
Richmond	78/62/t	81/64/t
Sacramento	85/56/pc	83/54/s
Salt Lake City	88/58/pc	77/44/pc
San Diego	69/59/f	68/60/f
San Francisco	63/52/f	65/50/s
	76/54/f	75/52/pc
	49/pc	89/48/pc

VANCOUVER, B.C. (AP) – An epidemic has broken out in Vancouver, B.C., killing at least 26 people and raising fears of a pandemic.

Schools, museums, libraries and theaters in the metropolitan area were closed today in an attempt to control the spread of what is thought to be a virus that authorities say may be linked to a further 65 deaths.

"This is a pathogen we haven't seen before," health minister Christopher Wilson said. "We're unclear about its exact nature and method of transmission."

Authorities confirmed they are investigating nearly 1,000 cases that may prove to be instances of the new disease. Most have occurred in the greater Vancouver area of 2.5 million people, although Victoria, White Rock, and Abbotsford have also been affected.

There have been 12 suspected cases reported in the United States—five in Seattle, Washington; three in Los Angeles, California; two in Portland, Oregon; and two in Las Veg

The sweating man's room smells like petroleum and he sits, rises, walks to the window, pulls back the drapes and there is nothing on the other side, nothing at all, just a blackout curtain behind a blackout curtain behind a blackout curtain, so he steps into the bathroom and turns on the faucets at the sink. Washing ... the idea of moving out into the city flu... He doesn't know

13 August

~~Don't get me~~

Don't get me wrong: it isn't that I don't know this is a world where it is possible for you to reach for your purse on the back of your chair in a café down in the Village and find it vanished, for a young housewife to take a nap on her couch in Sylacauga, Alabama, and be awakened by a three-pound meteor smashing through the roof.

It's just that our brains are wired to minimize such knowledge, blue-pencil it from species cognition.

It's just that we need to be reminded over and over.

Qibla direction? He lifts his head, scouts, locates a small arrow engraved on a copper coin pointing toward Mecca affixed to the upper left-hand corner of the make-believe-wood desk. He walks over and rubs it like a good-luck charm. Returns to the couch. Rises. Slides open the closet door, browses, slides closed the closet door. Turns the water on and off in the shower stall. Returns to the couch. Absorbs the room, takes in its densities and peculiarities. Stands. Sits. Stands. Rides the elevator down to the weakly illuminated lobby. The only person there is the tall receptionist minus a personality sitting behind the counter. He doesn't glance over when the elevator doors open. He doesn't glance over when the sweating man steps out, makes a slow circuit, steps back on.

14 August

no back support and reads because nothing else
comes to mind.
For more information, kindly dial 244.
Our room service staff will be happy to take any
special orders for our beloved children.
Qibla direction is placed on disk in your room.

Did you ever have the feeling our parents were uncomplicatedly nice people who may have loved us, but just didn't like us very much?

Okay, no, that's not quite fair. They were simply committed to living their lives, of which we were simply a very small part, a fact simply impossible for us to take in.

15 August

Landmarks create accounts, chronologies. ~~That's where I did this. That's where I did that.~~ In a ~~noun~~ non-landscape (in a landscape, i.e., where human gesture is absent, where there is no middle ground, time), it is difficult, if not impossible, to construct narrative buildings to house our ~~loves~~ lives in. And so we hover. Drift.

16 August

Hugh and I drove to REI this morning to pick me up an array of gloves.

through the metal detector. The alarm goes off but no one pays any attention.

At the front desk he asks the receptionist where the bar is. The receptionist, a tall bald man minus a personality, tells him there is no bar.

No beber, he says, grim. Kein trinken.

The sweating man's room smells like petroleum and he can't decide if the air-conditioning unit is cooling anything or just sucking in warm dry air from outside and strewing it.

On the desk he finds a directory in a pale blue plastic binder. He sits on the polyester couch with

The heaviest ~~piar, blok mount~~ — pair, black mountaineering mittens, for ~~sleet~~ sleep. A lighter pair, steel gray, to wear around the house and on errands. A pair of bike gloves, crimson high~~lites~~lights on a charcoal ~~blackgow~~ —back-ground, for greater dexterity ~~wen~~when working on the touch ~~sad~~ pad and ~~clay~~keyboard.

The frattish salesclerk with judiciously mussed ~~air~~hair and ~~pad~~ bad ~~base~~ case of ~~agnree~~agreeableness wore a pair of nitrile surgical gloves as if everyone had always worn, would ~~alre~~ ——— always wear, nitrile surgical gloves while operating a cash register in big box retail stores.

17 August

Or another waY of putting it:

no one pays any attention. The sweating man steps puts through his daypack. The alarm goes off but x-ray machine with his chin. The sweating man man in a white shirt and black pants indicates the as if lit by a single 40-watt bulb. Another heavyset Inside the main doors the marble lobby is dim

lifts. to the end of an aluminum pole. The striped bar the undercarriage of the car with a mirror attached steps out of the darkness and inattentively inspects A heavyset man in a white shirt and black pants

self. Nothing happens. They sit there. The sweating man repeats him-

He assumes they have arrived at someone's house, realizes it is a small hotel, realizes it is not the small hotel where he made reservations, not the one whose address he gave to the driver back at the airport.

He leans forward to explain this to the driver's thick neck, using as few words with as few syllables as possible. Like Tonto. His prostate feels enlarged or. The driver stares straight ahead as if t seat-ing man isn't speaking.

18 August

Hugh: consider what we can get used to.
How fast.

19 August

Tell yourself you have this to do, and then you have to do that, and it's as if your body can let itself evade memory for a while—the ~~tome~~ time it takes, say, to edit a couple frames, ~~here~~ hear yourself asking Hugh how so-and-so's relationship with so-and-so is progressing down at the bookstore—and then the recog~~in~~nition flies in from the edges.

looks up again he is rolling through some sort of in-between zone, neither city, nor desert: flat rocky ground interrupted by thistly brush interrupted by stone fences interrupted by a short row of more cinderblock houses interrupted by more flat rocky ground.

Nobody is outside. Nothing. No livestock. No cats or dogs or stars in the sky. Everyone is dead.

The sweating man has lost the names for everything.

He will take a short nap. When he wakes up he'll feel sharper, and that's when the taxi pulls up to a barrier, a simple striped horizontal bar across the road or maybe it is a driveway.

Bang: you're back.

You're here and absolutely nowhere else.

20 August

Doctor A supplied me with a pharmacy in a plain white paper sack. His strategy, he says: treat the ~~symptemati~~ symptoms. If my hands and feet sting and burn, stop them from ~~singing an~~ stinging and burning. If I feel worn down, pep me up.

Copper, cranberry, sand puink. Lavender, lilac, teal. Mint, plum, soft milk chocolate.

21 August

How do you remember to forget?

yoctosecond he believes he is in Indiana, Salt Lake, he has never left, no and his right foot won't stay still.

The taxi tortoises through unlit back streets lined with one- and two-story cinderblock buildings. Rebar juts from unfinished upper floors. The sweating man's calves are sore. His biceps. He deliberates upon his troubled foot and when he

Ludwig Wittgenstein: "One of the most misleading representational techniques in our language is the use of the word 'I.'"

The sweating man's eyes were shut.

His face tilted toward the ceiling, acutely intent on listening to the innumerable hearts beating around him.

Warm dry wind hits him through the rolled-down taxi window. Ten o'clock at night, ten-thirty: that's what he would guess. He has to squint to keep his eyes open. What he perceives is lack. He can't tell where atmosphere ends and sand begins, whether he is looking at desert or sky, flatness or dunes.

A green sign with white Arabic lettering on the top and white Western lettering on the bottom flies out of nowhere and vanishes.

It could be thirty minutes It could be an hour. Then he is on the outskirts of a city. The glary lights of a Pizza Hut and a Fuddruckers. For a

22 August

<u>Film #4</u>

<u>Title: Trace</u>

<u>Bloack & White</u>

<u>Running ~~Tomb~~Time: 22 minutes</u>

<u>(No Shot Longer Than 20 Frames.)</u>

Following Tehching Hsieh through ~~tje sturts of~~ the streets of lower ManhatTan the last few ~~mout~~months of his Thirteen Year Plan, the non-performance performance where he made art but didn't exhibit it publicly. Henever knew I was there.

I engineered the entire setup through his handlers In the city, its remarkably easy to be the ~~anoun~~anonymous tourist with the ~~fami~~ fanny pack and ~~canla~~ camcorder ~~tl~~ tucked~~onto a starefont in a into a storefront in the vVilla~~

into a storefront in the Village, recording a grainy gray glimpse of him cradling a ~~cpgf~~ coffee cup in a café window on ~~Lagau~~

Stubby men with five o'clock shadows clutched at his elbows, attempting to steer him through the crowd toward the exit. The sweating man shook them off, but they were determined. They kept coming at him. They kept pawing and pushing. At some point he gave in. Confused, achy, he let himself be carried along, secretly admiring their fortitude, their gameness for pulling this shit flight after flight, day after day.

He tried to imagine into them, but couldn't. He couldn't see himself from their point of view.

The airport smelled like tar and cardamom and then he was back in the movie, this time watching himself from a crane shot: the messed-up tourist hustled through a dense sea of bodies at an alien airport.

Claudia pointed out, curled in the papasan chair across the living room (my writing desk in front of the window looking onto a shady street lined with 1950s-era apartment blocks whose first-floor walls are spray-painted with colorful graffiti), plugged into her iPod, Weissbier in hand, that i'm spending way more time reading and rereading this thing than i am composing my next review for Berliner Kunst, whose deadline is ... let me check here ... 54 minutes away ... let alone getting interesting with her. Busted, absolutely, but

Which is to say John Cage: "Everyone is in the best seat."

Which is to say William Gass: "He knew why one normally didn't look. There were too many things to see."

~~Lob~~ Laguardia Place, surprisingly ~~livel~~ lonely, sealed against the xoam commotion around him, glaringly aware of going unnoticed. Or standing by himself outside The Film Forum, smoking, summer daylag ~~flda filtering~~ daylight faltering into evening, about to ~~stop into by a toket~~ stop in to buy a ticket for Last Night, that understated indie from 1998 in which a ~~grope~~group of people wonderswanders through Toronto in the ours leading up to the end of the world, sans explosions explanations sun ~~grow~~glowing larger & larger in the sk

24 August

How, when your 6, you believe love is one thing. How, when you're 16, you believe it;s something else. At 26, you think its too dumb to even think about. & next, for the rest of your life, you catch it flickerting from one thing into another, an earthwork of the changling heart.

American, or the only American who couldn't pass for a European, Australian, South African.

Moving through customs, he made eye contact with the screeners to show them he was a good guy who had scratch to hide.

A frosted-glass door slid open. He stepped into chaos. People were shouting at him, grabbing at his daypack. Why were people shouting and grabbing?

he would settle for two, he would settle for three, just enough to get him back on the ground, nothing more, except he keeps tapping and keeps watching himself tapping until the thumping on the folding door next to him commences, the flight attendant asking if he's all right, the folding door starting to rattle, a little at first, then more deliberately.

The plane began its controlled fall through the night. The sweating man lifted his shade and was startled to see perfect blankness, blackness, his own spirit face peering back at him.

The airport a small rectangular amber glow hanging in an immense lightless warehouse.

Where is the world?

He stood in line for his visa in a hall alarmed with fluorescent light, guessing he was the only

25 August

The Frost, they're referring to it as.

26 August

~~To rehearse: Smithson was born in Passaic, New Jersey, on 2 January 1938. Harold, his~~

27 August

35,000 feet. He would guess 35,000 feet, although there is no way to tell. He angles into the lavatory, engine drone inside him, outside him. Taps the bottom of the brown vial, trying to will a couple more colors and shapes into being. Not many, he wouldn't need many, he's not greedy or anything,

Yet i can´t name a friend
you had in college, not
because you didn´t have
any, of course, but because
i wasn´t one of them.

Let's say this is the nurse. Let's say this is Staten Island, circa 1943. Let's assume that someone (friend, coworker, cousin) snaps this fewer than 2 weeks, 10 days, before she draws back the hospital curtain to reveal a ~~march~~merchant marine in a metal-frame bed.

He drifted for 5 days in the middle of the Atlantic with 3 other seeseamen before a Navy destroyer spotted their lifeboat.

The nurse became someone else for the first time in her early 20s when she decided to move from a cotton farm

35,000 feet.

Okay, good, says the man, hanging up. Good.

We're all ears, the professor says.

We're listening, says the kid.

Are you listening? says the man. You're not listening.

There'll be no fucking off, says the kid.

Fuck off? the professor says.

It's not a turn of phrase, explains the man. I want you to fuck off.

We'd like to be part of your life, the professor says.

We'd like to share, says the kid.

That's just a turn of phrase, says the professor.

I do, says the man.

You don't mean that, the kid says, hurt.

going through, says the kid. You're angry. Upset. Who wouldn't be?

You feel overwhelmed, says the professor. That's what they call human nature. More or less.

I'm not going through anything.

Maybe we can help you with what you haven't been going through, then, the kid says.

We know how big it feels, says the professor.

You can trust us, says the kid.

We'd love to talk, the professor says.

We're talking, the man says.

We'd love to talk not over a phone, says the kid.

Can I ask you a favor? the man says.

Beer, the professor says. Tea. Whatever you'd like.

The man says: Leave me alone. Seriously. I don't need your help. I'm completely capable of failing on my own.

outside flat, soggy Ganado, TX, to college in Austin, and then on to NYC in search of the city's frantic hope.

She becomes someone else again when she parts her lips to greet this new patient, unaware in 6 summers shell be living with him in a north Jersey suburb in a little redbrick house with a large white magnolia out front.

In 12 giving birth to the person who will write the phrase: giving birth to the person who will write the phrase.

In 40 missing her recently late husband with an energy that makes words into light and noise.

In 50 being wheelchaired through the front doors of an assisted living complex to exhaust her last 6 months in the world.

Here, though, she's unaware of any of that, unaware the DNA (another sort of rattlesnake spiral) burrowed deep inside a single cell somewhere within her left breast has begun to ~~b;sdjes blo~~blunder.

Of getting where you're not, says the kid. The upward trend. It's a nice hotel. Not great. You could call it serviceable, right?

You know where I'm staying?

Except for the smell. Holy god. We're with you, is what I'm trying to convey here.

The man's prostate feels enlarged or maybe it's only that he has to urinate.

When he dies, the world will end: blink.

You're not, he says to the maybe it is the kid. You're obviously somewhere else, or you wouldn't be phoning.

We're in your room, says a second voice on the other end of the line, a full-toned female one, so full-toned it might be a male voice, but the man goes with female. Check your closet.

The man says: The professor.

The professor? repeats the professor.

Maybe we can help you with what you've been

Her eyes. Her pose. Notice how it's only pride's flush at being who she is, where she's come from, where she's arrived, her consciousness of the sunshine's slant on her face that you'll detect.

(The Spiral Jetty is a device designed to focus your attention on what isn't there.)

28 August

7 of 12 people at Fourth cookout showing symptoms.

Sorry about ditching you.

You know what one of the main factors in the upward trend of animal life has been over the last two billion years?

The man returns to studying himself in the full-length mirror. His beard needs trimming. Nobody would deny that. And it appears as if he has adopted one of those judiciously mussed hairstyles when in fact it is nothing more than his hair needing washing.

What kind of service? the man asks.

The power of wandering, says the kid, says the person the man takes to be the kid.

What?

29 August

And this morning: Canada: 7626. California: 2887. Arizona: 1963. Nevada: 940. Utah: 832.

30 August

Because you can't say you <u>look</u> at The Spiral Jetty. You have to say you <u>watch</u> it.

Acknowledge time's process in the perceptive act.

The longer you do, the stronger becomes the dislocation of every everyday thought.

I don't want to be part of it. What is it? I don't want to be part of it.

You can sense it out there.

I can sense exactly zip.

The voice misses a beat, pushes forward: You like your room?

The man surveys, considering. His room is too diminutive because in hotel rooms outside the States you have to plot your course before leaving bed. You have to concern yourself with your limbs. The bathrooms are designed for affiliates of a more compact species.

What pills? the man says. I don't take pills. It's hard to sleep. Isn't it hard to sleep? The information in your head drives you into the city.

31 August

Sometimes I Google other Alanas to discover what their lives aren't like.

I rename them.

I feel them renaming me.

2 September

Since the mid-1800s, about 500 towns have come and gone in Nevada.

You can be part of it.

You wanted to tell me there is something special going on. That's why you called me.

The voice misses a beat, pushes forward: There's something special going on.

The feeling, the man would say, of needing to invent a new language in order to start speaking about something you have never seen or heard before.

We? he asks.

Maybe we can be of assistance. Maybe we can help.

Is this the kid? he asks. This is the kid, right?

he hadn't noticed, he didn't know what he wanted and now he does, so he replaces the receiver in its cradle and steps into the bathroom.

The phone starts ringing. The man lets it wear itself out while he works with the special attachment on his nail clippers. The phone starts ringing. He folds down the special attachment, slips the clippers back into a pocket on the outside of his daypack, returns to the chair, lowers himself (scooping the black dress under him to avoid wrinkling and bunching), and lifts the receiver.

Don't hang up, the voice says.

I'm not hanging up, says the man. I'm sitting here.

You need more pills?

The man remembers the plump woman crawling in the video. Was that yesterday? He enjoys looking at art he doesn't know how to look at. The feeling of being reduced to a five-year-old before something on a wall or on a page or in air.

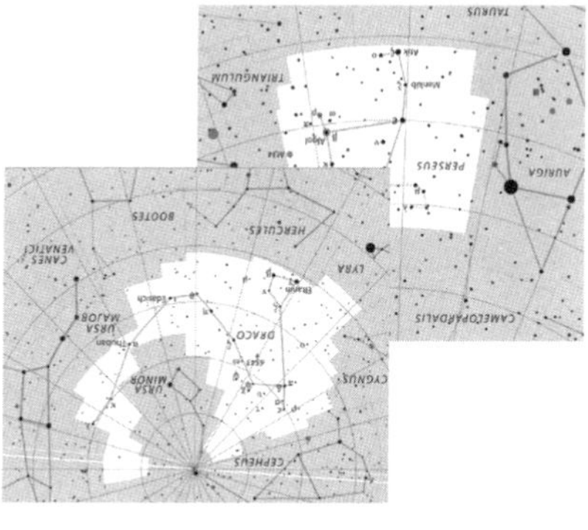

Hello derives from the word hallo (1840) via hollo (ca. 1400) (also holla, holloa, halloo, halloa), an exclamation originally shouted in a hunt when the quarry was spotted. The use of the word as a telephone greeting originates with Thomas Edison, who expressed surprise when he picked up for the first time & listened to what he had wrought. Alexander Graham Bell initially wanted to use the nautical ahoy as the telephone greeting.

[[See what happens when you begin tugging at a fact? it's all Theseus & thread.]]

3 September

Film #6
Title: Bare
Color; cartoonized.
Running Time: 13 minutes
Videoing German artist K. (just K., in a salute to Kafka), 25 years old, hair impossibly blond, face impossibly acne-wounded, approaching strangers in their 20s on the streets of Seattle, San Francisco, L.A., offering to purchase everything on them (jeans, shirts, coats, watches, wallets, rings, chains, knapsacks, keys, sex toys, cell phones, chocolate bars) on the spot.

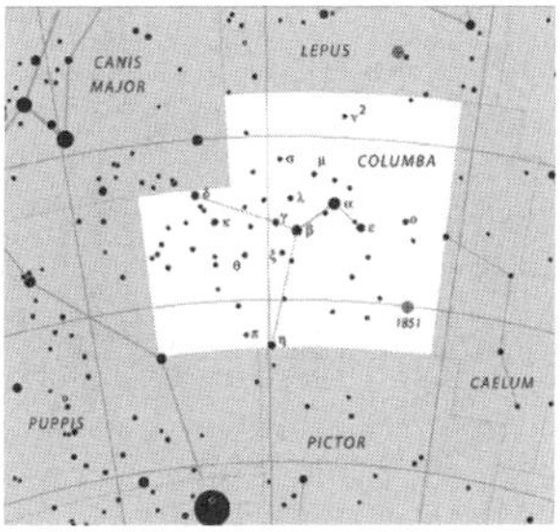

[Hello?]
Given its lack of clarity, its grayness, the man
concludes it might be originating from the U.S. or it
might be originating from the room next door.
Hello? it says again. Hello?
Examining his free hand, it strikes the man
that his cuticles need pushing back, they're a mess,

Michel Butor: "All the maps you have are of no use, all this work of discovery & surveying: you have to start off at random, like the first men on earth; you risk dying of hunger a few" miles from the richest stores.

Their expressions as they take in his proposal.

How some ~~yurn~~turn and walk away.

How others, smiling conspiratorially, let themselves be led into nearby department stores, coffee shops, clothing boutiques.

K. ~~weig wid lw~~ waiting near the changing areas or restrooms while they strip out of who they are and shrug into nondescript replacement clothes with which K. has provided them.

He doesn't say anything. He just listens. No one says anything on the other end of the line. It isn't uncomplicated figuring out if the person placing the call has already hung up, if what the man is hearing is the vague rustling of interstices, or if the person placing the call is still there, and what the man is hearing are the person's electrons disturbing space-time.

Examining his free hand, turning it over, rubbing its fingers with its thumb, the man stands by for the present situation to become a future one.

At last, a tiny fuzzy voice says into his ear:

K. returning to his temporary studio at the end of the day. Coating his subjects' possessions in gold paint. Arranging these objects on a series of black plinths with the care and precision of a model builder.

How, set out like that, the displays evoke taxonomical research, funereal rites, museum exhibits, pyramid treasures, acts of cultural anthropology.

K.'s subjects' actions speaking for themselves, the interior of each exchange able to be inferred by the exterior. We buy

The phone is ringing.

The phone has been ringing, the man would estimate, for two minutes.

He has a difficult time finding an appropriate way to occupy the chair. He tries to summon up how women in dresses do it. He can't get his mind around the mechanics and yet, repeatedly, women do it. They make it look congenital. For the first minute, the man assumed the ringing would stop, that the person on the other end of the line would give up and go away. He looks down at his hands in his lap and realizes his wristwatch is missing. Dismayed, he looks over at the desktop, the side table, the chest-of-drawers, and reminds himself, and reaches out and picks up the receiver.

ourselves off shelves, they are saying. We are what we own what we carry on our backs and in our pockets.

How, even as their gestures ~~seam~~

their gestures seem to argue for that position, they also intime intimate its opposite: unclothed, the subjects paling into semi-absences…and yet their bareness simultaneously hinting that they're so much more than what stuff has made of them.

Their possessions returning us to the commerce that produced them rather than to the people they might be.

Their bodies persisting as powerful contrary traces.

the phonebooth-sized elevator he holds his breath. The water in the hotel goes off at random. In the middle of the night, the afternoon, he rotates one or both of the knobs on the sink and nothing. Five seconds, three hours, and the water comes back on in a gurgling belch. When he asks about this at the front desk, the receptionist shrugs without looking up from his paperwork.

The shrug means the receptionist doesn't understand English. It means the man shouldn't be so impatient. It means nobody has anyone or anything for long.

This is the first time he has tried it on. He concentrates on the light material brushing his belly. The air coming up between his legs.

It doesn't bother him that the black dress won't zip in back.

Physics is physics.

He sits in a stuffed chenille chair the color of bologna. Had someone asked, he would have described the chair as Neo-Nursing Home. He studies himself in the full-length mirror affixed to the matching wall beside the cabinet housing the TV.

It's fascinating—how the material falls, how his hairy legs appear to be someone else's.

He can't stop paying attention.

In the hallway, the elaborate faux Oriental rug smells like asparagus piss. Every time he walks to

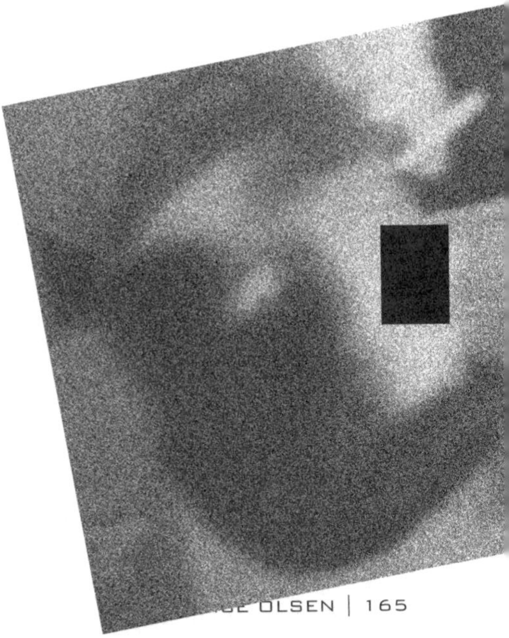

4 September

Or maybe it's not viral, ~~rjw qxgie—~~ the anchorwoman with the Ionic-capital hairdo is saying.

Maybe it's bacterial, fungal, something else altogether.

~~Brood~~casts whirr about nothing else anymore. Plane crashes, oil spills, financial monstrosities, serial rapes, Hollywood gossip, baby crib recalls, misbehaving Congressmen, obstinate peace talks, unwinnable wars: they're gone.

Now it's all breaking news and special reports and flustered graphics, even though no new news has in fact broken, there's nothing special to report, there's nothing spinning to show for the last 24 hours.

They're ~~lal~~ working around the clock, the achor-woman is saying they're saying.

They're doing everything they can.

Usually the man keeps the dress in his daypack. He simply likes to know it's there. Sometimes he takes it out and presses it to his face to inhale what is left of her, faint, fruity, dwelling in the fabric. It feels like he is in a corny movie and it doesn't matter, which sometimes he lays the dress out next to him on the queen-size bed or bunches it up on the second pillow at night. Sometimes he hugs it to his chest while he chases sleep.

5 September

The parts of our brians that analyze shapes and measure distances evOlved to help us survive in forests, navigate the mixed terrain ~~fo~~ of African plains. Step out of your 4WD along the rock-scattered shoreline of The Great Salt Lake, the Spiral Jetty frozen in the salt before you, water so blue it shocks, mountains harsh, uncanny land~~scope~~scape void of ~~very~~

everyone except you, and

you will intuit immediately that you are genetically

ill-equipped to perceive any of this correctly.

this place never feels like home. It never feels steady.

You have to think about it. you have to actively manage your ~~sinces~~ senses

The kid is gone and the professor is gone and the steps where they were sitting are empty.

The man slows, taking this in, speeds up, continuing to walk in the same direction, scanning the vicinity, trying to take in the undone scene: there is nobody there; there is another hot sunhazy morning burning in around him.

He appraises himself in his hotel-room mirror. Her dress is basic black with straps, cut just above the knee. She was never extravagant. She always went for a classic look. He admired that.

The kid notices him before he has taken ten steps. The man makes out recognition gathering through the kid's posture and he raises his right hand, palm open, waving at the man, and the professor glances over to see what the kid sees.

The man raises his right hand, palm open, to wave back, and, another step, the man enters a cloud of pigeons ascending.

The world briefly turns into grayblack vibration.

When his vision quells again, the kid is gone.

According to a 2011 discovery by Lynne Truss, a Cambridge manuscript expert, Syriac was the first language to use a question mark. Truss attributes an early form of the question mark to Alcuin of York, describing the punctus interrogativus of the late 8th century as "a lightning flash, striking from right to left."

6 September

Robert Smithson: <u>Look at any ~~worl whirl~~ word long enough and you will see it open up into a series of faults.</u>

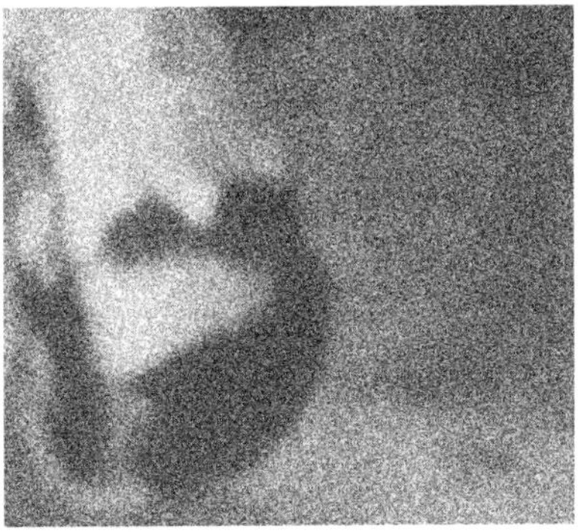

7 September

How, at times like this, you're always both with someone else and not.

~~To rehearse: Smithson wa~~

he is to see the kid. Why would he be pleased to see him? He wouldn't be able to say, if someone were to ask, but what he knows is that today he wants to sit down with him over a cup of tea and a what is the word baklava, a baklava, and catch up, discuss exactly nothing for as long as the kid can spare.

9 September

I was sitting on the deck with H., watching stars perforate the sky. I wasn't sitting there and then there was warm summer air dusty as an old house. Ive been okurring to myself like this mre & more.

Examining my gloved ~~houn~~hands, turning them over in my lap, rubbing the fingers of one with the fingers of the other, reversing the motion, trying to massaGe out the winter.

It's going to be OK, you know, said one of the voices that are him.

[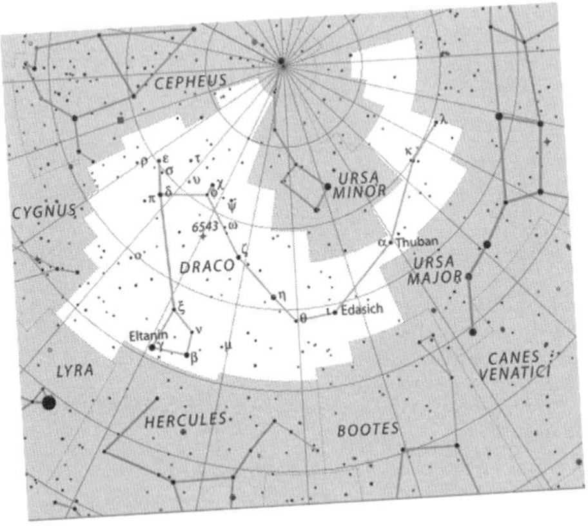]

Except the kid can't be attending classes. How can the kid be attending classes? He's just passing through.

The man rises and begins crossing the plaza in the couple's direction. It unsettles him how pleased

Your not allowed to say that, I said, rubbing. it's too early to make sentences like that sound sincere.

You're going to be fine.

You don't know that. How can you know that?

It's a semieducated guess. You've been healthy all your life. You've taken care of yourself. It's all good.

What's that? It's all good. Some of it's good. Some of it's bad. Mostly it's in the muddle. There's less prickling today, more ~~old~~ cold.

You need your heavier gloves.

(The light scent of our neighbor's floral fabric softener making the air exagggerate itself.) I'm sweating and it feels like January.

Sometimes I want to feed that dog hambeurger laced with zXanax. I shouldn't admit this. but thats pretty much what I want to do. I'd love to see him try to bark on a trip to East Orange in a car trunk.

Sometimes it's in my legs. Sometimes my fingers and sometimes my ~~logs~~ legs.

This is where he spots the kid the second time—across the plaza, sitting on the steps, talking to a woman in a business suit in her late forties, early fifties. A professor, the man supposes. The kid is talking to a professor, involved in making what appears to be an important point with his fragile hands.

We'll buy you snow pants.

Sometimes my chest. Sometimes it feels like I'm eating a Slurpee too fast.

We'll buy you a coat.

I've already got a coat.

You're not wearing it. You want I should go inside and get it? What does such a dog convey about its owners?

A pause, then I said: what I whant is I should not have to wear a coat in the goddamn middle of aUgust, is what I want. It seems like a reasonable request. To me.

two-story boxes, electrical lines swaybacking between them.

Turn off the main roads, and everything became still and compelling.

He lounged on the same bench near the same snack cart selling grilled corn-on-the-cob in the plaza in front of the university's main gates. Old women rested on their heels before blankets spread with coiled belts, cheap jewelry, handbags, shoes, fezzes for the tourists, used CDs. Even the female students here looked like American students in Phoenix with their black jeans and death-metal t-shirts and Nikes and baseball caps, only somehow tidier, better groomed, as if they were wearing identities borrowed from reruns.

From my point of view. I'd like to make a deal with somebody

A deal?

If this is as bad as it gets, okay. I can do this.

Who can argue with that?

But absolutely, positively nothing beyond this point. Which I really want to be clear about this. The symptoms stop here, and I'm content. More or less.

You think maybe it's ~~tome~~ time to call the kids?

The kids have lives. appointments They don't need to hear about this. It is what it is, is all I'm saying. Sounding, apparently, like a Buddhist myself all of a s~~o~~udden. become what it isn't, and the dealss off"

(We sat there, assimilating into the evening's silence.)

Love: the sense no score in tennis dates from 1742 from the motion of playing for love, i.e. playing for nothing.

Every night unable to sleep, he stood at the window and watched the city wind down. He propped himself up in bed and read her diary. He didn't read paragraph by paragraph, or sentence by sentence, or even word by word, but letter by letter, how she formed each one, how the lines made their adventures across the page, the lopped l's, the slants.

He dressed and walked out into the non-hours, hoping the oncoming sensations would tire him.

Turn off the main roads, and within half a block modern European buildings gave way to bare-wood

J. M. Coetzee: "All autobiography is autre-biography."

flicking around them like white aphids.

Families picnicked in a park fringing the ruins of a long Roman wall.

Every evening he went to the same local eatery and ordered the same dish: shaved lamb slices in a wrap, yogurt on top, a bowl of red lentil soup on the side. Shawarma: that's what you call the shaved slices in bread. He couldn't get enough. He couldn't believe how good it was.

Outside mosques, men in rows on raised marble stools, trousers rolled to knees, washing their feet.

Sometimes the man had the feeling he had misplaced himself.

(I wanted to see something shocking take place in the sky.)

(E.g.: heat lightning's sudden blush and vanish.)

(Hugh sipped his scotch, ice chinkling in ~~thi~~ his glass.)

You want we should go in to bed? Bill's sick. Rita. I've got to get up early to cover.

I think Ill sit out here a little longer

You sure?

I think I'll just sit out here.

I love you. I love you and I hate that fucking dog. I wish that fucking dog were a fucking cat. What fucking cat would embarrass itself with ~~ssodo bl~~

such behavior? I insist on another 40 years from you.

40 years is 40 years.

You want I should tell you how our story will end?

Our story?

You'll live to be a 101 and die peacefully in your ~~weep~~ sleep. I'll live to be one year younger, because i can't stand the idea of a world without you in it, and die buried beneath an avalanche of my own books.

supertankers anchored out in the bay, sailboats

On the taxi ride in from the airport, he saw

horizon serrated by mountains.

some reason, he had expected parched land, orange

the green hills undulating across countryside. For

afternoon. The man lifted his shade, startled by

The plane began its controlled fall through the

feet.

stowed upon cats the ability always to land on their

It was the prophet, goes the legend, who be-

scissors to cut off the sleeve.

his robe. Rather than wake her, he used a pair of

awoke to discover a tabby sleeping on the sleeve of

One morning, the legend goes, Mohammed

City of minarets. City of cats.

The clarity, the consistency.

[[it occurs to me: if you &
i have nothing else in common,
dear bro, we at least share the
obsession to keep moving,
checking out what's up the next
flight of stairs, around the next
corner. Which is to say we're
our parents' children--which
is deeply ironic, if you think
about it, since we're living in
a way they couldn't because
we existed in the first place.]]

. . .

. . .

. . .

. . . .?

. . . .?

I don't hear you promising.

. . .

. . . ?

. . .

. . . ?

. . .

. . . . . .

. . . . ?

. . . .

. . . . ?

. . . .

. . . .?

. . . .

. . . .?

Inside her head, she is saying I love you, I love you, I
love you. Inside her head, she is saying this is mine,
and this is mine, and this is mine, too.

He wants to thank Bruce Rogers for in 1917 reviv-
ing the font named after its creator, John Basker-
ville, in 1757.
The sharper serifs.
The more vertical axis to the rounded letters.

10 September

It grows like this: a match flicked into a lake of kerosene.

Europe: 10,476.
New York: 6,234.
~~Xmas~~ Texas: 5,991.
Utah: 4,295.

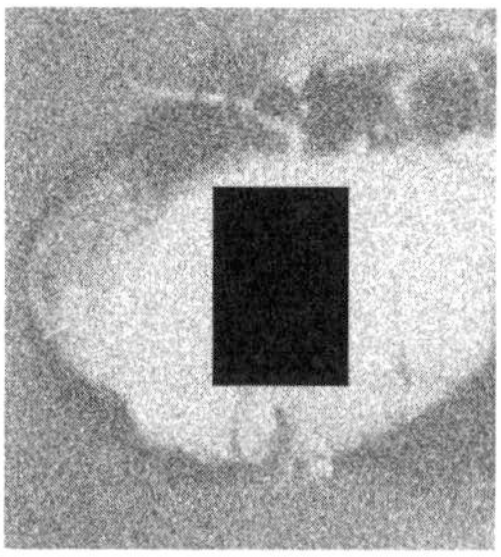

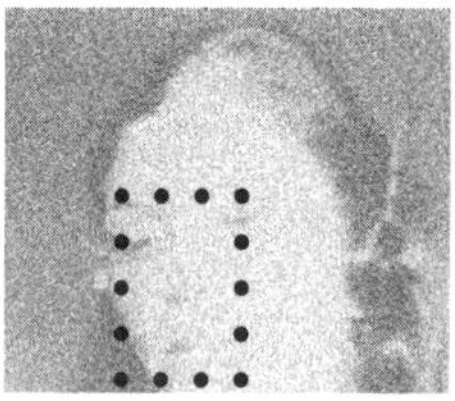

isn't thinking about anything. He finds this a relief. She has a specific job to do and she is doing it. Her movements are methodical, reverent. Her name is Alara. No, it is Harika. No, it is Alannah. Let's call her Leyla. Leyla's knees are killing her. Fist-sized dark bruises will cover them for weeks. She resists allowing the pain to seep up into her expression. Instead, she loses herself in each epiphanic kiss, cherishes every plane, texture, the idea of being deep among the thingnesses of the world, in marking every item, like a male dog, only with her lips.

skimpy maid's outfit crawling through her apartment, and yet so much is going on it makes the man dizzy. He never realized how much energy, how much concentration, it takes to see something. Each pill he swallows tints the video with a different effect. Maroon, tan, white with blue specks. Elliptical, pentagonal, kidney-shaped. Now and then he locates a detail he hasn't located before, or a familiar detail from a completely novel angle. After his visit, he will return to his hotel room to take a nap, the encounter will have so exhausted him. But now he is watching, trying to take in everything at once. He feels himself leaking into the woman's mind. The first knowledge that reaches him is that she

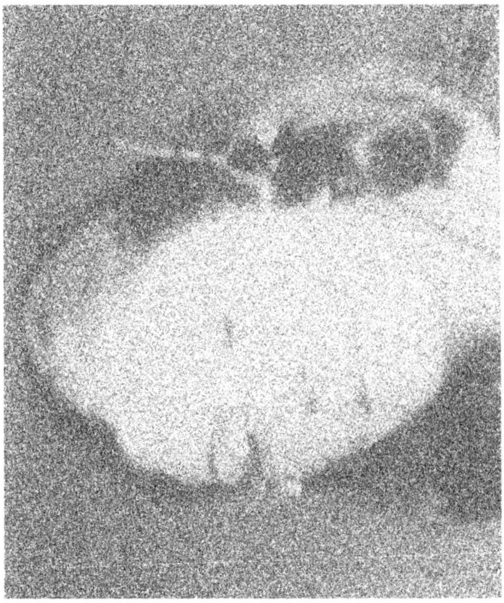

11 September

Robert Smithson: Every object, if it is art, is charged with the ~~rich~~ rush of time.

she traverses the apartment, her apartment, he would imagine, and sometimes her breathing, and sometimes the kisses themselves. Every so often the camera draws in for a close-up of her profile as her lips touch something and pulls back again. The feeling is like watching porn in slow motion. The feeling is unlike anything. It is like experiencing pure time. It is like what a minute feels like. The more the man looks, the more he sees. Nothing is going on in the video save for this woman in a

12 September

This morning alone, 5 voicemails for Anastasia.

~~Their~~ There have been more almost dailysince that first ~~massa~~message materialized. People no longer request spiritual amphetamines regarding financial matters or relation~~dyof~~ships. They're talking plagues and visions. The wReckoning.

Telemarketing from the end of the world.

I ask the ~~f~~phone company representative on the other end of the line why stranglers are leaving these dispatches for me, especially in light of the fact that my husband and I pay extra for an unlisted number

Her name is Sparrow, the representative says. Sparrow or Sbarro.

There's simply no uncheerfuling her inflections.

side table. The glass side table. The white chair. Both white chairs, one on either end of the coffee table. The white rug with the purple spiral woven into it. Periodically, she pauses to apply more lipstick. Then she carries on. She kisses every leaf on the large rhododendron in the corner. She kisses a vast white wall, moves to the window flooded with white light, moves back to the wall. The video runs without dialogue, without music. There is no soundtrack except for the small raspings parts of her make as

Sparrow Sbarro takes down my information and ~~ups M~~ puts me on hold. Muzak that used to be reereal songs by 173 Dead Nuns replaces her.

When she returns, she informs me there are 2 probable culprits: either someone named Anastasia has had our number at some point in the past, & what weve been recieving have been residual bulletins intended four her, or the lines have gotten ~~cri~~ossed somewhere in the system.

May we send smone over to take a look-see? SS asks. We'll give you a jingle and let you know what we find.

times. It is possible the video is hours long and he has just begun. In it, a plump woman with bobbed black hair crawls on her hands and knees through an airy modern apartment, kissing everything in her path. She kisses every article, every surface, leaving a mosaic of Marilyn Monroe red lipstick traces behind. She wears a skimpy maid's costume, black with white lacy trim, the sort you buy in an adult boutique, and shiny black fuck-me pumps. She kisses every inch of the glass coffee table, the glass candlesticks atop it, the blocky glass ashtray, the table's brushed bronze legs, the book whose cover is a photograph of the bridge the man stood on that morning. She kisses the streamlined white couch. The tall rectangular white lamp on the glass

Sure, I say, lacking out the kitn window at the backyard, the orange tabby wandering among the tomato plants in the vegetable garden, considering the cattle & ranch hands in the Great Basin that developed radiation burns on their exposed skin from the fallout aftr te nuclear tests in Nevada, the dogs & sheep that went ~~blon=~~ blind, locals who lost their hair.

<u>A look-see?</u>
<u>a jungle?</u>

† Cf. www.lanceolsen.com/tof.html —Ed.

And now he is in the modern art museum, standing in front of a video monitor.† He has been standing in front of it for the last half hour. People enter the spacious white room in twos or threes, usually talking about subjects irrelevant to the artwork around them. They wander from object to object, barely stopping long enough to become aware of their presence, ten seconds, twenty, paying the man in front of the video monitor no attention, then wandering into the next spacious white room. Sometimes they speak English flexed with enigmatic accents. Sometimes they speak languages that sound like those heard in dreams. The man can't take his eyes off the screen in front of him. It is possible he has already watched the video several

has never seen before: teahouses and restaurants lining the lower level, and, on the upper, cars, busses, trucks, vendors, and pedestrians gliding by anglers flocked along the railing, buckets at their feet animate with silver flashes, fishing poles a jumble of antennae above them.

This is where the man stalls out. All this seeing. All this relentless taking in. He reaches into his pocket for the brown vial. He looks down at the boats dragging white isosceles triangles behind them. He looks up at the unbelievable sky.

He thinks: This is where I am.

He thinks: Sometimes this is me.

13 September

~~O3t~~ Let's say this is the merchant marine. Let's say this is circa 1943. Lets say someone snaps this photo fewer than 2 weeks before the torpedo rips into a cabin down the corridor from where hes sleeping, its detonation heaving him from his bunk into a disoriented scrum scramble through smoke, csscreams, flames, water already hip-deep. Or another way of putting it: he goes to sleep barely 20 years old and wakes up 45, 55, 60. Slogging, he can't beg~~u~~in to imagine me here, more than half a century in his future, middle-aged, freezing

decker bridge spanning the strait—something he mosque, across a busy main road, onto a double- until one emits him onto a large square before a him somewhere, strays, rounds this corner, that,

him. He senses himself losing mass and substance, the goodness of himself becoming inconsequential again.

He doesn't look back until he has taken another left, right. By then it is as if the kid has never occurred to his day. The man idles, sweating, taking pleasure in the light lostness in his belly. Diesel, dust, curry. How without warning the call to prayer seems to be emanating from everywhere at once. How the quavering incantation filling these narrow back streets somehow reminds him of a rescued place. It creolizes the distant traffic sounds, the nearby shopping sounds, the ongoing conversations.

He figures he will let these alleyways convey him somewhere, strays, rounds this corner, that, until one emits him onto a large square before a mosque, across a busy main road, onto a double-decker bridge spanning the strait—something he

-> nostalgia, the longing for a presence that was never present, a returning to a home that was never built. Think of this all as a kind of parsing instead. A translation. i'm not trying to make anything work. i'm just trying to explain why it never will.

in some weird act of empathy; How sleet has ~~mgsatrf ip~~, migrated up my arms, across my shoulders, into my neck and jawbone. How it makes every swallow a conscious performance. ~~kslf ajslie w;cpx~~ how i woke last night to sheets spongy with perspiration heart fieldmousing breath short as the lieu~~tin~~tenant's must have been as he pushed toward what he must half understood were bursts of machinegun fire,

earnest coming-of-age-through-globe-trotting films)...which is when the kid surprises him, says out of the blue that to wake up alone in a strange place is one of the most gratifying sensations there is, at which point the man glances over, checking him out, startled (as he is continuously these days) by how little any two people on earth really have in common.

The café emerges out of the disturbance of people ahead of them. An open storefront with three or four men sitting on stools around blue plastic dollhouse tables outside.

The kid's hand drops away from the man's arm and the man only notices the hand's presence by its absence.

A few paces short of their goal, the alley they are in intersects another. The man blinks and with an easy motion turns the corner. Hands in pockets, he keeps strolling at a lazy pace, the throng before him opening, engulfing him, currenting around

Another way of saying this is to point out that to narrate comes from a Latin word, <u>narrare</u>, to tell, which ultimately derives from the Proto-indo-European root <u>gno</u>, which comes into our language as <u>to know</u>, the place no narrative can ever arrive at. For instance, our perfunctory birthday/holiday calls. They feel like opening the phonebook, picking out a stranger's name at random, & ringing to ask how he's doing. i honestly don't mean this as an insult or accusation. You know that. i'm just trying to figure it out, reach the heart of the heart of a relationship. i understand i can't reach the heart of the heart of. i'm not suggesting we give a shot at bridging the great divide, etc. i want to be clear about this. That's a fool's errand, unsullied

knowing it was either that or it was nothing. How, when I tried to stand, ~~dis~~dizziness sat me ~~dun~~ down again on the edge of our bed. How it went on that way 30 seconds 40 & then quik as it came flipped away   how I made my way into the bathroom & ~~brake~~braced against the sunk sink, door shut light on waiting while I caught up with myself watching versions of me rise thru dark water & merge with my body, with this body, and then I WAs back, was there, & you were standing behind me, sweetheart, groggy, palm lingering atop your scruffy head, ~~anticc~~anticipating, taking me in, waiting for reports from the front.

though, honestly, the man concludes, it probably hasn't been much), how remade he feels, how he sees everything now with brand-new eyes (even though the kid probably isn't all that unlike the person he used to be, is probably the same suburban kid [except, maybe, for a new diary choked with clichés, a new map dry-mounted over his bed bristling with a bunch of colorful pins], believes the narrative the kid is telling would be substantially the same as any other kid with a backpack and a couple of credit cards would tell because the kid is clearly committed to reenacting a certain boilerplate worldliness he has read about in the novels everyone reads outside the classroom in high school and college, has seen in dozens of overly

14 September

Editing all dAy, puffed up in front of my computer like a firefrighter in a HazMat suite: new parka (hood raised), scarf, ski pants, thermal boots, gloves, gloom.

15 September

In order to ~~rw~~ wrap up the film: one more visit. [[[Robert Smithson: One is liable to see things in maps that are not there.]]]

beginning somewhere and opening your eyes and being somewhere else and opening your eyes and being somewhere else and isn't that how living should come at you?

At some point the man loses track of what the kid is talking about and instead begins paying attention to his intonations—his exercise of pitch, stress, rhythm. It is obvious the kid has been alone a long time, that it is an enormous relief to locate himself in the company of another American, a temporary comrade, even if only for the length of time it takes to enjoy a cup of coffee, that it is exciting to be able to share who he has become with someone, the life that has happened to him (even

16 September

central and south america: 78321 california: 15448. flor: 13931. dC: 12762.

utah: 10686

17 September

Robert ~~Smithsin~~ Smithson: Levi-Strauss suggested that they change the word anthropology to entro

by a pack of feral juveniles that descended on him in the middle of a street in Athens, all smiles and shoves and quick fingers, but that that's what this is all about, isn't it, the Ur-story, that's the reason for starting out in the first place: the sensation of entropology, meaning highly developed structures in a ~~straight~~ state of disintegration. I think ~~thit's pset~~ that's part of the attraction of people going to visit obsolete civilizations. They get gratification from the collapse of these things.

18 September

Robert Smithson: when I was a kid i used to love to watch the ~~hurtl~~hurricanes come and blow the trees down and rip up the s~~l~~idewalks.

providing him with any positive reinforcement whatsoever—nodding, for instance, saying uh-huh, asking a follow-up question every once in a while to show some kind of attentiveness in play.

The kid is busy explaining how he, the kid, has been traveling for almost three months, sometimes by Eurrail, sometimes by ferry or foot, seeing how far he can stretch his money, which isn't nearly as far as he would have bet, it never is, that's how the Ur-story goes, sleeping in youth hostels and train stations and sometimes on the trains or ferries themselves, explaining how he got some sort of gnarly intestinal incubus for a week in Bucharest, got the cash he was carrying pickpocketed

19 September

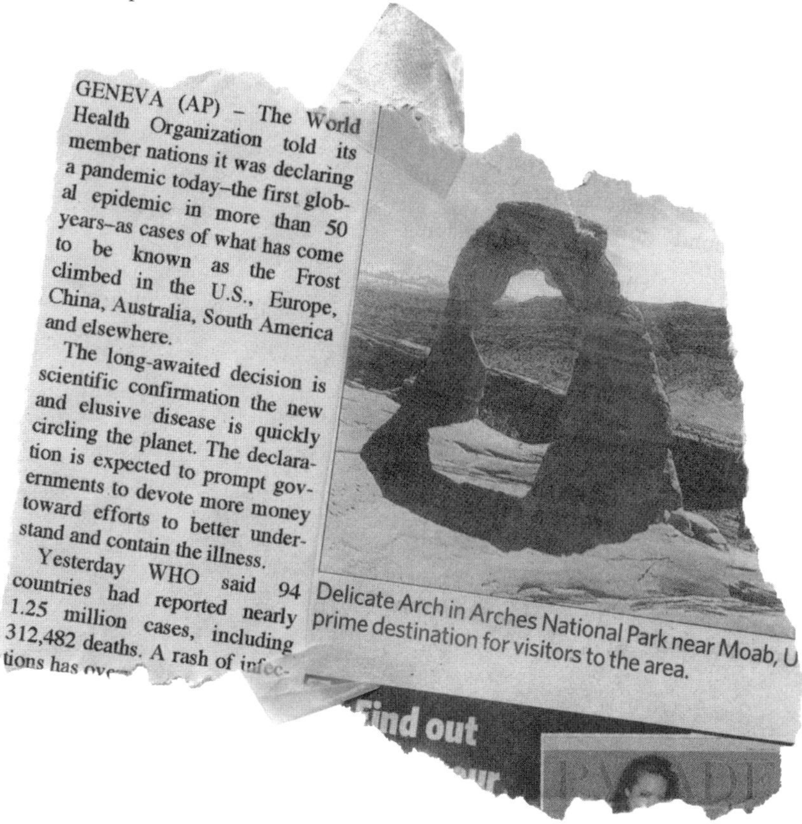

GENEVA (AP) – The World Health Organization told its member nations it was declaring a pandemic today–the first global epidemic in more than 50 years–as cases of what has come to be known as the Frost climbed in the U.S., Europe, China, Australia, South America and elsewhere.

The long-awaited decision is scientific confirmation the new and elusive disease is quickly circling the planet. The declaration is expected to prompt governments to devote more money toward efforts to better understand and contain the illness.

Yesterday WHO said 94 countries had reported nearly 1.25 million cases, including 312,482 deaths. A rash of infections has ove-

Delicate Arch in Arches National Park near Moab, U
prime destination for visitors to the area.

Find out

chessboards, tubs of cashews, tubs of walnuts, brass
hookahs, stuffed animals, fluorescent Raggedy Ann
dolls, wicker baskets, all this visual clamor.
The man has to give it to him: the kid is carrying on the conversation singlehandedly, undeterred
by the fact that the man isn't contributing, isn't

Alfred Korzybski: "The map is
not the territory."

Baudrillard: "The map
precedes the territory."

Swedish army manual: "if the terrain
and the map do not agree, follow the
terrain."

20 September

~~all these yrs together, Hugh, & look where we r~~

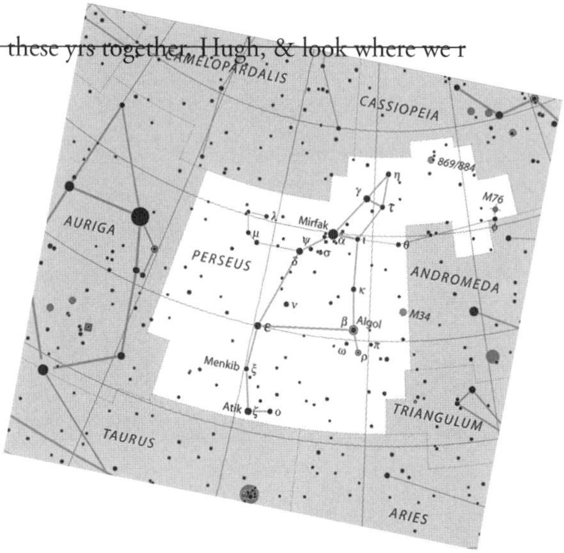

arguing on cellphones and thick older men in striped shirts with rolled-up sleeves crouching on low stools, hands on knees, walking their eyes over pedestrians passing.

And now the man recalls: yes, that's where he is.

Here.

Not the other place. This one. What he is doing is making his way among alleys of the vast bazaar spilling down the hillside toward the electric turquoise strait dividing this city, which city, the city he is in, in two, peasant skirts on clotheslines, men's tan jackets, green and white balloons, shiny pots and pans, strings of dried vegetables,

According to a Berkeley
study, a person touches his or
her face on average 16
times an hour. Perhaps,
i'm guessing, to make sure
it's still there.

21 September

Which is to say the central obsession holding together Smithson's diverse body of work—~~plaint~~ paintings, poems, essays, ~~fl~~——————> philosophy, photographs, land art—hits u with every frame: time and times relentless restlessness.

The weigh today will always be just a little more dog-eared than yesterday.

Let's get you something to drink. You like Turkish coffee? I know this café. Next corner up. Although, I mean, I could definitely do without the sludge-at-the-bottom thing, you know?

He laughs, rambles on. Chicago? The man would guess Chicago. Milwaukee. The man would guess somewhere in the nasal Midwest and guess, as well, that he, the man, has absolutely zip to say to him, this kid, but he, this kid, nevertheless reaches over and palms his, the man's, arm in a companionable gesture intended to aim him, the man, in the right direction, and then they are navigating through the noisy crush together, moving past thick women in light formless black topcoats and white headscarves grabbing through bins, sampling candied fruits, pointing to things at the back of stalls, past thin younger men in sweater vests

22 September

1. How ~~unrab~~ unraveled you can still find yourself before the memory of your mothers legs crumpling up under her 1 afternoon as she shuffled beside H. & you along the hall @ the assisted living center. how she came down on the railing with her chin. hard.

2. How one sentence you write will be your last although you probably won't know it.

3. How every video you make, that anyone will make, will have its final viewer the ~~some~~same way every book in the Used Appendix will have its final page-turner.

4. how our species will have its last delegate; our planet its last rain; our galaxy its ~~lost~~ last H atom;

5. ~~How it won't matter.~~ how, in the end, there will be no one left for it to matter to.

innately trustworthy and uncorrupt, that that's the human hub: believing every story has more or less the same beginning and the same ending, the same bedrock and architecture.

Yeah, he is saying, this kid is saying, the nice guy standing in front of him, as if the man has already responded to his original question, which, the man is almost (but not wholly) sure, he hasn't.

You need to sit down for a minute? it is saying.

The man studies the changing mouth changing and is interested to discover he has zip he wants to communicate to this kid, zero enthusiasm in talking with him, even though it is apparent the kid is a nice enough guy, attentive, empathetic, one of those countless naïve collegiate Americans who instinctively wants to help confused strangers on unfamiliar streets in unfamiliar cities, believing, you would learn if you had one of those late-night bull sessions with him back in his dorm room, that everyone is basically good at heart, reliable,

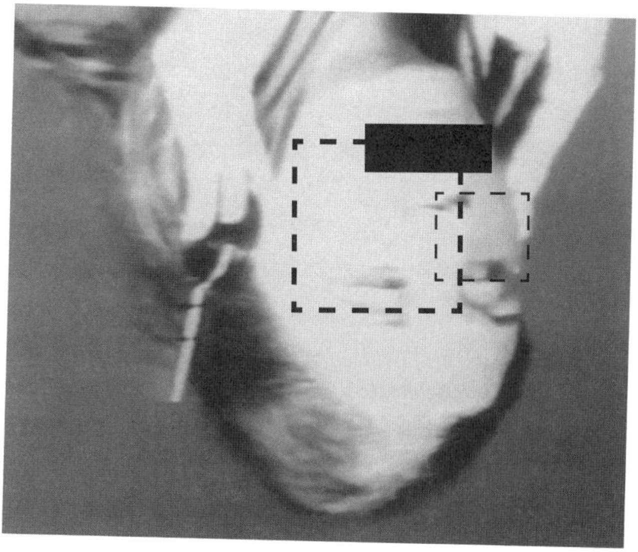

23 September

~~Slske ald vakkwszr~~

Sparrow Sbarro called ~~wile I wu~~ while I was ~~et~~editing to let me know a phone crew had been sent into our neighborhood yesterday afternoon

~~Smle all sj the The~~

The problem, they determined, was the wiring. Something was this when it should have been that.

But everythinkings working like a charm now, Sparrow Sbarro said.

in his early twenties traveling through any foreign country anywhere.

The man understands these data first and then that this person, this kid, he conceptualizes him as a kid, has a sewn-up cleft lip he has tried to disguise with his non-beard beard that appears vaguely insolent no matter what you do to it.

Dude, the kid says. Dude, you don't look so good.

The man isn't sure if he hears the kid's voice coming from inside or outside and the kid is also wearing a dirty blond ponytail and wire-rimmed glasses and his mouth is continuing to change.

i than;~~ds~~ked her, inspecting the ~~plum~~ palm of my free gloved hand. It didn't feel like my hand anymore. It felt like someone else's had been sewn onto the end of my arm. fSo-mestimes it felt shot full of Novocain. sometimes it winced for no reason like a little man with Tourette's

Sparrow Sbarro urged me to ~~cull~~ call her should I have any further questions or concerns.

Inspecting, I thanked her for that too.

She gave me her special access code

~~Pn velaf of atw f~~

To begin with, the man's eyes don't fall on a full face. They fall on a mouth ringed by reddish blond beard. The mouth in the process of changing and only after a few seconds does the man hear the sounds the changing has invented.

You okay? the mouth is saying. Hey, you okay?

He is in his twenties, his early twenties, this guy who was standing beside the man but is now standing in front of him, in his early twenties and in a lived-in t-shirt, raggedy sandals, baggy safari shorts that make his legs into knobby straws, and a backpack that makes him look like everybody else

People are shouldering past him and everyone is talking and it is loud and animated and someone standing beside him has asked him a question.

That's what finally captures his attention: the person standing beside him waiting for an answer to a question the man has failed to assimilate. The person too close, almost touching, and the man can't make out what the question was, and the person has just asked it again, or maybe asked a different version of it, or maybe a different question altogether, and the man has another glinting half-idea, although it disperses as soon as he tries to adjust it into solidity, and he feels himself raising his head, turning to see what all this vocabulary taking place beside him is about.

On behalf of the phone company she said she wanted to make sure I fully ~~gasp~~ grasped what an honor it had been serv1ing me,

Inspecting, I told her I did.

it's quite possible some time passed. It's quite possible it didn't. When I dialed in to what she was ~~slayi~~ saying again, I heard her explaining in the next day or two in the mail I would receive a form concerning our encounter she used the word encounter. She would appreciate it if I would take a moment to fill out said form and returnit in the addressed, stamped envelope~~m~~, which would accompany it   she used the word <u>said</u>

she added: we knw you have a choice of providers. Our telecommunications family thanks you for choosing us. Have a <u>GREAT DAY!!!</u>

24 September

Two hours after Sparrow Sbarro hung up, this on voice-mail: <u>We're all witnesses. It's like someone's peeled back our eyelids.</u>

The man is lingering in a crowded alley, inspecting exotic orange and green sweets piled in pyramids on a plank in a stall jammed among other stalls in a web of roofless passageways.

Maybe, the man half-reflects, the concoctions involve figs, apricots, pistachios. Maybe he believed by coming here, where, here, something major would happen. Something extensive inside him would recalibrate. Vision would be washed clean. Except the thing is this: the thing is he feels pretty much the same as he felt yesterday, if it is yesterday he is remembering, and not, say, last week.

The tang of spicy meat grilling. Ginger and dill.
Leather and cigarettes.

A nondescript white pill blurs his tongue.

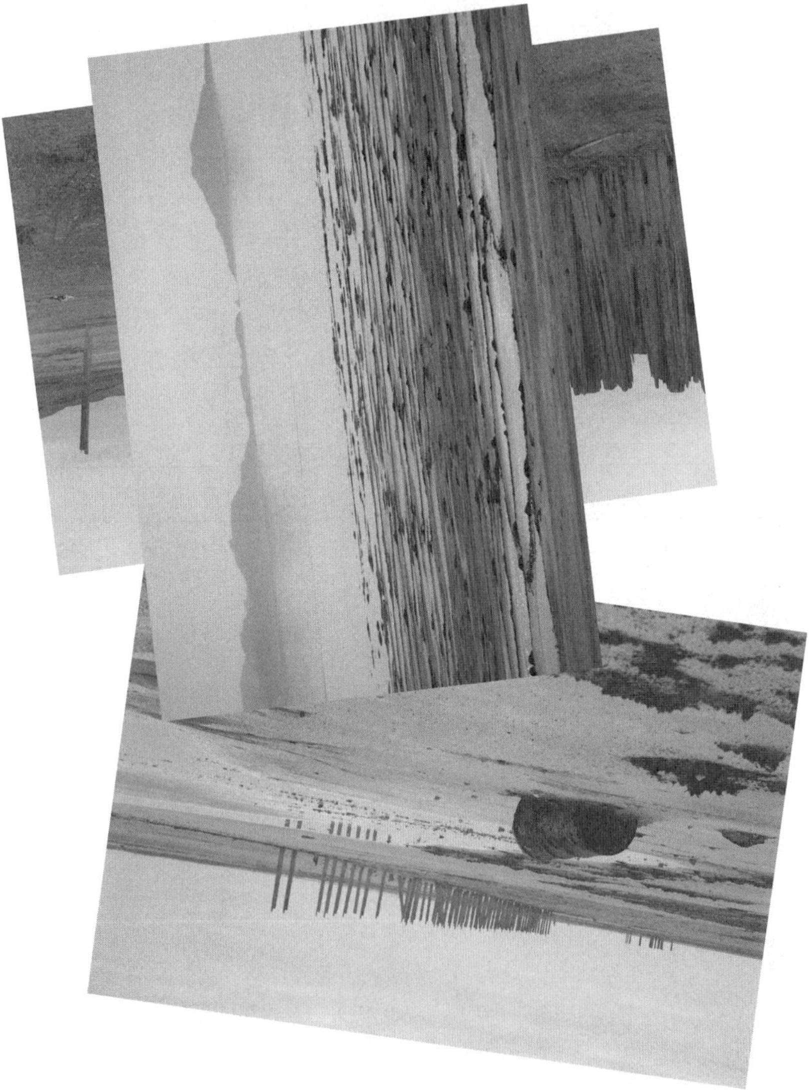

the supermarket back home by himself for the first time, at a loss what to buy, how much, where anything was, why all the other shoppers seemed to be so comfortable piloting the abstruse aisles and employing the merciless self-checkout machines, which is a feeling similar to the one that overwhelms him almost every night lately, the adrenaline scramble among the lungs reminding him it no longer matters when he eats, or showers, or goes to bed or gets up in the morning, because his gestures are meshed with precisely no one else's.

He is lingering in a crowded alley in a crowded city, what city, not that one, another, he isn't sure which.

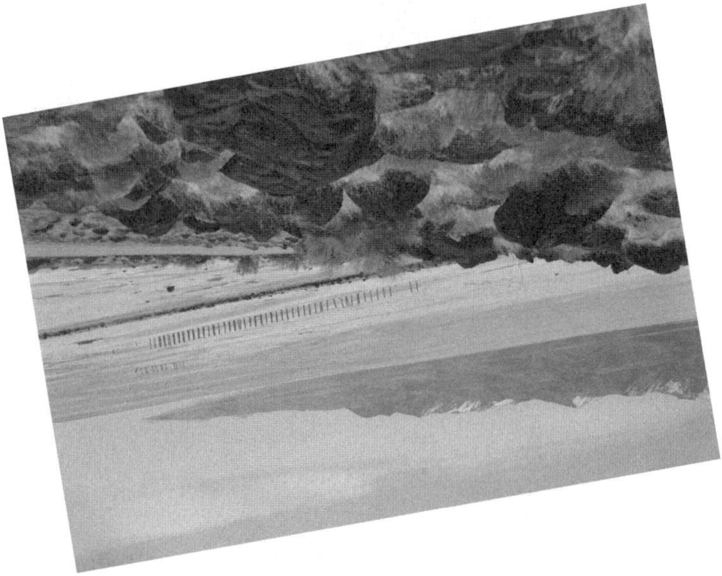

i called the phone company and ~~aksed~~ asked for sparrow

Sparrow? said the representative whose vocal cords strained to modulate into manhood.

Sparrow or Sbarro, I said.

Like the pizza chain?

I have her access code.

excYse me maam?

Her special access code. Would you like it?

We…uh…i dont think we have any special access codes here, ma'am?

Sparrow Sbarro does. She gave it to me.

A sustained suspension, then he continued as if I hadn't spoken:

May I ask for yr phone number?

I heard him ~~intern~~entering it into his computer.

Address?

More clicking.

& would you please summarize the nature of your problem

to him, he is riding the Circle Line, which is when he notices his wristwatch is missing and, dismayed, begins patting himself down, checking the zipper pouches in his daypack, the pockets of his jeans, the zipper pouches in his daypack, stopping somewhere in the middle of the commotion that is himself to ask what it is he's looking for, which is a feeling similar to the one that overwhelmed him entering

He asked me to hold a minute. Muzak that used to be real songs by Controlled Bleeding cycled. I shut my eyes & pictured another earthwork: the Toole Army Depot

Sometimes, she says, when I close my eyes, I forget what the color red should look like.

One morning the man notices what he takes to be a shopping list magneted to the refrigerator. He unfastens it. Because he isn't wearing his glasses, he holds the list close to his face and is therefore doubly bewildered by what he reads:

1. Die.
2. The only future becomes the only past.
3. Apply clown nose, black silk scarf, black dress.
4. Cremation.
5. Cremation.
6.

And now he is sliding along a moving sidewalk in the Denver airport. And now a male flight attendant is handing him a landing card. And now he is sitting on the steps of the big black statue in Piccadilly Circus, knees to chest, sweating, he can't stop sweating, traffic ant-farming around him, and now rattling in a tube carriage...the Circle Line, it comes

Chemical Demilitarization Facility. You can pick out its menacing gleam down in the valley when hiking the Oquirrh Mountains. What u cant see are the millions of pounds of mustard gas, Sarin, and VX awaiting incineration inside the bunker complex, or any sign of the nerve gas testing accident that in 1968 left thousands of Skull Valley sheep dead.

This is really wierd? the representative said returning but we don't seem to have a record of your first call??

But Sparrow Sbarro sent out a ~~clue~~crew.

We don't actually have a record of anybody by either of those names working here?

There was a crew in my neighborhood yesterday. She said so.

smear as a negligible problem that can be solved and the next shit smear as a negligible problem that can be solved and so forth, and part of him is trying to take in the fact that this is where he is and this is what he is doing: all this living, and here they are; all this living, and there is nowhere else.

It gets worse and worse, she says.

He frames himself from a distance, from outside the bathroom window, from two feet above it, looking down, looking in, clinically, this skinny bearded guy touching a towel to his beshitted wife's face in the shrill light in the middle of the night in this cramped room, and he adds: No, it doesn't.

I'm really sorry about this, ma'am? But we can have another crew out there Tuesday afternoon? Between two and five? Will that work for you?

Two and five?

Your situation should be pretty easy to resolve. I mean, Either someone by that name had your number before you, & what youre receiving are residual dispatches intended for her, or …

Or the lines have gotten crossed somewhere in the system.

…

…

Hello?

…

I'm still here, I said, hanging up.

He studies their reflections in the mirror.

He studies their reflections in the mirror.

Sometimes this is me, she says.

He releases her fingers from the eyeliner stick and sets it down on the sink edge. Wets a corner of towel. Dabs at the shit smear on her cheek. She closes her eyes, tilts her face up like a little girl to allow him easier access. She appears pleased at the attention she is receiving.

Where you are standing is never a place, he realizes, not thinking, thinking, but a new way of seeing things.

Part of him is remembering the dream of the memory and part of him is perceiving this shit

25 September

Q: Why is the Spiral Jetty so beautiful?
A: Because it is in the perpetual process of misremembering itself.

oil to the churning white. Tests the temperature. Rises and steps over to her and, side by side, lays a palm against her lower back, rubs in slow circles while with his free hand he reaches for a towel on the rack by the sink.

He experiences her stench as a physical object: hard, spiky, perpetual suddenness.

You know what? she says.

26 September

Health volunteers fanned out across the sity at dawn, monitoring.

Their wearing white armbands stamped w/ red candles ~~crowed~~crowned with red flames & amped-up Mormon smile-reproductions.

They're contemptibly outgoing, the kind of people you wish would learn to be a little less considerate of others.

On your ~~error~~errands, you notice them loitering at tram~~p~~ stops, in front of cafes & restaurants & the public library, wandering through aisles of supermarkets & department stores.

The local news ran footage of them taking up pasts outside the University library, the union, the ~~rat~~ art museum,

the faucets. He adds a capful of patchouli-scented

clawfoot tub, squats, fidgets with the stopper, rotates

Carefully not thinking, he steps past her to the

You know what? she asks.

to go back to sleep?

Aren't you tired? I bet you're tired. Don't you want

Come on, he says. Let's get you cleaned up.

Honey.

she is approximating what she sees in his face.

what her face just happens to be doing, or because

Honey, she mimics, smiling because that is

the stadium, strolling through classroom buildings and dorms.

Everywhere you look, they remind you your living in a rented world.

27 September

~~Pixure a father taki~~

Not today.

has trickled down her inner thighs, the backs of her legs.

The swampy stink of it slaps him.

There are smears of shit across the backs of her hands, her neck, her cheek, along the wall by the mirror.

A dark green chunk of it in a henna puddle on the tiles by her heels.

The man becomes aware of a sound and it dawns on him that he is the one producing it. The woman hears it and half turns. She has been applying black eyeliner, but missing. Her red lipstick has sometimes touched her lips and sometimes not.

Honey, he says.

28 September

Willaim F. Fox: This is another reason science ~~fix~~fiction plays so well when Hllywd sets it in the desert. Not only are we conditioned to see it there by almost a century of conventions—the moJave arm of the Great Basin being the nearest and most open space available to L.A., hence the cheapest setting for alien funtasies—but there are few other visual referents to get in the way of the action, intrude everyday scale and normality into the deliberate disorientation of te audience that makes them more susceptible to accepting the suspension of logic.

He awakes with a jolt. Because it should be dark. It should be the middle of the night—two thirty, three: that's what he would guess. Because it should be dark, yet a shrill rhombus of light jags from the bathroom.

The sibilance of running water.

The resonance of human movement.

He realizes he is lying on the floor beside her bed. He has been dreaming about swimming in Halong Bay. In the dream everything was lukewarm and sun.

In the bathroom dazzle he finds her leaning over the sink, applying makeup. She is naked, which he understands this information first, understands she is naked and that shit mixed with urine

Their trip of a lifetime, which makes me think: did you ever feel, if even just a little, that they held us responsible for never being able to take another?

out the front door and just keep going? I don't mean I don't know the answer. It's like...I'm trying to picture it, is all, and I can't. I'm...okay...so...okay... I'm going to hang up now. I'll call again soon. This makes me happy. Isn't that remarkable?

Helvetica's provocative sans-serif Swiss cleanness.

[[

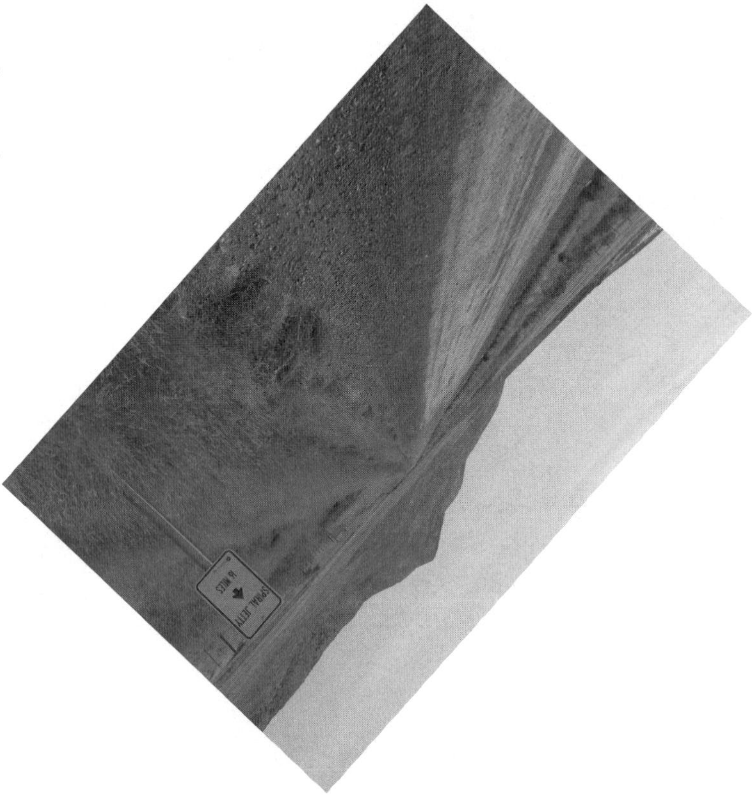

29 Septmber

brutally tired

30 Septmr

China: 384,211. Pensylvania: 41,967. Wisconsen: 37,180. Nebraska: 22,542. Utah: 21,339.

1 October

RS: The monument was a bridge over the Passaic Rvr that connected ~~begu~~Bergen County with Passaic County. Noon sunshine cinematized the sight, turning the bridge and the

couldn't stay awake. I turned on the TV. You didn't want any channel for long. I massaged your hands. You chewed and swallowed automatically, more concerned with what was on the screen than what was in your mouth. It...I mean, I almost never use this number. I couldn't even remember it. I'm sitting here going: What's my phone number? But we always used to know where the other one was, right? So why call? Anyhow, I'm trying to understand how it works from here on out. Do I get up and walk to the kitchen and rinse off the dirty dishes and load them into the dishwasher, or do I get up and walk

Part of what i mean, i guess, is, looking back, i can see how his anger inhabited you. The way you wrench-stopped the swing i was on for yucks, smuck up behind me when i was playing dolls in front of the TV & snipped off a wad of my hair, then swore i'd done it myself. You sounded so sincere, they almost believed you.

i was the take-home message,
the note in the bottle.

river into an over-exposed picture. Photographing it with my Instamatic 400 was like photographing a photograph. When I walked on the bridge, it was as if I were walking on an enormous photograph that was made of would and steel. The river beneath existed as an enormous film that showed nothing but continuous blank.

2 October

~~fosxture~~ Picture a father taking his wife and 8-yr-old sonon a roadtrip thru the astonishments called the Black Hills the Badlands Yellowtsstone Redwood Na'l Park the Grand

had commenced. It was matter-of-factly rehearsing what voices on machines matter-of-factly rehearse everywhere. The man waited for the second click, the click signaling the end of the time in which to deposit his digital trace, and hung up, then dialed again. Two more beeps, and he was curious about what he had to say. What he had to say was I know you're not there. I just wanted to hear your voice. I, um...I'm...where am I? Down the hall. On the futon in the guest room. I'm sitting on the futon. I was standing and now I'm sitting. You're in your room, sleeping. You were sleeping when I left. It's... when is it? Past midnight. You had a rough day. You didn't want to eat. You couldn't slip under and you

i've wanted to write this sentence from the start, Lance: it's not like you & i were ever close. i understand that. i'm assuming you do, too. it kind of hurts, but mostly it doesn't. On the one hand, it's somehow profoundly sad to articulate. On the other, the expression is nothing more than a statement of fact, as if i were citing the boiling point for water. it's not like at some stage we began drifting apart, is the thing. We were simply hardwired to move in different directions. i wonder what one says to carry on the conversation after that.

Canyon. pixture tht boy upon his return building a cardboard nqthi boooth to display the postcards he stockpiled along the way. There he is charging neighborhood kids a dime a show. There he is 8 years later entering the Art Students League in NYC on a ~~skul~~scholarship to study in the evenings. Picture him mimicking Abstract Expressionism: the ~~jes~~gestural brushstrokes, the surrealist impulse, the mythic undercurrents. Picture him experimenting with collages comprising homoerotic clippings from beefcake magazines, SF films, Pop Art. There he is squatting among ~~rea~~eds on the banks of the Passaic, fresh out of high school,

Had someone asked, he would have said [he didn't know] why he did it. He shouldn't have done it, he wasn't going to do it, but then he was doing it. Having fed her for the evening—a sip of tomato soup, a tiny bite of chicken, a napkin blot, repeat—he was walking down the hall to the kitchen with the tray. Next he was angling off into the guest bedroom, the one that used to be the boy's, setting down the tray on the carpet, dialing their home number on his cell. Listening to the other phone ring, their phone, both down the hall and in the center of his skull, examining his free hand, turning it over, rubbing its fingers with its thumb. The click on the line, her voice, the one speaking from before the subtraction

cigarette between his lips, curious about what will happen next. Picture himentering the Army Reserves for no other reason than to dodge boredom a little while. Picture him

It's this easy, he thinks, swimming lazily ahead.
This straightforwardly, uncomplicatedly effortless.

undergoing basic training and taking up his post as artist-in-residaence at Fort Knox, Ky, to paint watercolors of local installations for the mess hall. There he is 1 year later hitchhiking southwest, visiting a Hopei Indian reservation, hiking the Canyon de Chelly, dropping down from Arizona into Mexico and peyote visions, a string of acid revelations, the idea drawi dawning on him: who the fuck needs college when you can live like this, travel lik this, learn like this, read everything that falls into your hands? At 19 hes meandering through his first one-man show at the Artists Gallery in Manhattan, at 21 striking up a conversation with

When the junk dropped anchor late in the afternoon, they were the only tourists on board to take up the captain on his offer. They changed into their bathing suits, dove overboard, and are now doing undemanding sidestrokes toward the thin white brightness of beach several hundred yards away. The beach fringes one of the limestone islets that cones sharply out of the water into vaporous sunshine.

A sea of tall hats, it crosses his mind, water lapping.

She is swimming next to him, laughing at their gesture's outlandishness. The man knows the woman knows he would never try such a stunt back home because the possibility no longer remains in his repertoire. Over the weeks here, he has adopted a new range of personalities.

Nancy Holt at a ~~pre~~arty in a friend's loft. what does he see in the understated woman with dark brown hair and Buddha smile he'd known as a kid back in Jersey? What does her presence in his story mean? She'd gone off to study at Tufts and returned a post-minimalist and maybe she provides

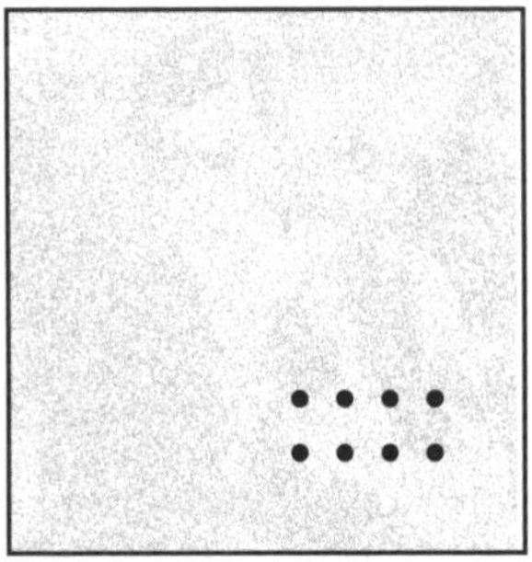

him like falling through weightless space, like the sound of doors slamming everywhere at once, angry at their children for pretending they had more important lives to live, that he couldn't have predicted any of this six months ago, he couldn't predict the next five minutes, and then bare-nerved, reptilian-brain fear.

What he is doing is swimming away from the side of a junk in Halong Bay.

This is a dream of a memory.

The tepid milky green sea slipping along his flanks.

There are photographs somewhere.
i remember seeing them as a child.

him historical continuity and mabye she's the kindred spirit and maybe the foil and maybe the ground. Picture the ineluctable relationship developing between them. Picture her his perpetual straight man, him the irascible autodidact with a bad Elvis haircut. Picture them heading to Italyto explore Byzantine art together. There he is chewing through

he couldn't be sure. In her diary, she implicated him without implicating him. She became scared, and then slowly less scared, and then the writing trailed off into some sort of asemic scribble among a welter of taped-in photographs. The circumstances led him to outbursts of willed inattention, angry at not being able to fend off what was swarming them, at her for becoming someone else, at himself for being angry, for pretending none of this was taking place, for being too serious about it, not serious enough, detached, too close, calm, too anxious, for not knowing what to be, for not wanting to be himself anymore, for being someone he wasn't, which felt to

Kerouac, Ginsberg, Burrow~~s~~ughs, Freud, Jung, and asking for more. Picture him in ~~91~~

1963

startlingly married, resolving to shed painting and turn to plastic sculptures that are about nothing except their own shapes and colors and the materials they are made of because such things are beauty without baggage, without any dense reasons for being beautiful. And there he is, his ~~k~~career starting to solidify ~~arin~~ around him, participating in a transformative

Sometimes she claimed one of her children hadn't phoned for weeks when in fact she had just hung up after a conversation with him or her. In the woman's subsequent corrective narratives, she was never the person at fault. One day he came across her halted inside their closet, head back, eyes squinched, deep inside the act of trying to recall why she had been transported to this uncanny spot. Her laptop materialized in the oven. The man started wondering if maybe he were the one whose memories were glitching. Who could say? Who could be used to triangulate the situation? Maybe he was the one getting existence wrong. He wasn't, of course, except possibly he was. He wasn't, except

undertaking that will never come to fruition at the Dallas-Fort Worth Airport: a huge (yes) spiral configuration on the fringes of a runaway that would only become recognizable as art from the air. Picture him looking, ~~willf~~ wildly, everywhere, at everything, struggling to discover a way to arrest attention in the midst of diversion and disturbance, appropriating and reinventing 18th- and 19th-century conceptions of landscape architecture, examining how Lancelot ~~Cabap~~ Capability Brown remodeled the great estate p~~l~~arks of the English gentry to resemble neat micro-versions, not of nature, but of nature's Platonic ideal, how Eliot tourned The Waste Land into a decaying 3D object what Cézanne did to trees mountains clouds' There he is installing Non-Sites first into this gallery and then into that: earth-&-rock-&-mirror-&-glass assemblages whose constituent parts he

Maurice Blanchot: "Literature begins at the moment when literature becomes a question."

Engram: to no one.

There was how this person he had known better, longer, than he had known any other person began forgetting things that no one should begin forgetting. Smudging facts, gumming up details, redrafting events that occurred three hours ago. Sometimes she believed something had happened to someone else when it had happened to her.

collected from specific geologic areas across the country. And suddenly the Spiral Jetty is there. And suddenly it is behind him. And there he is collaborating with Nancy ~~.s a gilw ;sers~~

on a movie about its construction. And there he is one year earlier documenting a walk they took through a muddy swamp in Bergen County, she filming with her Bolex camera, guided only by what she can

pinkish translucent bird with dark spots where its eyes should have been under a tree on the asphalt playground. How his teacher delicately picked it up in a wad of Kleenex and undelicately threw it into a nearby trashcan because, she explained, the lid slapping down, it was too small to save.

see through the lens & hear him instruct her to do. Why are these movies? What are they about? Maybe the act of ~~perfec~~perception itself, about what constitutes determined noticing. maybe how existence is always process, a way of moving, rather than a coming to rest. There he is several ~~mouths~~months later sitting on a bench facing the fountain in Washington Square, hazily anxious, cigarette between lips, curious about what an artist does after he has already done what his entire life has prepared him to do. What does an artist become after he has already become himself? Picture the man visiting one strip-mining company after another, presenting drawings & proposals for future earthworks, and picture each being graciously rejected.

Bill, he thinks, nodding. A Bill. My Billness.

Jim.

Dan. Patrick.

What would the end of the world look like without the exquisite capital Q of 16th-century Garamond?

He awakes with a jolt. The woman beside him still engrossed in the lives of hot teenage vampires. The plane he is on still thundering through ionizing radiation. Disoriented, he closes his eyes and is in elementary school, stumbling upon the aura of fabric softener seeping into the street from dryer exhaust ducts.

In the city, he thinks, nothing hurts.

He glances up in order to greet the first dog walkers. Waves at the severe man troweling his flowerbed. Nods to the patrol car crawling by, a different one, he can tell, with a different pair of cops inside.

Yes, he is sure of it.

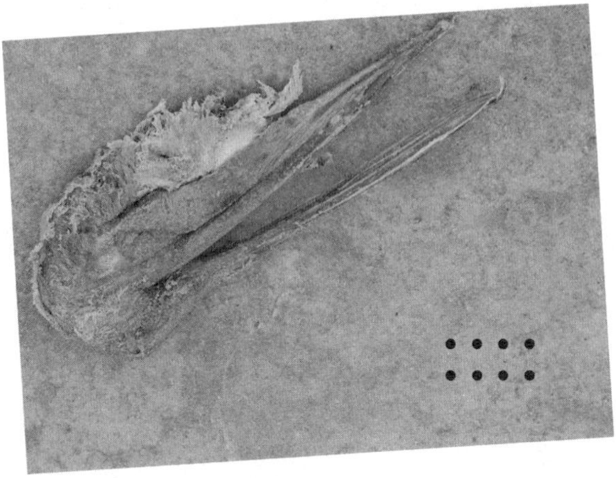

And now?

What direction will he go now?

and now he is belted into a small plane, pilot beside him, photographer behind, 15 miles northwest of Amarillo, Texas, on 20 July 1973, in the midst of a naked blue day, documenting his newly staked-out project in an artificial ~~lick~~ lake (these days dry, virtually unvisited) in the middle of the blasted desert: a 140-foot diameter rock (yes) spiral that will rise 15 feet from the water, commissioned by Stanley Marsh—local rancher, fellow artist, millionaire, and ~~bone-~~ bon vivant who with his wife owns over 200 square miles of the Lone Star State.

Picture something going quickly, furiously wrong. Maybe it's an unfamiliar noise that catches his attention, an abrupt shift in weight. Maybe he perceives the line of the horizon pitch without warning, feels a shudder running through the cabin.

The young pinkpeach daylight accumulating.

After a while his knees twinge. His lower back. He stands, stretches, cracks his vertebrae with an abrupt twist.

A breath, and he is strolling along the sidewalk, this average-looking guy in a plain white t-shirt, saggy worn jeans, blue baseball cap, pair of new white sneakers, just like everybody else out at this hour of day.

Strolling, he reviews the footage on his cell-phone. Sprinklers hiss to life around him. Moist grass. Chemical fertilizer. The overly sweet floral

Viz.: Theories of Forgetting, about S's Spiral Jetty. She didn't get a chance to complete it, but he showed me what she'd done. Everything's there. it just needs another month or 2 of work. Less documentary than series of visual meditations coalescing around S's artifact . . . a succession of entropic fadings mimicking the temporal wear of the thing itself, but also a demonstration of its strangely productive effects. As much as she's building into her contemplations a participation in dissipation, she's also working against that pressure, both in S's own project & in the various ones his inspires. So she theorizes decay, not merely as a process of emptying and exhaustion, but also as one of relay & salvage. in those terms art, body, & life become the mark of progress as well as a sign of passage, a means of building anew with constantly depleting remnants.

What is he thinking now?

And now?

What is moving through his mind as the rocky hillside a few hundred feet away reaches up to touch him?

He shot the contents of her refrigerator. Yellow mustard bottle. Two pickles in the cloudy pickle jar. He shot the spines of the books in her upstairs library (there were twenty-seven: not twenty-six, not twenty-eight) and the bric-a-brac congesting the top of her dresser and side tables.

The idea was to understand what kind of person she was when she wasn't the kind of person who confronted him at dawn in the kitchen.

The man viewed himself as a domestic anthropologist: what are her practices, her values, her technologies, her economies?

How does she live the way she lives, and why?

He videos the cops when they reappear out front. When they disappear around the side of the house. When they reappear out front.

3 October

sh~~i~~opping basket on arm, circumnavigating bright knolls of apples, oranges, peaches, pears, ~~plumes~~ plums, pineapples.

An irresponsibly tall health volunteer in a surgical ~~msku~~ mask steps in front of me as I round a bin of boxed blueberries. She asks me what I think I'm doing. I tell her I think I'm hunting for ripe bananas that are ripe but not too ripe. She points at my gloves.

I look down, look up, realizing I forgot to take them off before getting out of the car.

The woman in the terrycloth robe ushers them into the foyer. The door closes behind.

Earlier, he shot her sleeping. He stood above her, recording. The important thing was how her face kept changing. That's what he would have said had someone asked. Had someone asked, the man would have said he couldn't get over it. How her lips, nose, cheeks, forehead, eyes became other people's: an older woman's, a younger, a more thoughtful, a less, an elderly man's.

He decided she might find the footage illuminating at some point. Considering her through his screen, he concluded we should all see ourselves like this, in this condition of as if.

He concluded if you're living, you don't stand a chance.

I'm afraid I'm going to have to ask you to leave, she says.

Oh, I say. Oh. Okay. I'll just pick up a few things, and

I'm afraid I'm going to have to ask you to leave, she ~~sla~~ says.

A young pregnant mother and her little whiteblond ~~gril-~~ girl with a blobby portwine stain across her face who've been fishing for grapefruit an aisle over raise their ~~herds~~, sniffing the recycled air for danger.

4 October

Maps between 1740 and 1790 designated the Great Basin as The Sea of the W~~ors~~est, a Pacific gulf extending inland to the Rockies.

restroom, searching in his pocket with one hand while waving the other before the glowing red pupil on the paper towel dispenser.

He has always wanted to thank Stanley Morison and Victor Lardent for inventing Times New Roman for a British newspaper in 1931.

Filming the cops from his ex-neighbor's hedge. He is impressed by the clarity of the image his cellphone captures even in this silvering light. He shoots them rapping on what used to be his front door. He shoots them ringing what used to be his bell.

reaches down and lifts, tucks it into her chest, holds the animal to her like that.

Sways, almost undetectably.

The man experiences the nostalgia he isn't feeling, but will feel sometime in the future, perceives his memory of the event as a thumb-sized image wobbling on a small screen, and it is over, and the cat somewhere else, and his wife back at work, and the whole clip lasts fewer than forty seconds.

if i could go back to the times i wasted, i'd love to waste them again

He examines that clip at least once a day, unused to this person he has become, unable to think beyond the tiny scene moving in his palm, and now he is pausing at the row of sinks in the Salt Lake airport

Wat happened to Sunday?

He just told me today is Monday.

5 October

The nearly 250 mpsa of North America drawn between 1622 and 1800 uniformly represented California as a paradisal island.

She doesn't remark the cat's presence and then she does. Lowers her laptop. Extends her left arm. The tabby hesitates. The tabby hesitates. The tabby samples her scent.

Nothing changes, nothing changes, and then the cat deigns to approach, assessing her fingertips to establish if they warrant attention, and she

Rinsing out his coffee mug at the kitchen sink, the man catches sight of her on the deck. The dusty gold desert morning. How she takes a sip from her own mug, sets it down beside her lawn chair, returns to her laptop.

Summer glare, his remove, and his angle of perception prevent him from making out what occupies her screen, although he assumes it is the film she is editing.

He becomes aware of himself reaching into his pocket, extracting his cellphone, starting to video the videographer for no reason other than it seems like that's what he should be doing.

Thinking: I want to save her.

Nothing changes, nothing changes, she takes another sip, and the neighbor's orange tabby enters the frame. Surprised, the man looks over his cellphone's screen. The cat pads toward her, settles back on its haunches, Egyptian style, evaluating her through lazy green half-closed cat eyes. The man looks down at his screen again.

6 October

Let's say this is H., this A., somewhere inside Angkor Wat. The Ta Prohm temple, let's say, although it could always be somewhere else. This ~~photogap~~ photo represents the trip they'd been designing for years: the one that would fly them first to Bangkok via L.A., & next by plane, by train, by car, and by foot from Thailand to Cambodia, Cambodia to and thru Vietnam. I cant ~~rmrnk~~ remember what they are thinking. I can't remember where they were the day before this shot was taken or where they were the day after. I don't ~~gno~~ what might have been going through their hearts as whoever snapped this instant snapped it, don't recall what scents dominated the morning, the afternoon, what textures, what they had eaten lost, what they would eat next, who they imagined they would become over the course of the next decade. They don't know me. I barely know them. Or I do, but in the sense you know someone you used to hang out

What he is doing is remembering how he accidentally dropped and fractured the spine of his hardback copy of Ulysses—the Gabler edition, 1986 corrected text, 650 pages, clay-colored cover with orange, blue, and yellow highlights, the copy palimpsested with fussy marginalia carried over from the earlier editions he had used in college and graduate school. They spent $123.56 they didn't have to get it rebound, even though the original had cost him $21.00. In part this was to salvage the notes, every one an important transcript of who he had been. In part he just wanted to show a book it mattered. When he picked it up from the binder, his wife and he threw it a small homecoming party.

Champagne. Chocolate-covered marzipans.

Talking? They're people, sweetheart.

No. When are we?

He lets the camera run several seconds, concentrating on her puzzled face, then says: You're somewhere else, honey. Where are you? I'd like to be there with you.

She lies in bed watching him, computing, her eyes sparking among various emotions—embarrassment, exasperation, anger—trying to determine if he is crazy or just playing some kind of joke on her, trying to place who in the world this curious man could be, why he is sharing her room with her, holding that cellphone of his all wrong.

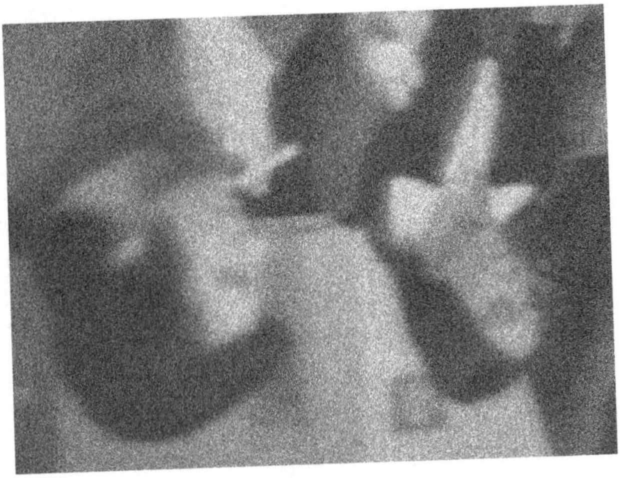

with in high school once in a whle & then never heard from again. they look like nice people, essentially optimistic, a couple w/ whom I might enjoy a drink. Only a drink; nothing more. Take a close look at their expressions: they appear to believe they have a # of interesting stories to tell. I'm sure they're right, though most escape me right now. I'm sure many had humorous endings on the far side of narrative's bridge, or possibly shiny ironic ones, or maybe led to brief illuminations about, say, the ~~tempest~~ temper of travel, or how people in the world really behave when they turn away from the camera.

I'm sure this was an important minute for them. I'm sure for the life of me I can't remember why.

Their room is tidy, even sparse: chest of drawers, large recliner, side table, reading lamp, throw rug. The woman's bed takes up most of the space, its adjustable metal frame cocked at an angle so her head remains slightly raised. Nights, he sleeps on a foam pad on the floor beside it.

And now he looks up, reaches over for his cellphone on the side table. Videoing, he asks: What mammals, honey?

These. Hear.

Where?

No. Listen. They're doing that thing animals do with their chlorides.

Screeching? Roaring?

The other.

[[<u>Paralipsis</u>, rhetoricians call it ->
the speaker/writer invoking a
subject by denying that it should
be invoked.]]

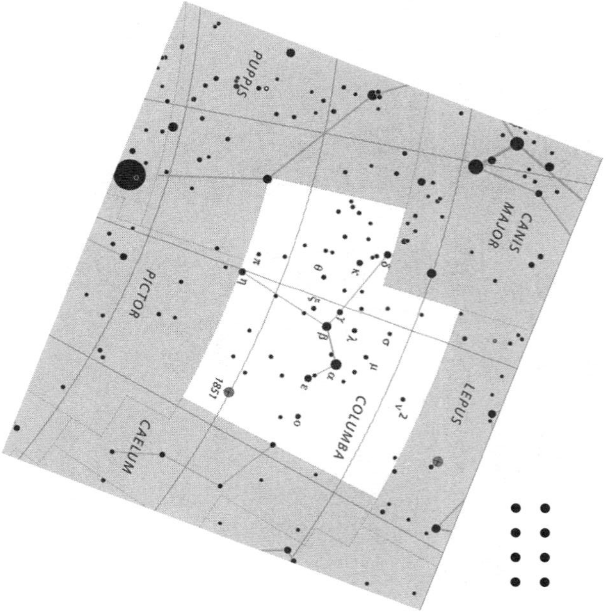

7 October

Because, 3 years later, Nancy Holt arranged 4 18-ft-long, 9-ft-in-diameter concrete Sun Tunnels in the wind-badgered Great Salt Lake Desert outside the nearly non-town of Lucin. They ~~flor~~ formed a great X, 2 aligned with the angles of the rising sun on the winter/summer solstices, 2 with the setting, small holes drilled atop each making a light constellation: Draco, Perseus, Columba, Capricorn.

Draw a line connecting those tunnels on the NW side of the lake w/ the Spiral Jetty on the NE, & you discover it is almost level, the former endpoint (Nancy's) dipping just slightly south of the latter (Robert's).

He has been reading, has been trying to read, sometimes the [diary] she used to keep because it was like visiting with someone he once knew but doesn't anymore, sometimes about the journalist gone missing in Burma. The journalist, never imagining things would take place the way they did, jotted notes in the pad he carried, tore them out, and wrapped them around Polaroid snapshots he clicked, tucked the packets into envelopes, and sent them to a woman back in the States who wasn't quite his girlfriend. He vanished crossing into India. Eventually the woman who wasn't quite his girlfriend edited what he had sent her and found a small publisher. A sign of gratefulness, she said in the foreword.

No sign when i helped him sort through her things . . .

this person with a high-pitched voice. The person's high-pitched voice rehearsed how somebody's wife had passed away recently and the husband whose wife it was hadn't used a machine like these since he was in grad school, and so, yes, if it weren't too much trouble, maybe she could show him what to do, how it operated, and the teenager did, gently, methodically, whites with whites, reds and pinks and oranges together, as if she were attempting to teach a person with an information processing disorder, as if the miniature box of Tide she cradled to her pelvis contained the souls of little murdered girls.

Who are these mammals? asks the woman—the other woman—one night from the hospital bed installed in their room.

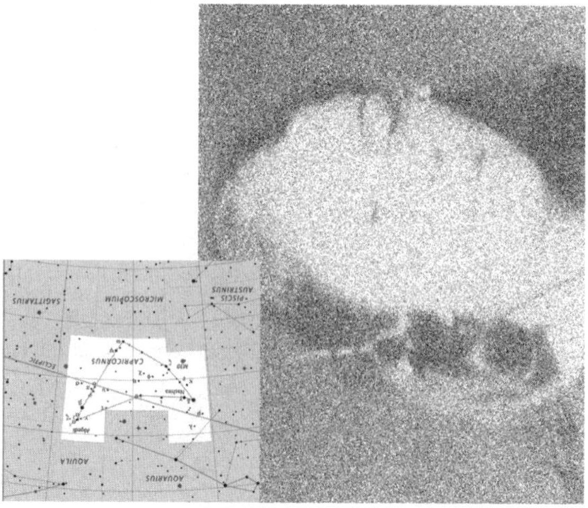

tHe tunnels, she once said, attempt to bring the sky down to earth.

8 October

I want to say I feel better today.

9 October

Spiral Jetty = inverse of distraction.

was the dream and which the other thing. The air in the house seemed to develop swerves, torques. Opening the washing machine several days later, he encountered her clothes clumped with his in the tub—dark, stiff. He tried to figure out how long the clothes must have been bunched in there like that. Then he lowered the lid and walked away. A week, and a certain fish-oily smell evolved. He returned, wadded the clothes into a large white garbage bag, and drove to the Second Avenue Laundry. He loitered before one of the industrial stainless steel washers until a teenager with long white-blond hair and pastel pink plaid shirt actualized beside him, asking if she could help him with something. The man heard somebody else nearby do the talking,

10 October

because, afterward, ~~Jonatha~~ James Turrell purchased the 400000-yr-old, three-km-wide crater of an extinct volcano outside Flagstag on the western edGe of the painted Desert, and began reapportioning tunes of earth in order to create various kinds of viewing chambers & tunnels within it employing as his media photons, sky, & celestial events, while Richard long commenced recording his solitary strolls through remote areas in Britain, Canada, Mongolia, and ~~Baz~~golivia, never making significant alterations to the landscapes he traversed, leaving oNly modest traces in his wake, ones you could almost muss, if you weren't plying attention—up-ending stones, or each day placing a single rock by

Scree.

What he is doing is sliding along a moving sidewalk through a vast airport.

What he is doing is appreciating the sensation of his body pressing back into foam as the plane rushes down the runway.

The thing everybody else knew was going to happen happened between 6:00 and 6:30 one otherwise flat November evening. The following morning her alarm clock went off at 7:30, just like always. At first the man couldn't understand, couldn't place which

the side of the path he took, transforming the act of walking into artowrk

11 October

~~Breikak~~

Breakfast on the deck:

I had this ~~drum~~dream last night, i said, poking at my granola and strawberry yogurt.

A dream? he said.

I was washing my hands in the restroom at the ~~mull~~ mill. The woman next to me glanced at my arm and asked me if I was okay.

he is another man, one they've never met before, while the man tries to work out what to look at, how to make it appear he's not thinking about being thought about, what he's doing with his feet.

On the street again, shaken, he ducks into an alley behind the All Star Travel Inn and uncaps the brown plastic bottle.

His fingers are doing things he doesn't mean them to.

He considers his right palm, studies this new variety of pill: the configuration of a Chiclets, the color of sage.

And you weren't.

She was wearing plum lipstick. That's all I remember. The top my arm was pockmarky, the bottom splotched purple and green.

You reached down & ~~robbed~~ rubbed it.

Which is when I noticed the skin moving. No, that's not it. There was something moving underneath the skin. These worms. Each an inch long. Flat. The closer I looked, the more of them there were.

~~But thi~~ that's not all, right?

I cld feel them wriggling across my back, too, into my spinal chord, up my neck into my brain. Miniature electric eels.

I ~~spin~~spooned in a mouthful of yogurt, recalling.

He watched me the way one person watches another when expecting a second act.

short chunky waiter leads Mike and Sandii to a table two over from the man.

The table between is empty.

The man smiles at Mike and Sandii as they take their seats and returns to his meal.

Two tables?

Instinctively the man speeds up eating, pretending he's not hurrying, he's not eavesdropping on Mike and Sandii's conversation, while the couple pretends the man isn't sitting as close as he is sitting, or maybe that the man is no longer this man,

What? I said.

That's it? he said.

What? I said.

You don't remember? he said.

What don't I remember?

It's not your dream, honey. Its mine.

...

...

...

The one I told you about last ~~wea~~week? On the deck? Like this?

...

Alana?

...

...

...

Lana? Lan? Honey?

You sure we can't twist your arm? Sandii asks.

In anticipation, she ducks her head under an invisible rafter.

Everyone misses you down at the store, Mike says.

You're sweet, says the man. Tell them I'll be back soon.

He isn't standing and he is, the trio in the interior of a social hug exchange—ineptly, as if each person were negotiating too many arms—and the

12 October

Because, afterward, Christo and Jeanne-Claude surrensurrounded the Reichstag w/ more than 100000 square mtrs of fireproof aluminum material. 11 islands in Miamis Biscayne Bay with 603850 ~~squir~~ square meters of pink polypropylene floating fabric. Set up 1340 giant blue umbrellas in Ibarki, Japan, ~~klasw to 592~~ another 1760 giant yellow ones at the Tejon Ranch, 75 miles north of L.A., eateach 6 mtrs tall, 8 in diameter. 3 million people visited & of those llf alewj two died: a giant yellow umbrella crushing a woman named Lori Mathews against rocks when a freak gust of wind blew it over; a crane operator named Masaaki Nakamura electrocuted when a blue one he was helping take down patted a 65000-volt power line. Art, then death.

How you doing? Mike asks, tone modulating into concern. Seriously, I mean.

We think about you all the time, says Sandii.

The man explains it's complicated. He explains how everything he says—he believes he could also say the opposite and it would sound equally true. He explains how everything cancels out everything else, or jumbles it up, or something. In mid-sentence, he laughs.

Look at me, he says. I don't know what I'm talking about. I'm fine. I'm getting by. It's great to see you guys.

13 October

i was standing on the sidewalk outside my front door, facing my house, sobbing, occurring to mybself. This is how the news gets through: a little, then a little more.

14 October

15 October? 16?

austrailia: 1674021. Oregin: 664252. Iwa: 539758. MS: 522130. Utah: 498794.

Rumor has it Mike was a Lost Boy, one of those kids banished from a fundamentalist Mormon compound in southern Utah for talking to a girl, watching a movie, who every once in a while turns up wandering around inside the downtown library.

We'd love to have a chance to catch up, Sandii adds.

Thanks, the man says. But it's good. Really.

The couple trades convivial coded expressions, which dissolve into overly compassionate ones, which they re-aim at him.

Didn't you love how dad used to refer to them as the L.S.D. -> Little Soul Deaths?

[[The man had one estimable bullshit detector.]]

18? 20?

~~Becawse, afterward, Michael Heizer~~

???

Robert Smithson: & each ~~ku~~cubic salt crystal echoes the spirul jetty in terms of the crystal's molecular latice. Growth in a crystal advances around a dis~~ou~~location point in the manner of a screw. TSJ could be considered 1 layer w/in the spiraling crystal lattice, magnified trillions of ~~tombs~~

???

Fractal aesthetics.

~~i dont~~

He specializes in environmental tracts. The man can't remember what Sandii does. He wants to say yoga instructor. Accountant. Yoga instructor. Mike is shaggily blond, bearded and stomached like an ex-logger. Sandii is flimsily blond, bony and mar-ginally stooped like an ex-dancer with an eating disorder. They wear matching jeans and powder-blue t-shirts that say: God's Little Bitch.

& then your packing the car with my vidoe gaer & a lunch cooler, propping me on the edge of our ~~bad~~ bed & helping me into my ski pants, sweater, scarf, socks, thermal boots, parka, gloves. (My ~~mucsl~~ muscles aren't working weel tod

Effexor?

& then We're crawling ~~dun~~down through the Avenues, health volunteers in blue surgical masks the only people mullmilling around outside.

Wellbutrin?

Rushing north on interstate 15 past oil refineries, suburbs scrambling into foothills, vast lake flickering into substance to our ~~lift~~

Zoloft?

Vicodin?

will make him do, and, looking up, encounters Mike from the bookstore.

Prozac?

Mike is standing there hand in hand with his what is her name his girlfriend, no, his wife, Helen, no, Sandy, Sandii, with two i's, beaming down at him with apprehensive brightness, inviting him to join them for lunch.

Luvox?

Hey, guys, the man says agreeably.

The pill is burning his esophagus. He asks how they're doing, thanks them for inviting him. Except, he says, he wouldn't want to intrude. Except they should enjoy themselves.

Paxil?

Intrude? says Mike. Jesus. Come on.

Mike works evenings behind the main register.

Angling off the highway at Corinne 60 miles north, the road tumbling into 2 lanes the ~~wur~~world shedding away oatmeal mountains and rusty scrub grass pitching up

Like driving into a Western.

You expect covered wagons cowboys

War parties collecting along the ridgeli

~~25 miles father~~

25 miles farther, just beyond the visitor center commemorating the completion of the 1st transcontinental railroad in 1869, ~~asfalt rums pir~~ asphalt

By the time the short chunky waiter with the flat-footed lumber shows him to a table, the man is sweating fiercely.

It is only 3:30 and already the restaurant is crowded and rackety.

Sweating fiercely, the man tries to concentrate on the menu amid chatter and chinkle and the hiss coming off freshly delivered fajita platters. He tries to concentrate as if he might choose something out of the ordinary, then orders what he always orders: a Corona and sopa de frijol negro. He extracts the vial from his pocket. Ticks out a pill (peach, pentagonal), slips it between his lips, curious about what it

Ortega: "To think is to ask for trouble." A piece of paper with this line on it taped above my word processor.

runs out & progress devolves into following markers a little bigger than your hand instructions tucked into odd crannies on the Web: take the gravel road 6 miles ~~worst~~ west to intersection w/ white sign for Promontory Ranch; turn south & continue another mile ~~& 1/2~~

crossroads near an ab~~un~~andoned corral; curve southwest 9 miles on the deteriorating packeddirt road hodgepodged with stones & erosion fissu

sometimes, I re~~mumm~~member thinking, we used to pass a lone car tortoising back from its pilgrimage. He used to lower his window & flag down the driver to confirm we were on the right track. ~~Slkanwlsd~~

It takes him nearly forty-five minutes, even though he was sure when he began that the restaurant was only two blocks away, two or three, which he crosses a wide intersection, thinks he may be off-course, retraces his steps, strikes out again, passes a shabby service station, a low-slung strip mall from the fifties, a Pizza Hut, a tobacco shop, an adult boutique. He is the only pedestrian out in the open. A steady sibilation of traffic, but he is the only pedestrian except for the man in a badly fitting business suit pumping gas into his Honda Accord, except for the woman with the platinum beehive staring up at the unoccupied sky between drags on her cigarette in front of the dry cleaners.

i saw you step out one afternoon as i was driving by. You were squinting, my exposed mole-brother.

Waiting for the creeping wash of pleasure, the man reclines his seat and closes his eyes and observes his mind trying to do things, first this thing and then that, but less and less well, at a greater and greater distance, believing at some point it is still wide awake when it isn't, not really, not at all.

What he is doing is sitting on the edge of the bed, motel room filamenting with shower steam, listening to children noises on the far side of the door.

Next he is dressing in the same clothes he wore to the airport.

Next he is striking out on North Temple.

(Sometimes at the end
of what could no longer
quiet be referred to as the
road we used to discover
a solitary Jeep or Bronco
overlooking the remnants
of the oilrigs & a few 100
yards past them down
a brief steep hill clotted
with sagebrush the thing
it

~~today you dont~~

~~Today no one;s here ex~~

the sky a noisy blu, the lake an electric
turquoise amazement the suns a fanatic, the atmosphere scorched the salt flat @ the edge of which the jetty
now lies so white ~~at stgg~~ it staggers

he's rolling to a stop, throwing on the emergency brake
throwing open the door walking around the car to
help me out & we're standing there stretching
our spines working our knees

The woman in the seat beside him is reading
too fast. She is one of those people who in her twenties applied sexy black eyeliner with the precision
of a French model, but now, in her late forties, has
gotten sloppy, the eyeliner all smeary, awobble, and
she's turning the pages too quickly.
Who could read like that?
The point of such an act would be what, exactly?

He had been reading. He had been trying to read...some book about a journalist who went missing in Burma. A kind of memoir. There are no such things as memoirs. They are ingenuously written novels disguised as memoirs. The last line, he remembered, came as a surprise: "[NOTE TORN, TEXT MISSING]"

What mammals, honey? he asked, raising his head.

He swallows the pair of pills with another long chug from the water bottle. He takes his time with the scotch over ice, which tastes lightly of the plastic cup it inhabits. He orders another.

two tin men after a downpour

were arranging our gear   slowshuffling down to what's
left of Smithson's idea   & next im videoing, ~~ju g99rs sew~~
boots wetcrunching through glassy crust   interested in the
long shotsm   the ones that take in the jarring sweep of
water

grayblue mountains serrating the low horizon

[[basalt chunks rickracking the shoreline among prickly paleyellow weeds & ~~viscous~~viciously green blushes]]

[[the saline tang in the mouth]]

[sulfurous rot on the breeze]]

Because this countertop was new to him. The palms of his hands, too. How doorknobs received his grip. How her bank records scrolled down her laptop's screen in the office that used to be a girl's room, turning her into a procession of evocative numbers.

He would sometimes lie on the floor next to the sleeping woman's bed and, hands cupped behind his skull, pass time looking up at the ceiling through light textured like the static on a rabbit-eared TV set.

One night she asked—not that woman, no, the other: Who are these mammals?

Inside the first bag, twenty-three peanuts.

Inside the second, twenty-seven.

His backpack had no identification on or in it. No luggage tags, no journal, no travelers' checks. He watched it glide through the dangling black flaps behind the check-in counter and dematerialize.

It was there. It was gone.

On the far side of security, a man in Hawaiian shirt, shorts, and white socks almost reaching his knees rode up the escalator, down, facing backward, holding a large blue Slurpee to his chest with distractingly short arms.

What the light is making
happen around me is almost
overwhelming.

i'm interested in a series of close-ups:
the miniscule translucent brine shrimp
pinking the waters edge the ~~slat~~salt
crystals furring the jetty's rocks the
desiccated nearly colorless bardbird
carcasses strewn across the flats.

It's unclear how they died.

The impression: the very intensity of the environment in which they tried living murdered them.

two, three, each a different shape, shade, deliberates, changes his mind, slips one back in, clicks the cap back on.

When the flight attendants jangle and bang to a stop beside him, he pays for a scaled-down scotch bottle. With it he receives two shiny blue bags of peanuts and one tiny square white napkin with a maybe it is a polyethylene gloss.

Had someone asked, he would have said he wanted her to experience the same thing he did, more or less, roughly speaking, if only for a minute.

He wanted to share.

Scree: his mouth mouthing.

The man ferrets through the zipper pouches in his daypack between his legs until he locates the brown prescription vial, taps out a pill the color of California swimming pools, changes his mind, taps out

Czeslaw Milosz: "The purpose of poetry is to remind us how difficult it is to remain just one person."

he wanders farther & farther out till soon hes nothing except
a thin dark squiggle wobbling against whiteblue shimmer

even with my gloves on even in
this ~~glow~~growing heat, my sausage fingers are so numb i'm
~~k~~clownclumsy with the equipment

friends already knew what he would say, and he already knew what they would say, and there was only so much language developed for an occurrence of this kind, and then everything became repetition, the groove at the end of the record where the needle refuses to lift.

What he was doing was rearranging. Transposing toothpaste tube and mouthwash bottle, face cream jar and deodorant stick, tweezers and scissors, nail filer and floss dispenser.

Before he misplaced the Pepto-Bismol, he unscrewed the top and took two chalky wintergreen swigs.

He wanted her to know what it felt like, he would have said had someone asked.

Not a hand slap or anything. More a sharp nip.

[[[And ours. He stopped picking up -- when? Maybe 2 weeks after the cremation. it took me a while to figure what that meant, then one day i rang him up to discover his phone had been disconnected.]]]

I remember thinking ::::

I remember thinking :::: the way the jetty assembles itself with the atmosphere, the micro-glittering water, this estranging landscape.

[[its remarkable the human eye doesn't fail more quickly, given all it lets in during a lifetime]]

the stillness making each klip seem photo~~grphai~~graphic—inhaling exhaling inhaling again before detecting the most evanescent movement through the viewfinder: a shadow shifting in air, current unsettling the lake &

What he was doing was opening the cap on every plastic prescription bottle, tapping all but three or four pills from each into his palm, snicking the cap back on, replacing the bottle where he found it. There was the way at some stage he stopped returning friends' calls, although he can't bring to mind precisely when that point was, it seemed always in some perplexing past tense, because his

Remember the time he slapped me when the glass of milk i was carrying from fridge to breakfast table slipped out of my hands? His fingertips were done with me before either of us had a chance to register the happening. Then it was over, and mom and you were sitting there, & i was standing in front of him, and he was appalled at himself, at what his body had tried to get away with behind his back.

Later we heard them shouting in their bedroom. it was one of those Kid moments when you realize with a rush that no one outside the airtight box called Family could possibly understand who you are.

& motionlessness thats really a succession of nearly indiscernible motions soundlessness thats steady background wind

i won't forget this remembering thinking
    i promise
    i won't let this morning ~~gut~~ away

~~Was apon a th~~

we used to swim legs & arms buoying bodies unable to sink even if they tried & afterward the fine salt residue crusting your skin your ~~what is the wor~~ wet clothes drying into rumpled mannequins how you washed & washed them before you could convince them to deflate back into themselves

And so: I should leave, he thought. He knew he should leave. He decided: I will. He would. That's what he was doing. Except that wasn't what he was doing. What he was doing was entering the bathroom with the clawfoot tub. What he was doing was cautiously unlatching the medicine cabinet, cupping his hand beneath it in case anything clattered out.

There was touching this item for the last time, touching that. The slow recognition about how his coworkers had started treating him with disquieting attention, as if he were somehow fragile, injured, exposed, which he was, of course, he wouldn't disagree, but which he didn't want to be, did and didn't want to be perceived and treated as.

The man remained motionless next to the desk until his lumbar vertebrae pounded. His knees began to lock. It wasn't interesting anymore and, halfway down the hallway himself, he heard her snore recommence. He stopped to make sure. It sounded like what is the word comfort, no, reprieve, it sounded like the word reprieve, that's what it sounded like.

Time emptying out from the morning.

Time corrupting.

raising my head over the viewfinder to ankchor myself
spotting him hanging crosslegged far out in the middle of a
white dream

he is doing. He isn't. He didn't. What he did was stay put, stall to see what she would do next so he could determine what he should do next, and what she did next was remove something from the fridge, clank it back inside again, thunk shut the door.

She drifted upstairs. She drifted downstairs. She drifted along the hallway, back to bed.

There was how at some point waking in the morning became physically painful, unexpected, a surge of fright. How he would wrench out of sleep with his chest fluttery as a twilight swallow.

There was selling the house. There was purging the closets.

Never told you how i met Claudia,
did i? 3 a.m. in this uber-Berlinish
club Ackerkeller on Bergstrasse.
Lacuna Amnesia playing. All pixie &
pink-haired. 6 years younger than me.
Sharply intuitive.

We woke up next afternoon in my place
& have been living here ever since.

~~wat i mean to~~

crut~~chn~~ching ~~bank~~
to the shoreline up the hill to pee among large basalt buffalo humps Rounding a boulder the size of an ~~uprhgt~~ upright refrigerator, this: 10 or 12 people scattered across the rocky ground in front of me, some curled against one another, some into th~~ume~~mselves, some stretched out on their backs, hands folded on their stomachs. most in their teens, early 20s, but theres also a mna in John Lennon glasses & cropped graying hair who could pass as a prof & several away a scrawny woman in her 30s with pointy features & tiny mouth who could pass as a biker. The little whiteblond girl with the portwine stain from the ~~stuper~~supermarket tucked into the arms of a shirtless mulleted man in voluminous beige shorts his face grease-painted silver like at a football game

my 1st thought: how could ~~thse plep~~ these people possibly sleep so diligently on scuh inhospitable earth?

My sekond: they're all dead.

This unfolding thought: I can easily take her.
And this: I could sprint up behind her, knock
her to the floor, sweep up my sneakers, become bad
memory before she knew what hit her.
He could do that. It would be weirdly easy. He
wouldn't need to employ a utensil. A vase. A potted
plant. He could do that. He is doing that. That's what

theyre not all dead. you can see ribcages ~~ripen~~rising and falling. The prof making clacking noises at the back of his throat. the scrawny woman twitching negligibly, a ~~god~~dog napping itself into a flock of lifting geese

its the teenager outs~~t~~ide the library, multiplied

a hive

the calm hand calming on my shoulder i flinch ducking out from ~~unnerv~~

under it turning all in one to find him standing beside me explaining he's followed me to make sure everythings okay only everything isnt okay

nothing is okay

this is the thing wE both know

[[imagine: you & i, dear bro, exist as 4 words in the hem of this
narrative. Remarkable how noisy
silence can be.]]

how we find ourselves waiting, taking in the ~~fract~~ fact together

i reed the flash at the corner of my
vision as a rogue floater & than I get
it: <u>a flake</u>

to confirm it was the original, when he heard the
woman's snore cut short.

A breath, and the sound of her throwing off the
sheets.

A breath, and the disturbance of her rising.

Maybe she had heard him. Maybe she was simply on her way to pee. Maybe she was having trouble sleeping, too.

Motionless by the desk, he saw her dark form drift past the doorway. Heard her move down the hall into the kitchen where he had left his sneakers neatly aligned inside the sliding doors.

hovering in the air   another. large shavings sifting down around us, sparsely at first, &, within a fEw pulses, thicker, more persistent

Are we seeing this? i ask.
I don't think so, you say.

its ~~slow~~ snowing yet the sky remains its tactless blue

milky fish scales tapping sleepers
faces chests legs arresting winking out and next

and next a strange man hovering at the foot of my bed.

The room, my room, I'm fairly sure, smutched in grays, the mans face staticky as an old black+white television set left on at 3 in the mourning

who are these people? I ask him

what people?

When did they go to school?

When did they rest?

Families grilling. Rat dogs fighting. Sitcoms blaring from open windows.

The man sits on the edge of the bed in his damp underwear and damp socks, feet flat on the carpet, hands flat on the bedspread, inhaling, remembering the time he was in the office that used to be the girl's room, prying at the shaggy non-colored rug these. here.

the strange man hovers in the slatey air contemplating. out of the static he says: where are you, honey?

tkaing to you

no, he replies. you're somewhere else. where are you? i'd like to be there with you. tell me where u r

[[i want to say i am writing this]]

[[i want to say i am dreaming it]]

him while the flight attendants commence unbuckling, rising to prepare the snack and beverage carts, brew the coffee, busy themselves with gossip in the galley.

Take a picture of me, a teenage girl says to her mother behind him, not the fucking hills.

He can hear the kids from the trailer park playing outside. Constantly. In the parking lot, behind the motel.

the light, the trace of beery apricot within it you cant tell me this isnt late october you cant tell me were not ~~all~~already living in the future

[[maybe some time is passing]]

sweat pants and hoodie has released a novel with a hot teenage vampire on the cover and begun reading while people strike up conversations around

in my diary, I write: <u>People don't take trips. Trips take people.</u>

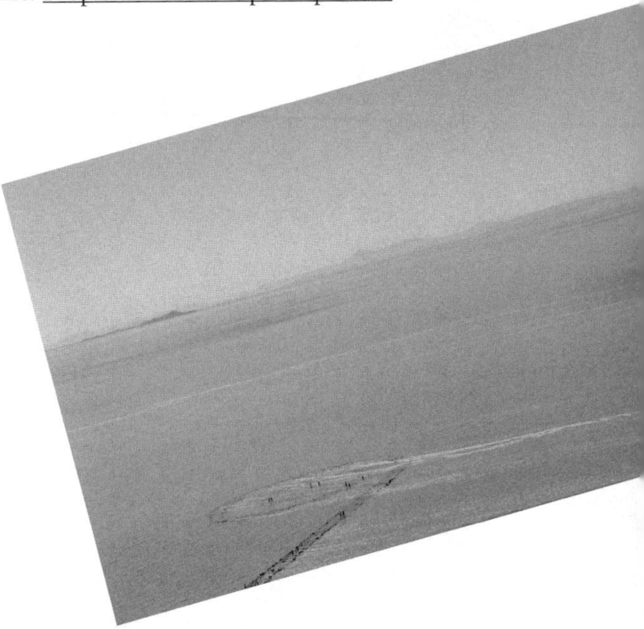

body was sleeping next to yours or watching something with you on the Discovery Channel about the
history of maps or how beer possibly dates back to
9500 B.C. when cereal was first farmed.

The point that was important was that nothing
was important.

This was the important point.

The significance was precisely the lack of significance.

Beside him, a chubby woman in pink Juicy

[[maybe all the nights are the same night]]
in the waiting area outside the doctors office i fail three people quizzes about celebrity love lives   which british actor was arrested in july for assaulting his mother & sister   which american start met and fell for prince william dur

thats your memory again

There were two people living together, day after
day, dicing carrots hip-to-hip in the kitchen.
Strolling up the street after dinner to watch
evening glitter on across the valley.
There was the uninvolved knowing that another

wn my diary, I right: theirs so much time my eyes hurt

~~what are they doing? I ask the strange man.~~

Who?

he is sitting in a chair next to my
bed reading The title of the ~~beak~~ in
his hands is Theories of Forgetting.
His face is well lit yet I can't place him
he seems like a good person, someone
I can count on, but i dont trust him

All the people, I tell him.
where are you new he asks

Disappointed, he discovers someone has already filled out the in-flight magazine's crossword
puzzle.

How can it be snowing? It can't be snowing on a day like this. It's crazy.

would you like your diary? u can write it down u can read what youre ~~thank~~thinking. Would you like that?

inn my ~~rdai~~diary I rite she cried a little bit every day—not becs she was sad, but becs the whirled was so beautiful and life so ~~shot~~short

~~what I mean to~~

A minute, five. He turns from the awareness of lying on his side half a mile above ragged cliffs and scree slopes to lowering his shade and reaching for the water bottle in the seatback in front of him.

i know your not there the man on
the answering machine says i just
wanted to here yr voice on this thing
i'm   where am I? I'm down the
hall.   leaning against the counter
in the kithcen its   when is it? Past
midnight I think. just hit me i
almost never used this number. Isn't
that odd? couldn't even remember
if it's the right one we always knew
where the other one would be so
why call anyway i want to know how
it works from here on out i mean
how do I get up and walk to our
bedroom i'm trying to picture it but
uh   okay   Ii'm going to hang
up now ill call you back   i
promise

A spangling tug in his lower abdomen and tarmac
dropping away below him.
The hazy khaki desert. Rapidly contracting
roads. White-fringed salt marshes.
Fuselage creaking and swaying.
He closes his eyes and opens them and sees
brutal blue lake, sunstorm, complicated city, the
flagrant shock of mountains.

Performing ahistorical activities generates a sphere of silence around him, of what is the word salvation, no, cessation, a sphere of cessation around him, yes, sometimes in his socks, his sneakers neatly aligned inside the sliding doors, the buttery sensation of the floorboards beneath him, how he can slide across the living room in a slo-mo skate, elbows pumping, or sometimes lean back against the kitchen countertop, cool black granite against hot dry palms, staring into accruing luminescence, head blank as snow blindness, spooning up granola and yogurt and banana coins.

Hers: his.

in mi diary i write: im freezing

Keep an i on the television set. the information it radiates.

youll be watching a ~~worm~~worn-
out sitcom star selling a rejuvenating
face cream…flipping between her and
reruns of a crime show set in miami
during the eighties black man white
man skimming across blue bay in a
speedboat & the sitcom star will look
up at the camera from her product the
black man turn away from the chase

Bill's gone she will tell you thru electromagnetic waves

rita's left us he will say

i'm very sorry she will say

vanitys cheap he will say you know its always the first to go

stepping into and out of the clawfoot tub, running his fingertips along the spines of the books in the library upstairs that used to be somebody's office. He bends forward, arches his neck delicately, touches his tongue to a faux leather binding, resumes his usual posture.

An email i received from mom
shortly after she was diagnosed
-- "Please don't worry too much
about my medical news, sweetheart.
it's just the way it is living
inside a human body."

About the time i assumed
she was too far gone to write
again, another email --
"There is a 100% chance i
will die of something sometime,
and it is a good and holy
thing to be mindful of this,
to live each day with joy +
gratitude." Who wrote that?

candles, antique perfume bottles, decorated eggs, miniature ceramic elves issuing from miniature ceramic huts.

Who wants to pass the night under such alarming conditions?

It gives him the impression he is snorkeling and someone reaches over and pinches off the top of his rubber tube.

No. That would be your room.

It feels all right standing there, simply standing, except it feels even better wandering through the rest of the place, visiting the tiny office that used to be a girl's room two doors down with the heavy desk and the laptop with amebic rainbow screen-saver. The tiny bathroom, which it feels even better

Even the dogs have given in until morning.

He steps onto the deck and lifts the window with the broken catch and is blind-manning through the living room, the hallway, arms extended in front of him in case she has re-orchestrated the furniture again. He doesn't like the uncertainty. He doesn't like it yet somehow he does. It makes him feel like he can inhale sleep and the lack of color in this house.

These days the bedroom is all off. He barely recognizes it, which is everything has been redistributed, jumboed and stuffed and fluffed in there like some nightmare rococo painting. The top of her dresser and side ta[illegible] crowded with knickknacks,

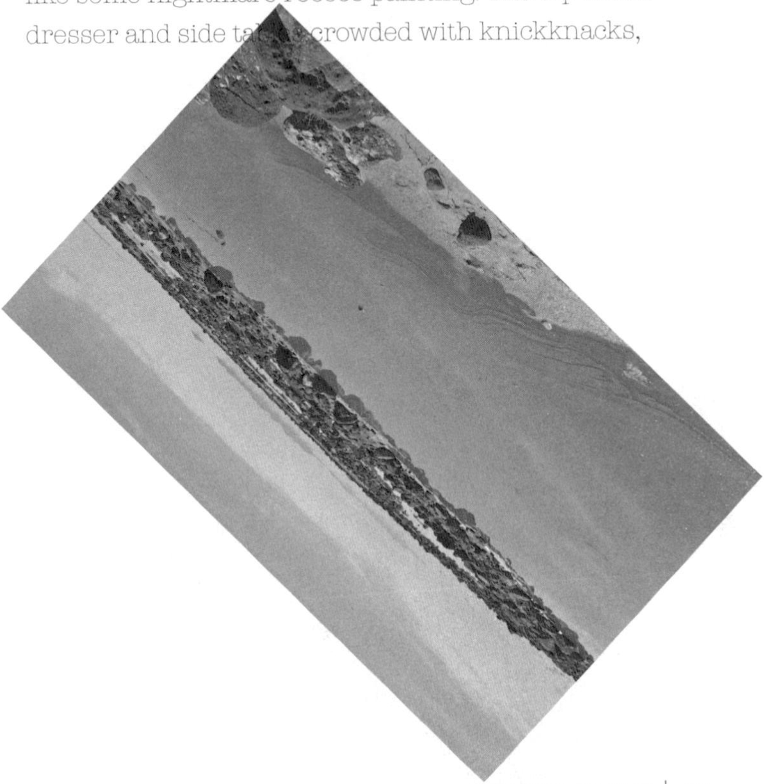

[ick up the voice says

who looks like a girl I used to know
sits crosslegged beneath cloudlarge trees on the collage lawn

boy in wirerimmed glasses standing behind her peering over her shoulder at her sketches

this is how your bones break sweetheart he says affectionately

he says

listen to the crackles

The street behind him is one-hundred-percent empty, the neighborhood one-hundred-percent aphasic.

strolling along the sidewalk in front of the bungalow. Reaching the end of the block, he turns and strolls the other way.

Streetlamps shifting light frequencies and white brick dirtying into pewter, gray trim into blackish blue.

A breath, and he veers, cuts across the front yard, alongside the house, past the whirring air-conditioning unit in the bedroom window, up the pile of cinderblocks, over the slatted wooden fence.

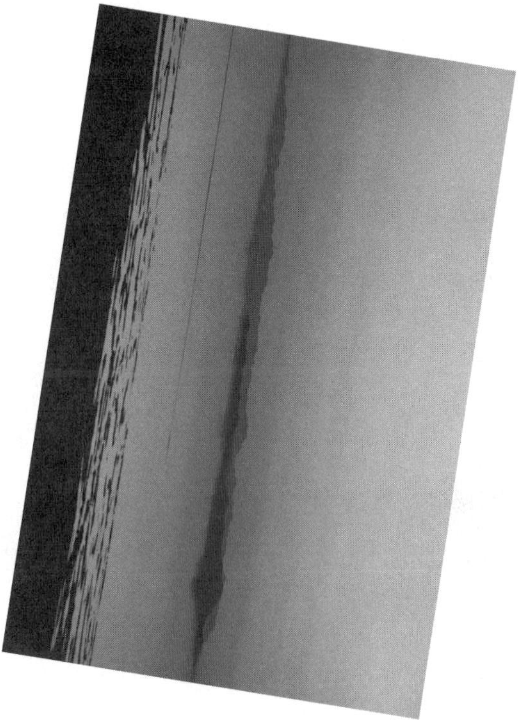

<u>Ppick up</u> the voice on the answering machine says

hello i say.

<u>Pick up if you're there.</u>

who are they i ask the strange man

lids don't quite make contact with her lower ones. He can see the whites, thin slices of unnerving.

The flight is happening around him, the plane rushing down the runway, his body pressing back into foam.

Sometimes several hours before dawn he ends up

appear older when they are unconscious. On their backs, mouths open a little, chins tilted up, they aren't the same people as when ordering a burger at McDonald's, removing a book from a shelf down at the store. The woman beneath him seems dead except for her snore and it doesn't help that her eyes aren't fully shut, a fact that startles him when he first realizes it, causes him to suspect maybe she is really awake, staring up at him, stalling to determine what he will do next so she can work out what she will do next. Only the more his own eyes acclimate, the more he can see it is just that her upper

his damp underwear and damp socks, feet flat on the carpet, hands flat on the bedspread, breathing machine-cooled air smelling of mildew and maybe it is someone else's body odor or sadness.

Teflon sheen leaks from around the blinds in her room. There isn't Teflon sheen and his eyes adjust then there is and he crosses to her bed gingerly. Hovering over her, he appreciates how people

[[

this is enough

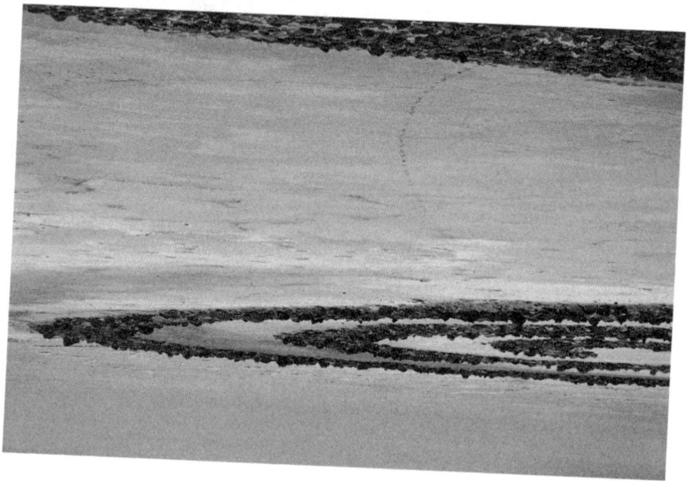

Chateau Motel and Trailer Court,
1999 West North Temple. No Record.

At the front desk the man asks the toad-bellied clerk in shapeless beige shorts and Lynyrd Skynyrd t-shirt for the same room he has been living in for however long he has been living in it.

Loose-faced, the clerk processes him as if he had never seen him before.

Door locked, bolted, do-not-disturb tag on the outside handle, he pulls the plastic-backed curtains and sets down his daypack on the chair in the corner and waits beside the laminate desk, then takes a shower because nothing else comes to mind. Afterward, he sits on the edge of the bed in

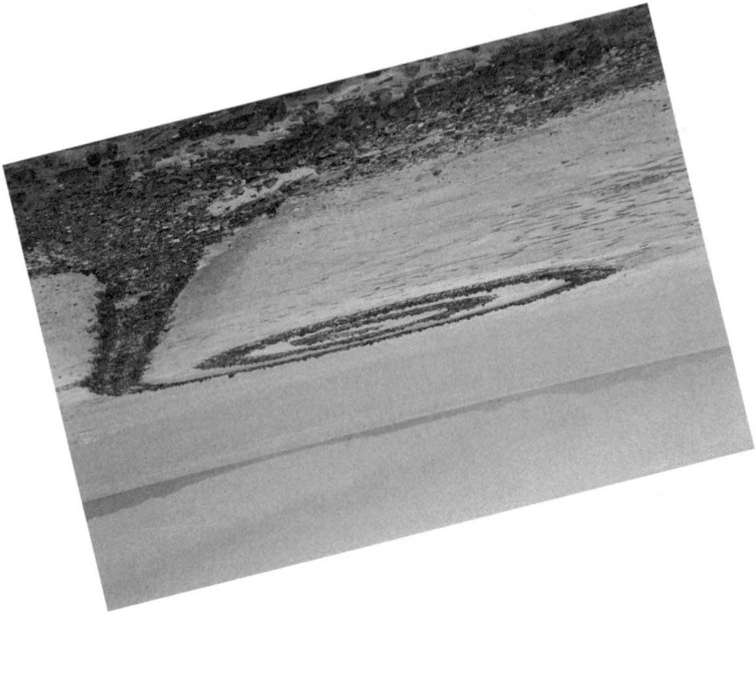

how come we never made videos of us asks the voice on the answering machine

it waz always this person
that thing where were we

i take the diary from the strange man and write

i'm hear

He doesn't return to his gate. He continues walking—past the row of fast-food restaurants, the security checkpoint, down the escalator into baggage claim, out of the terminal.

A yellow taxi at the pickup stand, its windows rolled down, its trunk already ajar: this is what he rides to the motel and trailer park just beyond the noisy 215 overpass.

Google: Route 215 everywhere (Arkansas, North Carolina, Maine, Missouri, etc.), with motels/trailer parks in the vicinity of more than dozen.

It is here, like this, and not on the plane, not at 38,000 feet, that he initially experiences time-blear. He is in this place but he is anywhere and it could be two in the afternoon and it could be four in the morning.

Another day, another week.

In the restroom he removes his cellphone from his pocket, turns it on, holds it under the faucet for sixty seconds, ninety, bunches it up in paper toweling, drops it in the trashcan below the hole in the countertop.

Jack, he thinks, exiting. I look like a Jack.

Beautiful turn: "time-blear."

Yet here's the problem: i don't remember him writing. As in EVER. He was always the family's book man, but only in the sense of reader/collector/page lover--never author.

any more than he can, they keep watching, keep anticipating the next story, which will, they believe, he believes, always be more interesting than the one they're actually watching.

Enormous planes settle onto the runway like clumsy pelicans a lake. His forehead nearly touching the window wall. Behind, an agitation of mothers, fathers, grandparents, uncles, aunts involved in the pastime of trying to distract children on the verge of tears, boredom, pules, chases, ruin. Businessmen talking to spirits on ear-bud headphones. Passengers scattered among seats, knitting, reading, dozing, studying maps, playing video games, typing on computers, iPads, Blackberrys, listening to music, examining palms, staring at the CNN Airport Network on the screen suspended from the ceiling. Although they can't hear what's being said

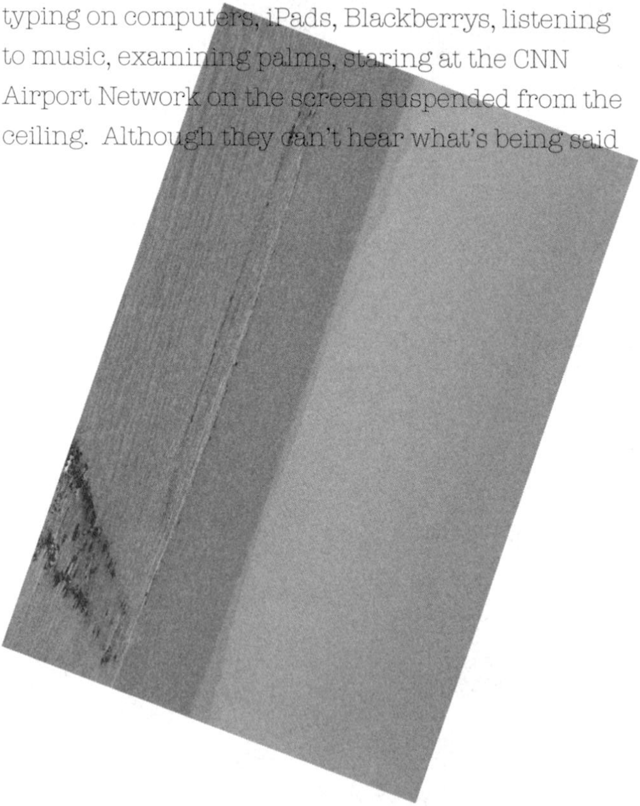

He wanders the airport for hours. Coke and slice of pizza at Sbarro. Latte and slice of banana walnut bread at Starbucks. He thumbs through travel guides at the bookstore, rides past photographs of implausible orange rock formations on the moving walkway.

There were his children and then that was something else.

(Look quick. There we are.)

But let me back up and start again, dear bro. Anja's waiting for me after work one evening with a message the manager stuffed under our door: Sie haben ein Paket. i run down to pick it up only to find this, postmarked Amman, half a year after the fact, addressed in a hand i don't recognize (see enclosed), no name of sender, addressee, just the address itself.

it's not his voice, and, even if it were, why the weird use of 3rd person? Written sometime before he left the States? Journal in the form of some invisible future-perfect thought experiment? it doesn't make any sense -- or as he would say: it does & it doesn't. Help me out here, okay? What are you seeing?

dangling black flaps into a dimension he can't quite bring to mind. He watches where it used to be until the airline agent with milky oversized midwestern glasses hands him his boarding pass and tells him the gate number, which he forgets before he has stepped away from the counter.

His daypack waiting in a gray tub on an aluminum table.

White sneakers. Cellphone. Brown belt.

The man holds up his ticket in front of him like a mug shot. The tall, slender, black, modernist TSA screener on the other side of the metal detector waves him through, focusing, not on him,
but on the LED panel above his head.

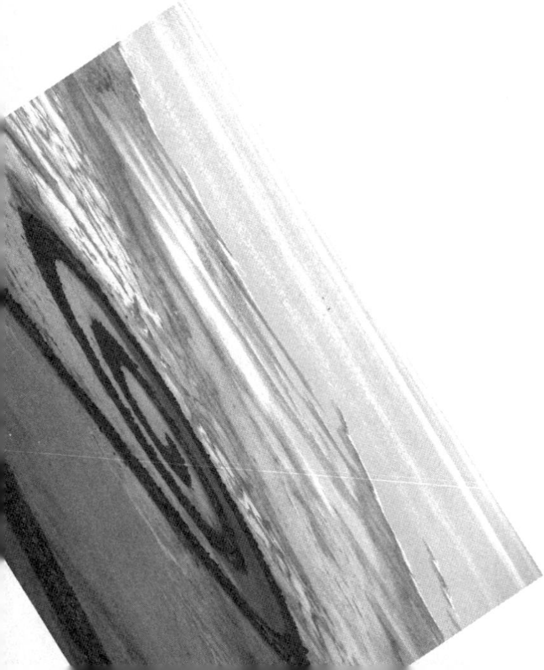

glass door, glances back at the woman who is now raising the phone to her ear and parting her lips to speak.

See you soon, he mouths, models her a smile, steps through.

A moment later, maybe a week, he is watching his backpack slide down the conveyor belt behind the check-in counter and disappear through

evaluating, which is when he understands he no
longer has anything to add.

He does have something to add and then he
doesn't and in a quick relaxed series of gestures he
pivots, cuts across the kitchen, unlocks the sliding

No: that was someone else.

I love its attention to detail, he says. You don't get that anymore, do you. The twenties. The thirties. But not these days. Crown moldings. Wall niches. The what do you call them corbels. Not in this price range.

He sees the woman's cellphone is on. A fuzzy, radiant phosphorescence meaning the line is open, meaning somewhere out there a 911 operator is listening in on their conversation, recording,

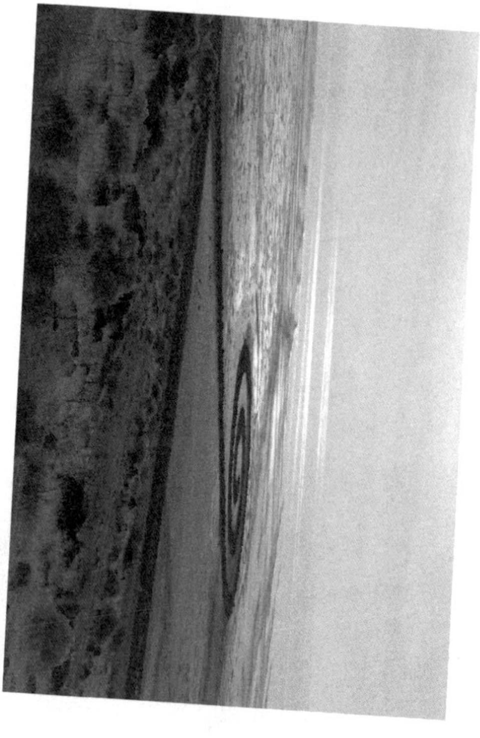

Just so you know.

Do you like the house? he asks.

Before I came out. From the bedroom.

Its character. What do you think of its character?

They'll be here any minute. Like on one of those reality cop shows. And it's June.

June? he says.

I'm a florist. I make flowers look flowery. I bother exactly no one. What have I got you could possibly want?

The word bungalow.

Her face, he sees: she is wearing a surgical mask.

You get this bit with the mask?
Me, i'm clueless.

What the fuck happened over there?

toward what is the word legibility. The light surrounding him is resolving toward legibility. Colors rising out of the room's complex aspects.

No, her robe isn't pink. It is a difficult shade of blue. Blue or gray, but not pink or quilted.

Terrycloth.

The word for what it is is terrycloth.

He wants to say the woman is wearing matching slippers and all at once she isn't suspended anymore. She is planted on the floor just like he is, planted in this room, this neighborhood, speaking to him like he is speaking to her.

I've already called the police, she is saying.

i shudder every time i reach this section.

he hovered over her sleeping body in her bed. Her face kept changing. He couldn't get over it. Her face kept becoming other people's faces as he watched. He remembers being mildly impressed by the resonance, the tenacity, of her snore. It wasn't loud, just persistent. She had a white scar over her left eyebrow suggesting a grain of rice or a flatworm. He can't make it out now, which is when he becomes aware that the light surrounding him is resolving

Clean the plates? Put them away? What sort of burglary is this?

The man dries the bowl and spoon with the luminous dishtowel on the stove front, replaces the bowl in the cabinet, the spoon in the drawer.

I eat off the plates you've eaten off? she asks. Adds: The doors are locked. The windows.

The one that looks onto the deck? he says, facing her again, leaning back against the granite countertop. The lock only feels like it looks.

You know this? i Know that window, right?

The catch. Of course i Know that window. That deck. That Kitchen.

He is moving effortlessly. Her kitchen. His. He squints and she grows younger. Squints and she grows older. He experienced the same effect when

You just come in? she says to his back. You just do this?

I don't take anything.

Food. You take food. And then...what? You eat?

You're asking me the questions? I'm asking you the questions.

They are both quiet, he recalling his dentist once explaining to him that teeth are perpetually adrift in your gums, migrating and modifying continuously, no matter who you are, what you try to do about it.

Three months, she says. Three and a half.

No, a cellphone.

Three and a half, he says. Five, six. It's April, right?

He steps over to the sink, spoons the contents of the black or gray bowl down the drain, flips on the water, the garbage disposal; flips off the garbage disposal, the water.

the heart is allways the least to go away

It's been months, she says. How many months
has it been?
No, a pistol.
When did you buy? he says.
Buy?
The house. When did you buy the house?

She is holding an object in her hand. A modest pistol. What they call a what is the word subcompact, with names like Bobcat, Cobra, and the way she enunciates makes him wonder how many bridges and crowns and caps have re-organized her mouth.

The pistol is pointed at him.

I'm thinking: mice, she says. Squirrels. Animal sounds. I'm thinking maybe my house wears down around me a little every time I go to sleep. I know it does, but I'm thinking maybe I can actually hear it as it's happening.

No, he decides, a pack of cigarettes.

She adds something he can't make out.

What? he says.

The noise, she says.

Her voice is younger than she looks. Someone in her thirties. Forties.

I'm not the noise, he says. You're the noise.

I hear things. I come out to check. Only there's never anything.

A woman. The woman. She is scrutinizing the stillness the man has become. He wonders if she can really see him or if she can only sense the accumulation of his body in space. The certain density. Second sight. Should he remain motionless? Continue eating?

She is smallish and several years older than he is and maybe she wears glasses and maybe she has left them on the bedside table when she got up to investigate the noises coming from her kitchen. His kitchen. Her kitchen. It used to be his. Now it is this gray hair, this shoulder-length gray hair, and he thinks kindergarten teacher in a pink quilted robe. He thinks: I can easily take her.

He feels rather than sees her part her lips to speak and recalls he is wearing a t-shirt, a plain white t-shirt, and saggy worn jeans and a pair of new white sneakers. The t-shirt and sneakers glow in the dimness, giving away his position, and she is saying: You're doing exactly what here?

He is in the process of lifting a spoonful of granola and yogurt and banana slices to his lips, semi-thinking about how a glass of orange juice would taste good with it, possibly recalling and possibly misrecalling seeing a carton on the shelf in the refrigerator among the calamity of white light, possibly behind a yellow plastic mustard bottle, a pickle jar with two pickles in it wafting in cloudy pea-green brine, an open can of peaches in sugar water covered loosely with a sheet of Saran wrap.

This thought happens to him and the man hears someone take a quick breath across the room and he raises his head: a stranger suspended in the doorway between the hall to the bedrooms and this place, the one the man finds himself occupying.

silverware and selects a knife, a steak knife, no, just a regular blunt-end one, with which he cuts up the peeled banana over the yogurt and granola and listens to the wet sound of slices tlicking into the mix.

Which is when he becomes aware of the spiky scent of ground coffee. He discovers a coffee maker beneath the cabinets near the microwave and the machine must be black because it blends in almost entirely with the countertop. He can see it and then he can't and then he can. The one they had was black, too. No, brushed aluminum. He would figure two tablespoons of ground beans in the wire mesh filter. He would figure the timer was set last night.

with different kinds of fruit in it. A pale white apple, which would appear green in daylight. One orange, which the man picks up, palms, sniffs, puts back down. Two bananas, one splotched with biomorphic stains, and he chooses the other. Opening drawers, closing drawers, opening drawers, he locates the

This thought happens to him and the man hears a noise and raises his head. He thinks cat before he remembers there isn't any cat before he remembers there was no cat, but maybe now there is. A few seconds, and he settles on the idea of floorboards adapting, a breeze bothering things outside, even though it is summer and he knows there aren't many breezes at this time of day at this time of year.

He scoops the yogurt from carton into bowl and stirs the granola from the bottom up. On the counter beneath the paper towel holder is a large fruit dish, except it is a different one, chrome grid, not glossy Norway maple, maple or maybe it was fir,

And then the man opens his eyes to find himself standing at the kitchen island. He is studying the cereal bowl on the granite countertop before him through light textured like the static on a rabbit-eared TV set. It must be morning—four, four thirty: that's what he would guess. The cereal bowl, black, black or gray, is half full of granola and the man realizes there is something in his left hand and something in his right. An open carton of strawberry yogurt. A spoon with aerodynamic design. To the best of his knowledge, he is making breakfast.

hugh

Theories of Forgetting